PRAISE FOR BEN ELTON'S
BLAST FROM THE PAST

"[*Blast from the Past*] is perfect Elton territory: non-sexist,
non-racist radical feminists, the absurdities of the Loony Left,
and a stalker thrown in for good measure. And . . . he turns
it into a humorous, comfortingly old-fashioned
and very readable love story."
—*Maxim*

"*Blast from the Past* is Elton at his most outrageously entertaining.
Elton is a master of the snappy one-liner, and here the witty
repartee hides a surprisingly romantic core."
—*Cosmopolitan* (UK)

"Ben Elton's in top form with this gripping black comedy, which
gets better with every turn of the page. And there's a sneaky
sting in the tail to round off a surefire hit."
—*New Woman* (UK)

"Riddled with intrigue and steamy, sexual tension, this is a lively
thriller of sexual politics and morality. Elton's best book yet."
—*Elle* (UK)

"*Blast from the Past* is a comedy, but an edgy comedy. Like Elton's
Popcorn, it is a slick moral satire that works as a hairy cliff-hanger."
—*The Sunday Times* (London)

Also by Ben Elton

Stark
Gridlock
This Other Eden
Popcorn

[Ben Elton]

BLAST

FROM THE

PAST

Delta
Trade Paperbacks

A Delta Book
Published by
Dell Publishing
a division of
Random House, Inc.
1540 Broadway
New York, New York 10036

This novel is a work of fiction. Names, characters, places, and incidents either are the product of the author's imagination or are used fictitiously. Any resemblance to actual persons, living or dead, events, or locales is entirely coincidental.

This work was first published in Great Britain by Bantam Press, a division of Transworld Publishers, Ltd.

Copyright © 1998 by Ben Elton
Cover design by Royce M. Becker
Photograph of Lips © Jeremy Wolff/Graphistock

Library of Congress Catalog Card Number: 99-35258

All rights reserved. No part of this book may be reproduced or transmitted in any form or by any means, electronic or mechanical, including photocopying, recording, or by any information storage and retrieval system, without the written permission of the Publisher, except where permitted by law. For information address: Delacorte Press

Delta® is a registered trademark of Random House, Inc., and the colophon is a trademark of Random House, Inc.

ISBN: 0-385-33452-4

Reprinted by arrangement with Delacorte Press
Manufactured in the United States of America

October 2000

10 9 8 7 6 5 4 3 2 1
BVG

For Sophie

BLAST

FROM THE

PAST

[1]

It was 2:15 in the morning when the telephone rang. Polly woke instantly. Her eyes were wide and her body tense before the phone had completed so much as a single ring. And as she woke, in the tiny moment between sleep and consciousness, before she was even aware of the telephone's bell, she felt scared. It was not the phone that jolted Polly so completely from her dreams, but fear.

And who could argue with the reasoning powers of Polly's subconscious self? Of course she was scared. After all, when the phone rings at 2:15 in the morning it's unlikely to be heralding something pleasant. What chance is there of its being good news? None. Only someone bad would ring at such an hour. Or someone good with bad news.

That telephone was sounding a warning bell. Something, somewhere, was wrong. So much was obvious. Particularly to a woman who lived alone, and Polly lived alone.

Of course it might be no more wrong than a wrong number. Something bad, but bad for someone else, something that would touch Polly's life only for a moment, utterly infuriate her, and then be gone.

"Got the Charlie?"

"There's no Charlie at this number."

"Don't bullshit me, arsehole."

"What number are you trying to call? This is three, four, zero, one . . ."

"Three, four, zero? I'm awfully sorry. I think I've dialed the wrong number."

That would be a good result. A wrong number would be the best possible result. To find yourself returning to bed furiously muttering, "Stupid bastard," while trying to pretend to yourself that you haven't actually woken up; that would be a good result. Polly hoped the warning bell was meant for someone else.

If your phone rings at 2:15 A.M. you'd better hope that too. Because if someone actually wants you you're in trouble.

If it's your mother she's going to tell you your dad died.

If it's some much-missed ex-lover who you'd been hoping would get back in contact he'll be calling drunkenly to inform you that he's just been diagnosed positive and that perhaps you'd better have things checked out.

The only time that bell might ring for something good is if you were actually expecting some news, news so important it might come at any time. If you have a relative in the throes of a difficult pregnancy, for instance, or a friend who's on the verge of being released from a foreign hostage situation. Then a person might leap from bed thinking, "At last! They've induced it!" or, "God bless the Foreign Office. He's free!" On the other hand, maybe the mother and baby didn't make it. Maybe the hostage got shot.

There is no doubt about it that under almost all normal circumstances a call in the middle of the night had to be bad. If not bad, at least weird, and, in a way, weird is worse. This is the reason why, when the phone rang in Polly's little attic flat at 2:15 A.M. and wrenched her from the womb of sleep, she felt scared.

Strange to be scared of a phone. Even if it's ringing. What can a ringing phone do to you? Leap up and bash you with its receiver? Strangle you with its cord? Nothing. Just ring, that's all.

Until you answer it.

Then, of course, it might ask you in a low growl if you're wearing any knickers. If you like them big and hard. If you've been a very naughty girl. Or it might say . . .

"I know where you live."

That was how it had all begun before.

"I'm watching you right now," the phone had hissed. "Standing there in only your nightdress. I'm going to tear it off you and make you pay for all the hurt you've done to me."

At the time Polly's friends had assured her that the man was lying. He had not been watching her. Pervert callers phone at random. They don't know where their victims live.

"He knew I was wearing my nightie," Polly had said. "He got that right. How did he know that? How did he know I was wearing my nightie?"

"It was the middle of the night, for heaven's sake!" her friends replied. "Got to be a pretty good chance you were wearing a nightie, hasn't there? Even a fool of a pervert could work that one out. He doesn't know where you live."

But Polly's friends had been wrong. The caller did know where Polly lived. He knew a lot about her because he was not a random pervert at all, but a most specific pervert. A stalker. That first call had been the start of a campaign of intimidation that had transformed Polly's life into a living hell. A hell from which the law had been unable to offer any protection.

"Our hands are tied, Ms. Slade. There's nothing actually illegal about making phone calls, writing letters, or ringing people's doorbells."

"Terrific," said Polly. "So I'll get back to you when I've been raped and murdered, then, shall I?"

The police assured her that it hardly ever came to that.

[2]

He'd been a client of hers. At the council office where she worked, the office that dealt with equal opportunities and discrimination. His was one of those depressing modern cases where sad white men who have failed to be promoted claim reverse discrimination, saying that they have been passed over for advancement in favor of less well qualified black lesbians. The problem is, of course, that often they are right: they have been passed over in favor of less well qualified black lesbians, that being the whole point of the policy. To positively discriminate in favor of groups that have been negatively discriminated against in the past.

"But now I'm being negatively discriminated against," the sad white men inevitably reply.

"Specifically, yes," the officers of the Office of Equal Opportunity (of whom Polly was one) would attempt to explain. "But not in general. Generally speaking, you are a member of a disproportionately successful group. There are any number of sad white men who achieve promotion. It's merely that you are not one of them. You're being negatively discriminated against positively, and you'll feel the benefits in a more socially cohesive society."

Not surprisingly, this argument was never much of a comfort, but Polly's failure to help her client did not cause the man to do as

5

so many disappointed clients had done before him and dump the entire weight of his confusion and impotent anger on top of Polly's innocent head. He had not called Polly a communist slut and stormed out of her office. He had not threatened to bring death and pestilence upon her. He had not promised to starve himself to death on the steps of the town hall until he got justice.

If only the man had behaved like that. How much better it would have been for Polly. Instead, he had become infatuated with her.

At first she had not been unduly alarmed. He sent one or two cards to her office and one day, on discovering that it was her birthday, he went out and returned with a single rose. On their final consultation he had given Polly a secondhand book, an anthology of postwar poetry, rather a tastefully chosen selection, Polly thought. He'd inscribed the book, "To dearest Polly. Beautiful words for a beautiful person." Polly had not much liked that, but since the gift could not have cost more than a pound or two she had felt it would be more trouble to refuse it than accept. Particularly considering that it was, she thought, to be the last time they would meet.

But the following evening the man knocked on the door of the house where she lived and greeted her as if he was a friend.

"Hi, Polly," he said. "Just thought I'd drop round and see what you thought of the book. Hope it's not inconvenient. I mean, if it is, just say."

Of course, Polly knew then that she had a problem. She just did not know how big. "Well, yes, it is inconvenient, actually, besides which . . ."

"Don't worry, don't worry at all. How about later? Maybe we could have a drink?"

"No, Peter," she said. Peter was the man's name. "That's not a good idea at all. Now I don't know how you got my home address, but you mustn't come here again. What you've got to understand is that we have a professional relationship. It's not at all acceptable for you to try to enter my private life."

"Oh dear." Peter looked surprised. "Sorry." And he turned and scurried off.

Five minutes later he was back.

The change in the man was shocking. His face seemed to have been physically transformed. The muscles and the contours appeared to do different things, point in different directions. He still looked pathetic but now he also looked demonic.

"And what you've got to understand, Polly, is that you can't just be fucking friends when *you* want to! All right? You can't just fucking use me—talk to me at the office and then refuse to speak when I call."

Now Polly knew who had been phoning her. The tone, the voice, they were unmistakable. Polly wondered how she'd failed to notice it before, but then he'd always been so mild to her face.

He was mild to her face no longer.

"You can't just take my fucking presents and then think you can make all the rules! A relationship cuts two ways, you know!"

That was the thing. The terrible, terrible thing. Right from the very beginning Peter had thought he and Polly had a relationship. His anger at her rejection was the vicious, righteous anger of one who felt betrayed. Peter had invested so much in his fantasies of Polly that it was impossible for him to believe that his feelings were not in some way reciprocated. Everything Peter did he did with Polly in mind, and in his unbalanced state he had come to believe that despite her denials Polly was equally conscious of him.

"*Dear Polly,*" he would write, "*I watched you at the bus stop. Thank you for wearing that blue jumper. I was so thrilled to think that you had remembered I liked it.*"

7

And Polly would rack her brains and remember the time back in her old life, when Peter had been just another sad case, when he had remarked on how much he liked the top she had been wearing.

The appalling thing was that after only a short period of harassment Polly did of course have a kind of relationship with Peter. Everything *she* did she did with Peter in mind. Thus the stalker feeds his need, becoming central in the life of someone who should be a stranger to him. For the victim—Polly—it was like being in love, except the emotion she felt was hate. Like a besotted lover, she thought about her torment the whole time. Of course to Peter this was only right. For he was giving everything—his time, his passion, his every living breath—so why should not the person he loved give something back? Surely a true and deep love is worth that at least?

Eventually Peter got his wish. He and Polly were brought together, if only in court. Bringing matters to such a pass had not been an easy process for Polly. Naturally the law had been as concerned for Peter's rights as it had been for hers, and, as the police had pointed out, you cannot prosecute people for being annoying and rude. The law at the time did not even recognize stalking as a crime.

Neither did it recognize the fact that Polly was being driven mad.

It was not, it seemed, illegal for Peter to repeatedly write to Polly expressing his wish that she would get AIDS (which was all a bitch like her deserved). It was not illegal for him to stand outside her house and stare up at her window until late into the night. It was not even illegal for him to ring her front doorbell in the small hours of the morning. Polly's distress was in fact almost irrelevant to the courts. What they wanted to know—what Polly was required to show—was that Peter's actions had dealt her *material harm*. Money, it seemed, was the bottom line. The law required Polly to establish that Peter's activities had left her out of pocket. Had the mental torment she was suffering rendered her unfit to work? Could she demonstrate that Peter was preventing her from making a living?

If she could, the law would be in a position to act; otherwise she would simply have to learn to live with her problem.

Polly produced her doctor's letter, her employer's testimonial, the diary of harassment the police had advised her to keep. She told of her sleepless nights, her clouded days, the tears and the anger that blighted her life.

Across the courtroom Peter luxuriated in every detail, thrilled, finally, to have proof that she was as obsessed with him as he was with her.

When it ended Polly had won a victory of sorts. The judge granted her an injunction. Peter was to neither approach nor contact Polly for an indefinite period, and should he try to do so he risked a custodial sentence. It did not stop him completely, but after further warnings from the police his hysterical intrusions on Polly's life slowly began to diminish and for Polly life started to resemble something like a nervous normality.

He was still with her, of course. She felt he always would be. She still glanced up and down the street when she left the house in the morning, still checked in the communal hallway when she got home at night. Still wondered as she had always wondered whether one day he would try to stick a knife into her for betraying his love.

"Actually, I don't think he would ever have turned violent," Polly would say to her friends.

"No, definitely not," they would reassure her. "Actually I read that those type of people almost never do."

But she always wondered.

And now, three months since he had last surfaced, it was 2:15 in the morning and Polly's phone was ringing.

[3]

On the previous evening, as the dark clouds had gathered over the grim hangars of RAF Brize Norton and an invisible sun had set behind them, a small party of military men (plus one or two civil servants) assembled in the grizzly, drizzly gloom. They were awaiting the arrival of an American plane.

Inside that plane, suspended high over England, sat a very senior American army officer, deep in thought. So preoccupied was the general that he had scarcely uttered a word in the five hours since his plane had left Washington. The general's staff imagined that he was considering the meeting that lay before him. They imagined that the general had been wrestling with the delicate problems of NATO, the ex-Soviet states, and the New World Order. After all, it was to debate such weighty issues that they had crossed the Atlantic. In fact, had the general's staff been mind readers, they would have been surprised to discover that their commander was thinking about nothing more momentously geopolitical than a young woman he had once known, scarcely a woman—almost a girl, in fact, a girl of seventeen.

Back on the ground the British coughed and stamped and longed for the bar. There were always mixed emotions involved for British officers when dealing with their American cousins. It was a thrill, of course. The undeniable thrill of being on nodding terms with such unimaginable power. Most of the officers standing waiting, shuffling their feet on the tarmac at Brize Norton, thought themselves lucky if they got the occasional use of a staff car. Their professional lives were couched in terms such as "limited response," "tactical objective," and "rapid deployment." When they described themselves and their martial capability they spoke of "an elite force," a "highly skilled, professional army." Everybody knew, of course, that these phrases were euphemisms for "not much money," "not many soldiers."

The Americans, on the other hand, measured their budgets in trillions.

"Can you believe that, old chap? *Trillions* of dollars. Makes you weep."

Their ships were like cities, their airplanes not only invincible but also apparently invisible. They had bombs and missiles capable of destroying the planet not once but many times over. Traditionally within the scope of human imagination only gods had wielded such mighty influence on the affairs of men. Now men themselves had the capacity, or at least some men, men from the Pentagon.

There was no denying that to other soldiers, soldiers of lesser armies such as the British who stood waiting on the cold, damp tarmac, such power was attractive. It was sexy and compelling. It was fun to be around. Fun to tell the fellows about.

"I read somewhere they were developing ray guns."

"Bloody hell!"

But alongside the sheepish admiration there was also jealousy. A deep, gnawing, cancerous jealousy born of grotesque inequality. The difference in scale between the American armed forces and those of its principal and most historic ally is so great as to render Britain's military contribution to the alliance an irrelevance. In truth,

Britain's role is nothing more than to add a spurious legitimacy of international consensus to U.S. foreign policy. That is why Britain has a special relationship. That is why Britain is special and why the Americans let it remain special. They certainly can't trust the French.

The general's plane was beginning its descent. Looking out of the window, he could just make out the fields below. Gray now, nearly black. No green and gold as he liked to remember them, as indeed they had been on that fabulous summer's day half an army lifetime ago. Before he'd blown his chance of happiness forever.

He took from his pocket a letter he had been writing to his brother, Harry. He often wrote to Harry. The general was a lonely man in a lonely job and he had few people in whom he could confide. Over the years he had got into the habit of using his brother as a kind of confessional, the only person to whom he showed anything like the whole of his self. His brother sometimes wished that he would unload his woes onto someone else. He always knew when he saw an airmail letter in his mailbox that somewhere in the world his celebrated and important brother was tormented about something.

"The little shit never writes to say he's happy," Harry would mutter as he slipped a knife into the envelope. "Like I care about his problems." Although of course Harry did care; that's what families are for.

As the plane began slowly to drop toward England, and its undercarriage emerged, rumbling and shaking from its belly, noisily pushing its way into the gathering night, the general took up his pen. Contrary to all accepted safety practices, he also lowered the tray table in front of him and laid the unfinished letter out before him.

"Olde England is outside of the window now, Harry," he wrote.

"Funny, me returning this way. Back in those sunny, glory days when I was last in this country, all I could think about was becoming a general. All I wanted was my own army. Now I'm a general, a great big general, the biggest fucking general in the European Theater. Strange then that all I can think about is those sunny, glory days. And her. I'll bet you're laughing."

General Kent paused, then put down his pen and tore the letter into pieces. He had never lied to Harry and he did not wish to start now. Not that anything he had written was untrue. Quite the opposite. His thoughts were indeed filled with memories of halcyon days long gone and the girl with whom he had shared them, and he was certainly cursing the army that had torn them apart. But that was only half the story of what was on General Kent's mind, and Harry would see that immediately. With Harry, omission was tantamount to deceit. Harry would know that his brother was holding out on him, as he always did. Harry had known that Jack wanted to be a soldier even before Jack had known it himself. It had been Harry who had broken the news to their parents after Jack had chickened out and left home without a word. Christ, what a scene that must have been.

The general stuffed the torn pieces of his letter into the ashtray that was no longer allowed to be an ashtray and returned to staring out of the window.

Down below, the chilly Brits were assuring each other that despite its undisputed position of global dominance, the American army was not what one would call a proper army.

"They're either screaming abuse at each other, singing silly spirituals, or bonding in a big hug. I mean really, I ask you, what a way to run a show."

The Brits all agreed that despite having more firepower than Satan and more influence than the God in whom they trusted, the

armed forces of the United States were not what one would call a formidable fighting machine. No, no, the damp, miserable khaki-clad
figures felt, much better to be lean. Lean and hungry, like the British
forces. Much better to be underfunded, undermanned, and under-
valued, like they were. That was character building. That was what
made a soldier a soldier.

"They can't even get the uniforms right," the jealous Brits assured each other. "They seem to be dressed either as Hell's Angels in
leather jackets and sunglasses or as Italian lift attendants with more
brass and braid than a colliery band."

Everybody agreed that it was a shocking state of affairs, but in
truth there was not a man amongst them, itching in his damp khaki
blouse, who would not have dearly loved to swap places and be
dressed half as stylishly as the Americans.

A far-off noise in the gloomy sky announced the imminent arrival of the loved and hated allies.

"On time, at least," remarked the senior British officer in his
best patronizing drawl. "Thankful for small mercies, eh?"

It started to rain.

"Look at them," said the general, staring out of the drizzle-
dotted window as his plane taxied toward the little RAF terminal
and the forlorn-looking British reception committee. "Nothing ever
changes in the British army, you know that? They're actually proud
of it."

One of the crew handed the general his coat.

"They always look the same. Down at heel but defiant. Like they
just got off the boat from Dunkirk. The worst thing about being a
great power is when you're not one anymore. It takes centuries to get
over it. Look at the Portuguese. They just gave up altogether."

"Sir! Yes, sir!" said the young airman, not having the faintest idea what the general was talking about.

Jack turned to General Schultz, his chief of staff, who was sitting respectfully two seats behind, playing on a Gameboy.

"Let's make this piece of bullshit as quick a piece of bullshit as any bull ever shitted. OK?"

[4]

Polly turned on her bedside lamp and felt her irises scream in protest at the sudden light.

The phone was on her desk, on the other side of the room. Polly had put it there so that if ever she booked an alarm call she would have to get up in order to answer it. It was too easy to just reach out from under the duvet and clunk the receiver up and down in its cradle. Polly had missed trains that way. You didn't wake up, your dreams just changed gear.

The phone rang again. Somehow it seemed to be getting louder.

Through Polly's watery eyes the room looked strange. The phone, her desk, the crumpled shape on the floor that was her jeans, everything looked different. It wasn't, of course, just as the phone wasn't getting any louder. Everything was exactly the same as it had been when she'd gone to sleep the previous evening.

The phone kept ringing.

Polly got out of bed and padded across the room toward it. Across almost her entire home, in fact. Polly's landlord claimed that Polly lived in a studio-style duplex and had set the rent accordingly. Polly thought she lived in a studio and that she was being ripped off.

The phone was set to ring six times before the answering machine kicked in. Polly watched the machine as it completed its cycle.

She was more angry than scared.

Very angry, terribly angry. Anger had seized hold of her whole body, which was the one thing she knew she must not let it do if she wished to get back to sleep before dawn. In vain she struggled to regain control of herself, but it was too late. The anger had released its chemicals and they were surging through her nervous system like a drug, making her muscles twitch, her stomach squirm, and her heart expand like a balloon against her ribs. An anger so powerful because it was born of fear.

The Bug was back. Great holy shit, hadn't the bastard had enough?

"The Bug" was what Polly called Peter. She had given him that title in an effort to depersonalize him. To resist the relationship that was growing between them. Polly had realized from the beginning, as every victim of an obsessive does, that the more she knew about her tormentor the more difficult it became to remember that he had absolutely nothing to do with her. Every extra detail that she accumulated of the man's hated existence clouded the basic fact that he had absolutely no business in her life at all. He was a stranger, an aggressive stranger of course, but that did not mean she had to get to know him.

Even when the whole ghastly business became a matter for the police and solicitors, Polly had strenuously avoided sharing in the information that was unearthed about her foe. She did not want to know what he was like or where he came from. She did not want to know if he had a job or friends. She had learned the bitter lesson that the more she knew about this man the more there was for her to think about, and the more she thought about him the greater was her sense of violation.

Which was why Peter had become the Bug. A bug is a thing that annoys you. It buzzes into your life and is difficult to get rid of, but it can't hurt you or kill you; all it can do is buzz. A bug is also a minor virus, a thing you accidentally pick up, like a cold or the flu. It could happen to anybody. If you catch one you're just unlucky, that's all. It has nothing to do with you.

Above all, it is not your fault.

A bug is something that you shake off. That you determine will not ruin your day and if you cannot shake it off you accept your misfortune philosophically and cope the best you can. You do not become obsessed with a bug. It does not cloud your thoughts and bleed an undercurrent of tension and unhappiness through your every waking moment.

A bug cannot own you.

The "thing" that was Peter was not a friend or an enemy, or an acquaintance, or even a man. He was a bug and only a fool rails and rants and weeps over a bug; only fools feeds its malignant symptoms with their anger and hurt.

Polly stood waiting for her answering machine message to start and struggled to control her fury.

She scarcely even noticed that she had begun to cry.

[5]

General Schultz, General Kent's chief of staff, was not a very good hustler and there followed what seemed to be an interminable period of introductions and handshaking as the British and American parties greeted each other on the tarmac. Eventually, just when Kent was beginning to suspect that he would be expected to bond even with the man who waved the Ping-Pong paddles, he found himself sitting alongside the senior British officer in the first of a convoy of army staff cars heading for London.

Kent was silent, preoccupied, deep in thought. Despite this, however, his host felt obliged to make some effort at conversation.

"I had the privilege of serving under a colleague of yours," the senior British officer said. "During the Gulf War. I was seconded to the staff of General Schwarzkopf. Your famous Stormin' Norman."

Kent did not reply.

"Splendid name, don't you think?" Actually the senior British officer thought it an absolutely pathetic name. He despised the way Americans felt the need to attach silly macho schoolboy nicknames to their leaders. "Iron" this, "Hell bugger" that; it was bloody childish.

General Kent knew exactly what his host was thinking and in his turn thought it was pathetic the way the British compensated for their massive inferiority complex by forever sneering at the Yanks.

There had once been a time when British soldiers were equally world famous and equally popularly revered, "Fighting Bobs Roberts" of the Boer War, the "Iron Duke" of Wellington himself, but that had been in another century, when . . . General Kent stopped his train of thought. He did not wish to be pondering the inanity of his companion's comments. He wished to be left alone to concentrate on his own deep and tormented feelings. To dwell once more upon the summer of his love.

What would she be like? Would she remember? Of course she would remember. She would have to be dead to have forgotten, and he knew she wasn't dead.

"Not your first trip to Britain, I imagine." Once more the senior British officer's voice crashed into Kent's thoughts. The man was not giving up. He had been instructed to make the American feel welcome and by hell he was going to make him feel welcome even if that also meant annoying him utterly.

"I said, not your first trip to Britain, I imagine," he repeated loudly. "Been here before, I suppose."

He had blundered into General Kent's very train of thought. General Kent had been in Britain before and it had changed his life forever.

"Yeah," Kent acknowledged at last. "I was here before." But his tone suggested that he did not wish to elaborate.

"I see. I see. Here before, you say? Well, I never. Splendid. Splendid."

Another few cold, dark miles slid by outside the windows of the car.

"Plenty of friends this side of the pond, then, I imagine. People to look up and all that. Old pals to visit?"

Again the Englishman had got it right. There certainly was an old pal to visit, but General Kent did not choose to discuss it. He had never once in over sixteen years discussed the one love of his life with anyone apart from his brother, Harry, not a soul, not ever and he certainly did not intend to start now. After this the British officer gave up and the conversation, such as it was, lapsed completely until the Englishman delivered his American through the gates of Downing Street.

"Well, good-bye, General. It's been a privilege and a pleasure to meet you," said the senior British officer.

"Yes, it's been very real," replied General Kent. "Thank you so much for the trouble you've taken."

"Not at all. Good-bye, then."

"Good-bye."

The two soldiers shook hands and parted.

"Surly bastard," thought the senior British officer.

"Pompous creep," thought General Kent.

Kent stood outside the famous front door for as long as he dared, breathing in the cold night air, attempting to marshal his thoughts. He must pull himself together. He had an important meeting ahead of him. It was his job to brief the British on White House plans for the eastward expansion of NATO. He needed to be thinking about Poland and the Czech Republic, not about making love in a sun-drenched field to a seventeen-year-old girl. He stamped his feet; he must concentrate! It was time to put away the past and think about the present. The past could wait. After all, it had waited these many long years; it could stand another few hours.

"General?"

Kent's party had now all assembled on the pavement and were awaiting their commander's lead. A bobby was standing expectantly, ready to open the door.

"OK, let's do it," Kent said, and led his officers across the familiar threshold.

[6]

Polly was smiling.

Polly was frowning.

She was yawning. She was walking. She was standing.

She was walking to her bus stop. She was standing at her bus stop. She was walking away from her bus stop. She was standing at her front door searching for her key.

A hundred tiny, near-identical moments from Polly's life, frozen in time, developed, printed, and stuck on Peter's wall.

"Well, I don't see as how it can do any great harm really," Peter's mother would say, more for her own comfort than that of the next-door neighbor with whom she would share the occasional pot of tea. "Lots of boys have pictures of their favorite women on their bedroom walls. Pamela Anderson or *Playboy* girls, stuff like that. In fact, I think Peter's more normal than those other boys because at least he's gone all funny over a real woman. Not just some fantasy figure."

Peter had taken the pictures in defiance of the court injunction against him.

He had not begun to lose interest over the previous three months as Polly had been hoping. Quite the opposite. He had acquired a different car from the one known to the police and he would

22

park it in Polly's street at about seven in the morning. There he would wait, hiding behind a copy of the *Daily Mirror* until he could watch and photograph Polly beginning her journey to work. Once she had boarded her bus he would start up his car and follow it until it got into the local main street, where Polly got off. Peter could not take any photographs at this end of her journey because there was too much traffic and too many people, and it was a red route, anyway, so he couldn't stop his car.

Once when Polly got off the bus Peter saw her throw a sucked-out Just Juice box into a dustbin.

Of course, he had to have that box, even if it meant getting a ticket. He put on his hazard lights, pulled over, and pushed his way across the crowded pavement toward the rubbish basket. When he got there a homeless person was already inspecting the contents of the bin in the hope of finding something to eat or read. The homeless person was not interested in Peter's box. Fortunately for him.

Sometimes before he went to sleep Peter caressed the box, putting his fingers where hers had been in that moment when she had squeezed it and crushed it up. He imagined her delicate fingers squeezing and crushing at him in the same way.

Then he would put his lips to the little bent straw and gently suck at it.

"I think she's still on his mind a bit," Peter's mother would tell her friend, "but he's not made contact, not since, not since . . ." Peter's court appearance remained a painful memory for his mother. Whenever she thought of it she became angry. Angry with Polly.

"That bitch. She didn't need to tell the police, did she? She could have come to me, talked to me. I could have stopped him. And anyway, what harm was he doing? He loved her, didn't he? It's not as if she had anything to be afraid of."

In fact, Peter's mother knew very well that from the tone of Peter's letters and messages Polly had had every reason to be afraid of him. He had never actually threatened her directly but the things he said about her and wished upon her would have scared anyone. Peter's mother had rationalized this. She reasoned that if the Bitch had only been pleasant—just said hello to her son and smiled occasionally, perhaps replied to one or two of his letters—then he would not have become upset. Peter's mother felt, as Peter did himself, that devotion such as Peter's deserved some sort of reward. After all, it isn't every girl who's worshiped the way Peter worshiped Polly.

"He brought her presents. Flowers and CDs. She never said thank you, not once. Not so much as an acknowledgment. Well, of course he was hurt. Of course he was upset. I don't blame him. I nearly wrote to the Bitch myself."

As far as the Bug's mother was concerned, Polly wasn't Polly anymore. She was "that woman" or, when she felt particularly distressed, "the Bitch."

"Anyway. He's promised me he'll let it go now, stop approaching her and all that. Well, he has to. Otherwise it's prison, and what would I do then? It's her loss, anyway. She doesn't deserve a boy like my Peter."

But Peter could not let it go. How could he? You can't just let love go. Love is something beyond a person's control. You don't ask it to come and you can't make it leave. Only iron discipline can control an obsession, and Peter had none.

Even as his mother spoke Peter was at his computer. Inside his computer, like the bug he was. It was exciting to reach out to her through the silence of cyberspace. He was banned from e-mailing Polly, but that didn't stop him making a connection. A palpable physical connection. His fingers touched the keyboard, the keyboard touched the modem, the modem touched the Telecom network, the network touched Polly's phone, and so he touched her!

He could hack into her.

He had read her Sainsbury's loyalty card account. He knew that she had bought most of her furniture at IKEA; he even knew the styles and colors she'd chosen. Likewise he knew the brand of abdominizing exerciser that she'd ordered in an insane moment of optimistic piety from the back of a color supplement. He imagined her rolling back and forth upon it in a leotard, though he'd got that wrong; she'd never even assembled it. He even knew her ex-directory telephone number. Sitting in his bedroom reading Polly's Telecom account on his computer screen had felt so good. It was a little invasion of her privacy, a violation of her secrets. Finding out the things she did not want him to know.

Peter's mother sometimes opined that Peter seemed to love that computer more than he loved the Bitch. She did not understand that to Peter his computer was an extension of Polly, a means of penetrating her.

[7]

General Kent's meeting had long since finished and he was alone, sitting at the wheel of a car parked in a small residential street in the Stoke Newington area of London. The car was unmarked, there were no military or diplomatic plates, no official driver, no bodyguard. Just Jack and the girl on his mind.

On Kent's lap was a file marked "General Kent: For sight of. Secure file. Absolute discretion required. No nonauthorized viewing whatsoever."

A few years before, it would have simply said "General Kent: Private." Kent reflected that military industrial complex bullshit was now expanding at such a rate that soon there would be no room on a file for the description of what was in it and they would have to attach extensions to the cover.

The contents of the file were biographical. Details about the life and current circumstances of a thirty-four-year-old Englishwoman: Polly Slade. There were photographs too, old ones and new. The new ones were very similar to those that had been taken by the Bug. Polly walking, Polly standing, Polly at the bus stop, etc. The pictures in the file were rather better than the Bug's blurry efforts, having been taken by professionals, but they were no more revealing. Just a woman on a street. That was all. Of course the Bug did not know of the general's photographs and the general did not know of the Bug's. How astonished they would have been to find out the other's existence. After all, the chances of the same woman being covertly photographed at the same time and in the same place by two completely separate and unconnected people must be millions to one. But that is what had happened.

General Kent looked at the face in the pictures. Such a nice face. A little careworn, perhaps, but very pretty. Not everyone would have thought the woman beautiful, but General Kent did, ravishingly so.

The file also contained a telephone number.

Kent carried a mobile phone, but this he left in his pocket. Instead he took up the little stock of ten-pence coins that his security contact had furnished him with and got out of the car. Nearby was a public phonebox. Not one of the solid red ones that Jack remembered, but a phonebox nonetheless, not merely a phone in a hood on a pole.

It was late and the street was quiet. Empty almost, save for one other man, a nervous-looking fellow loitering farther up the street. The other man appeared to have been making for the phone box himself, but when he saw Kent he stopped.

Kent wondered whether the man had been planning to call one of the extraordinary number of girls who advertised their sexual services on little cards inside the phone box. Judging by the pictures on the cards, some of the most impossibly glamorous and attractive women in Britain were advertising cheap fucks in Stoke Newington. Kent suspected that if the fellow ever did pluck up courage to call he would be disappointed.

He pushed twenty pence into the machine and dialed. It was 2:15 A.M.

[8]

The phone was on its fifth ring. After the next one Polly's answering machine would start. She sat on the floor and assumed the lotus position. When the Bug spoke she wanted to be ready.

Polly's yoga teacher, a Yorkshireman called Stanley, had said that yoga was the process whereby the superior, conscious element in a person was freed from involvement with the inferior material world. A tough trick to pull when you're being stalked in the small hours of the morning, but Polly was determined to give it a go. And so she sat, as the answering machine began to clunk, her feet crossed, her knees spread like a wing nut, her elbows on her knees, and her fingers and thumbs set in the required position.

She was calm, she was at ease, she was relaxed.

Her bottom was freezing.

The problem was her nightie. It was an old shirt of her father's and was too short for the situation; it did not properly cover her backside from the cold floorboards on which she sat. She did not wish to break position at this crucial moment of calm; on the other hand the whole point was to be comfortable, and a cold bum was not comfortable. Besides which, some ancient memory was whispering to her that this was the best way of getting piles. It was no good, she would have to move onto the rug. While remaining absolutely calm, at one with herself and in the lotus position, Polly shuffled over to the rug using only her buttock muscles to move.

"Hello," said Polly's voice as Polly shuffled. "Nobody's answering at the moment, but please leave a message after the tone. Thank you."

A defiantly unfunny and matter-of-fact message. Polly's days of using music, cracking gags, and pretending to be the Lithuanian Embassy had ended the day that the Bug had first discovered her phone number. During the worst period of harassment she had got a male friend to record her outgoing message, but this had just made genuine callers think they had the wrong number.

There was no incoming message.

The caller hung up and the answering machine clicked and clunked accordingly. Furious, Polly leaped up from her lotus position (an effort that nearly broke both her ankles), grabbed the phone off its cradle, and shouted, "Fuck off!" at the dial tone. Stanley would not have been pleased.

"Now, d'you think 'indu philosophers'd go abaht 'ollering 'Fook off!' into't pho-an?" he would have inquired. "No fookin' way."

Polly struggled to prevent her blood from boiling. Calm was required. Calm. She had work in the morning.

Perhaps it had been a wrong number after all.

Perhaps the drug baron on the other end of the line had heard Polly's voice on the machine, realized his mistake, and had gone on to deliver his threats elsewhere.

Inside the phonebox Jack put down the phone. He had been expecting her to answer personally; he hadn't prepared himself for an answering machine. She couldn't be out. He'd specifically had that checked. She must be screening her calls. Or else she had become a heavy sleeper over the years.

A little farther up the street Peter was watching Jack. For a moment he thought that the man must have finished his calls, but then, to Peter's fury, the man picked up the phone a second time.

Polly was just about to return to bed when the phone rang again. This time she didn't bother with the lotus position; she just stood in the middle of her room, shaking with anger and fear, and waited.

"Hello," said Polly's voice again. "Nobody's answering at the moment, but please leave a message after the tone. Thank you."

This time the machine did not clunk to a halt. Polly could hear the faint electric hiss of an open but silent line. He was there but he wasn't speaking. Standing there, alone in the night, Polly watched the phone like it was a hissing snake. Like it was going to pounce. She itched to grab up the receiver again and scream further obscenities, but she knew that she mustn't. If there was one sure way to give the Bug satisfaction it was to share her emotions with him. Do that, shout at him, let him hear your fear and he would be nursing an erection for a week.

"Polly?"

It wasn't the Bug. She knew that within those first two syllables.

"Polly. Are you there?"

Within four words she knew who it was.

"Are you there, Polly?"

It was the last voice in the world that she had expected to hear.

"Listen, don't freak out," said General Kent. "It's Jack, Jack Kent."

[9]

Jack and Polly had met many years before, in a roadside restaurant on the A34 near Newbury. Jack was a captain, serving with the American forces in Britain. Those were the days when the Cold War was still hot, which was more than could be said for most of the food in the restaurant. The moment he'd walked in, Jack had regretted his decision to stop off for a cup of coffee, and as he brushed the crumbs from the orange plastic seat he very nearly turned around and walked straight out again. His uniform had already attracted attention, however, and he did not wish to appear foolish. He was, after all, an ambassador for his country.

Jack cleared a space for his newspaper amongst the debris left by the previous occupants of his table. There was an election on, not that he cared much about British politics. Mrs. Thatcher was in the process of pulverizing some white-haired old boy in a donkey jacket. It didn't look like a very equal contest to Jack; he'd been under the impression that the Brits believed in a fair fight.

A hormonally imbalanced teenaged lad approached Jack's table and offered him a menu.

"Just coffee, please," Jack said.

"Coffee," the lad repeated, and Jack knew immediately that he would not be brought coffee. He would be brought that beverage the

British chose to call coffee but which the rest of the world recognized as the urine of the devil's dog. This dark and bitter brew would be accompanied by a small, sealed plastic pot of white liquid marked "UHT Cream," which Jack knew to have been squeezed straight from the colon of a sick seagull.

Jack took in his surroundings. Great Christ, what hellish imagination had conceived of such places? These "Little Shits" and "Crappy Cooks" and "Happy Pukers"? These pale imitations of another, more vibrant culture plucked from the highways and byways of America and dumped down, dowdy and deflated, upon the A roads of Britain? In the three years that Jack had been in the United Kingdom he had viewed the inexorable advance of these gastronomic ghettos with increasing alarm. They were everywhere. Every turn in the road seemed to reveal another ghastly vision of red, yellow, and orange prefab architecture plus a huge plastic elephant for the kiddies. Any day now Jack expected to find one of these cheery hellholes installed at the gates of his base, possibly even outside his office door.

Jack's "coffee" arrived, about half of it still in the cup, the rest in the saucer, lapping around the grimy thumb of Jack's server.

"One coffee," the server said. "Enjoy your meal."

The fact that Jack was clearly not having a meal was of no concern to this boy, whose instructions were to say "Enjoy your meal" on delivery of every order, and that was what he did. Jack reflected on the problems of imposing a corporate culture. There was simply no point attempting to make English kids into Americans. You could put the silly hat on the British teenager, but you still had a British teenager under the silly hat. You could make them say, "Enjoy your meal," "Have a nice day," and "Hi, my name is Cindy, how may I help you right now?" as much as you liked, but it still always came out sounding like "Fuck off."

Jack was restless. He could not be bothered with the newspaper.

Mrs. Thatcher would win the election and she would probably stay in power forever. The Brits weren't stupid; they had a winner there. Hadn't she just won a war, after all? A war! Even a year after the event Jack could still scarcely believe the good fortune of his British colleagues. It was so unfair. America was the world's policeman; they had the best army, they should have got to fight the wars. And yet all of a sudden, just when everybody least expected it, those lucky bastard British had arranged themselves a real live, proper, nonnuclear, blood-and-guts, old-fashioned war. Jack and his comrades had suffered agonies of jealousy when it happened and, of course, being in Britain at the time had made it a hundred times worse. There they were, young eager members of the most powerful army on earth, and they had had to sit around in Britain, of all places, guarding cruise missiles while the dusty, down-at-heel old British sailed off halfway round the world to defend the Queen's territory in the South Atlantic.

Jack put the frustrations of the previous year from his mind and took a sheet of writing paper from his pocket. Perhaps he would pass the time by writing to his brother. Jack had been meaning to write for some time but had kept putting it off because it was too depressing. What had he to say for himself? Only that it was starting to look as if Harry had been right all along. Harry had always said that joining the army was throwing your life away.

"OK, Harry, I admit it," Jack wrote in his small, precise hand. *"You were right all those years ago and you've been right ever since. The army is a pain in the ass. It's boring and there isn't any glory anymore. Are you pleased, you son of a bitch? Maybe you should put it in one of your damn poems!"*

This was a cheap shot. Harry no longer wrote poems, although for a brief period as a teenager he had attempted to. Jack had never, ever let Harry forget this.

"Yeah, I'll bet you're pleased," Jack continued. *"Tell Mom and Pa the black sheep is bored. Tell them they saw more action shouting slogans at LBJ and fighting cops in '68 than I've seen in the fifteen years since I joined the fucking army."*

This was not true at all. In fact Jack had seen plenty of action, having served with distinction in Vietnam, but Jack was in a sour mood. Besides, Jack's Southeast Asian service had been at the end of the war, beating the retreat, so to speak, a great power cutting its losses. The U.S. disengagement from that bloody adventure had not felt very glorious at the time and it still rankled with Jack. It was one of the many things for which he somehow managed to blame his parents, an attitude his brother Harry found pathetic.

"What?" Harry would exclaim. "It's Mom's fault you didn't get enough Vietcong to shoot at! Jesus, Jack, you are such an asshole."

"Well, it was the enemy at home that stopped the war, wasn't it?" Jack would counter. "Those students and hippies and campus fucking heroes! They had their Vietnam War, oh yeah! Outside the White House and on the steps of the Lincoln Memorial! And then they ruined it for me! I didn't get sixties' Vietnam, no, not me. I got seventies' Vietnam. I didn't get to play Beach Boys music and fight a jungle guerrilla war. No, I finally get out there in '73, just in time to help load a bunch of fat fucking failures onto helicopters in the compound of the Saigon Embassy. That was my introduction to the new global reality. Even the music was shit. You can't fight a war with Donny and Marie at number one."

Jack and Harry had fought all the time as kids and they still did whenever they got the chance. Harry certainly had no sympathy for Jack's frustrations with army life. He had never made any secret of the fact that he thought Jack's life choices incomprehensible. As far as Harry was concerned, in the army there could only be two states—bored and terrified—and neither seemed very attractive to him. Harry's theory of why Jack had chosen the course in life that he had was the old favorite that he had done it to spite their parents. They had been teenagers during the sixties and while their mother and father had not embraced the counterculture entirely, they had certainly inhaled. Being college teachers, it would have been almost impossible for them not to. The sixties had been a very difficult decade to opt out of. Even the Brady Bunch and the Partridge Family had hippie values. Almost overnight, unorthodox behavior had become the new orthodoxy, long-haired weirdos became the norm, and patriotic boys with crew cuts started to look like freaks. Jack felt like a stranger in his own home. He had wanted proper parents at a time when the concept of formal generations was breaking down. Anybody could be hip; gray-haired old men were on the TV extolling the glories of drugs, and grizzled beat poets and blues men were becoming folk heroes. Whereas traditionally adults had encouraged young people to act like grown-ups, suddenly grown-ups were acting like kids. Jack was fifteen and he felt like the only adult in his house. He had cringed away his teens while his mother swapped dresses for caftans and his father's thick wavy hair got longer and longer and stupider.

Jack's mind had wandered. He returned to his letter and current dissatisfaction with army life.

"*I bet you're laughing to read this,*" he wrote. "*I know you think I'm in this situation because I wanted to embarrass Mom and Pa. I still can't believe that. You actually think I joined the army because Mom wore a see-through blouse to my high school graduation! You're such a jerk, Harry. You just can't bear the simple fact that however bored I may feel right now I love the army. You hate the fact that somebody with virtually identical DNA to yours actually loves and respects the armed forces of his country. Just like you love your damn chairs or washstands or whatever it is you whittle out of trees in your stupid wood in Ohio. I didn't join the army because all the guys in*"

*my class got to see my mother's nipples. I joined because I want to kill people
in the cause of peace and freedom, OK? Something I am unlikely to get the
chance to do at RAF Greenham Common, the shithole of the planet. If England had hemorrhoids, believe me they'd be here."*

Jack had hated the Greenham base the day he had arrived, and
the three grim years he had spent there since had done nothing to
change his mind. Three grinding years. Years that lived in Jack's
memory as one long, wet miserable winter's afternoon. He supposed
that the sun must have shone at some point during the previous
thirty-six months but if it had it had made no impression on him.
Concrete and steel, steel and concrete, that was what the camp
meant to Jack, and the very sky itself seemed to be constructed of
the same joyless stuff. A Cold War sky, gray, flat, and impenetrable,
like the belly of a vast tank. Jack had spent a thousand ghastly hours
of duty staring up at that gloomy canopy. He often thought that if
ever the missiles for which he and his comrades were responsible
were to be fired, they would just bounce off that sky and fall right
back to earth, blowing them all to hell.

He took an absentminded sip at his coffee and immediately
wished he hadn't. He continued with his letter.

*"Then, of course, there's the singing. Harry, that awful, awful singing
beggars belief. Worse than when you were trying to learn 'The Times They
Are A-Changin' ' on the guitar. From dawn to dusk, and back again from
dusk till dawn. Whenever a guy gets remotely near to the wire his ears are
assaulted by those seemingly endless dirges. I cannot believe it, Harry. The
one thing I thought was when I got in the army I would not have to listen
to any more fucking hippies. Now I'm surrounded by them! They'll be
singing now, those appalling women, if singing isn't too grand a word for it.
Keening, I've heard them call it, which sounds to me like something cats do
in alleys, which would be about right as far as I'm concerned. They stop
around midnight, but some nights I still can't sleep for the din. Those damn*

dirges are still running around my brain, like a tone-deaf rat with a mega-phone is trapped inside my head. I can hear them even now, Harry, even as I try to concentrate on writing this letter. Here's what they were singing yes-terday. Show Mom. She'll probably think it's beautiful.

> *You can't kill the spirit.*
> *She is like a mountain.*
> *Old and strong.*
> *She goes on and on and on.*
> *You can't kill the spirit.*
> *She is like a mountain.*
> *Old and strong.*
> *She goes on and on and on.*
> *You can't kill the spirit . . .*

You get the idea, Harry. They repeat it ad nauseam, and believe me, the emphasis is on nauseam . . ."

A woman struggled past carrying two children and leading a third. One of them managed to spill orange fizzy stuff onto Jack's letter. He sighed and called for the check. He could sit in that restaurant no longer. The noise and the smell were getting on his nerves. Old chip fat and baby sick were competing for supremacy in his nostrils, and BBC Radio One was clashing with the dirges run-ning round his head. The song playing was called "Karma Chameleon," sung by some kind of transvestite called Boy George who seemed suddenly to have become more famous than God. Jack had noticed that when the British liked a song they liked to hear it a lot and "Karma Chameleon" had been number one forever. Jack had liked it at first, but in that depressing place it seemed as tinny and irritating as the three girls who were singing along to it while simultaneously drinking milkshakes and smoking cigarettes. Jack liked to smoke himself but he never ceased to be amazed at the smoking capacity of the British teenage girl. He bet they could do it underwater. Jack finally gave up on his grubby coffee cup, scarcely having tasted its gloomy contents, and got up to go. For all its soulless concrete and its dreadful women, RAF Greenham Common was beginning to look preferable to his current surroundings.

Then, rather abruptly, Jack sat down again.

An old couple looked up from their all-day breakfasts and stared. They were no doubt glad of a moment's diversion from eating their meal, from the unpleasant task of consuming the formless mess they had unwittingly ordered under the mistaken impression that they would be brought food. They were more than happy to take a break from rooting around on their plates to find a bit of bacon that had actually been cooked. They were grateful for the chance to look, if only for a moment, at something other than the snotlike puddles of raw egg white that surrounded the chilly yolks of their partially fried eggs. What a disaster. Yet they would no more have dreamed of complaining than of robbing a bank.

They stared at Jack for a moment and turned wearily back to their disappointing meals. Jack had not noticed them anyway. His attention was absorbed elsewhere. The reason he had sat down again was because, just as he had risen, a young woman had entered the restaurant. She was accompanied by a middle-aged couple, probably her parents, but Jack scarcely glanced at them. He was only interested in the girl. He recognized her the moment he saw her.

She was the interesting one. The beautiful one.

The one with the pink streaks in her hair. The one he always looked out for when he drove into the base, slowing his jeep down in plenty of time to make sure he got a good look. Each time Jack surprised himself at just how attractive he found this girl. He had certainly never been taken by any of that monstrous muddy regiment before, and the young woman in question was scarcely what he might have thought was his type. Her eyes were often surrounded by great dark purple circles of eye shadow, which made her look like a negative photograph of a panda. On some occasions she had the female gender symbol painted on both cheeks. Jack feared that she might be color blind because of the green lipstick she sometimes wore, although usually it was a garish, aggressive red. Nonetheless, despite all of this, the girl's fresh, sparkling beauty never failed to shine through. She had the sweetest face that Jack had ever seen, and the neatest of bodies, like a dancer. Jack always tried to get a good long look at her as he drove past and now fate had afforded him the opportunity to absorb her properly. The more Jack looked, the more absorbed he became. In fact it would not be putting it too strongly to say that he was transfixed. His mouth watered and his eyes became lost in dreamy contemplation.

The women at the till wondered if perhaps the coffee was improving.

[10]

"**Don't freak** out," his voice said. "It's Jack. Jack Kent."

Polly was freaking out. She stood shaking in her nightshirt, staring at the answering machine as it delivered a voice into her life that she had not heard for more than sixteen years.

She had met him in a roadside restaurant on the A34. She was seventeen and a committed political activist. What is more, she had been a committed political activist in a way that only a seventeen-year-old can be. More committed, more political, and more active than any committed political activist had ever been before her, or so she thought. She would have made the secret love child of Leon Trotsky and Margaret Thatcher look like an uncommitted, apolitical layabout.

Polly described herself as a feminist, a socialist, and an anarchist, which of course made her an extremely dull conversationalist. Small talk becomes wearisome when no two sentences can be negotiated without the words "fascist," "Thatcher," and "capitalist conspiracy" being crowbarred into them. So when Polly had announced her intention of joining the women's peace camp at Greenham Common her parents had secretly been extremely pleased.

"It's only for the summer," Polly assured them, under the impression that they would be devastated.

"Yes, dear, that's fine," her parents said.

"It's just something I feel I have to do," Polly continued. "You see, white male Eurocentric hegemony has developed a culture of violence, which . . ."

Polly's parents' eyes glazed over as she spoke at length about the sociopolitical development of her commitment to the anarcho-feminist peace movement. They had very much preferred it when she had been obsessed with ABBA.

The problem with idealism in the young is that like sex, they think that they are the first people to have thought of it. Polly's parents were lifelong liberals and would have assured anybody who cared to listen that they were very much against the world being destroyed by nuclear war. Yet their daughter bunched them in with Reagan and Genghis Khan and seemed to feel that it was her duty to convert them from the warmongering ways of all previous generations.

"Did you know that the U.S. defense budget for just one day would feed the whole Third World for a year?" Polly would tell them at breakfast over her fourth bowl of muesli, "and what are we doing about it?"

By "we" Polly's parents knew that really she meant them and the truth was that apart from maintaining a standing order to Oxfam, they were not doing very much.

Therefore, although they were certainly going to miss their beloved daughter, it was nonetheless going to be rather a relief to be able to enjoy breakfast again without feeling that by doing so they were shoring up the Pentagon and murdering African babies.

And of course Mr. and Mrs. Slade were very proud of their daughter. They admired her moral zeal. Other kids were going off grape picking in France or working in supermarkets to pay off the loan on their motorbikes, or having it off in Ibiza. Their daughter was saving the planet from complete annihilation. Mr. and Mrs. Slade felt that if she could do that and complete the prescribed reading for her A-level year then she would have spent a useful summer.

And, of course, one thing they did not have to worry about now was boys. Polly was a headstrong girl and between the ages of fourteen and sixteen had alarmed her parents by bringing any number of extremely off-putting young thugs home for tea. Cider-swilling, long-haired bumpkins who kept falling off their mopeds; snarling rude boys in sixteen-hole Doc Martens; cocky New Romantics who wore far too much makeup—and, for a brief, distressing period, a green-haired lad who called himself Johnny Motherfucker and claimed to have eaten a live pigeon. Mercifully, since Polly had discovered politics there had been fewer of these horrible youths hanging about the place, although Mr. and Mrs. Slade lived in fear that on some rally or other their daughter would get involved with an anarcho-squatter peacenik punk with a tattooed penis and rings through his scrotum.

There would be no risk of such disasters at Greenham Common. The Greenham Peace Camp was separatist, women only. Men were not allowed to stay overnight. Mr. and Mrs. Slade thought it all sounded splendid. Summer camping, with plenty of time for reading, in the company of serious and idealistic women, struck them as a very good idea indeed. Of course the first mass evictions and the sight of their daughter on the news being carried away by policemen was rather a shock, but still, better a bobby manhandling her than some dreadful yob who rode a motorbike and washed his jeans in urine.

[11]

Jack skulked behind his newspaper and watched the girl as her parents ordered tea and tea cakes. He watched as they attempted vainly to spread the lump of icy butter that had been crushed into the center of the bun by some joyless slacker in a stupid white hat, dry tea cakes with a bit of butter in the middle being a speciality of the restaurant chain they were in.

When they'd finished, the father figure asked for the bill. Jack sighed to himself, his pleasant diversion nearly over. The little ray of sunshine was about to be extinguished. He hoped the girl would be the last to leave so that he would be able to look at her legs as she walked out.

Then the two older people got up, kissed the girl, and left without her.

This was a surprise. Until that point Jack's interest had been entirely passive. He was merely passing a few minutes of his dull day on his dull tour of duty, eyeing up a pretty girl. Now things were different. The girl was alone and devilish thoughts were playing on his mind. Should he say hello? Of course it was madness. He was a U.S. army officer and she was a peace protester, dedicated to the confusion of all that he held dear. What was more, she was at least ten years his junior.

On the other hand, she was gorgeous and it could do no harm to say hello. She would probably tell him to shove it anyway and there would be an end to the matter.

Polly did not notice Jack approach. She was lost in her own thoughts and was feeling rather sad. This had been her parents' first visit since she had joined the camp and now that they had gone she suddenly felt rather homesick. Strange, she thought, that having spent most of the last five years imagining that all she desired was to leave home she was now discovering that home had its advantages. The devoted love and affection of her parents and a regular supply of clean knickers were two that sprang immediately to mind.

"Can I buy you a cup of coffee, ma'am?" said Jack. "If you can dignify the swill they serve in these places with such a name."

Polly couldn't believe it. An American soldier! She had only ever seen them at a distance before, or whizzing by in their cars. The Americans were a different, more glamorous breed, officers and technicians and the like. It was poor little teenage British squaddies who actually guarded the fence and got sung at.

Having overcome her initial shock, Polly asked Jack to sit down. She was certainly not going to let an opportunity like this go by. Here was her chance to convert the enemy. Jack ordered the coffee and asked if she'd eaten. Polly said that although she had, she'd be happy to do so again. In fact she was starving, having only allowed her parents to order a snack lest they think she was not eating properly at the camp.

If Jack had been at all concerned that his impulsive gesture would result in an awkward silence he need not have worried. While ordering the food the girl managed to call him a fascist, a mass murderer, and a zombie-brained automaton. She also asked him if he ever thought about what he did, appealed to him to desert the army, and inquired whether he knew the temperature at which a human body combusted. From there it was, of course, a short step to a detailed description of the Hiroshima shadows.

"Those people were burned into the walls, you know. Babies' skin peeled away like parchment while their eyeballs literally melted."

Vainly did Jack protest that he too wished only for a peaceful world and that it was his opinion that the vigilance and armored might of NATO's forces had prevented such horrors occurring more often.

"Oh, sure," Polly sneered. "You want to stop nuclear war so you build more bombs. Brilliant. That's like fucking for virginity. You're just a bunch of sweet old peace-loving hippies, aren't you? Do you realize that one day's budget for the U.S. military would feed the entire Third World for an entire year?"

Polly had ordered a three-course meal at Jack's invitation and at this point the tomato soup arrived. Jack was impressed to discover that this girl could even be furious about that. She had good cause to be. This was the time when microwave ovens were still a relatively recent invention, when the microwaves actually continued to be generated even when the door was open, thus making it possible for teenage wage slaves to contract bone cancer while at the same time failing to heat up the food.

"It's hot on the top and cold in the middle. With a skin on it! I mean, how do you do that? It's almost as if it was deliberate."

Jack just nodded and stared. He simply could not get worked up about the soup. He was feeling too happy. She really was beautiful, this wild English rose, and so angry. He loved how angry she was, passionately angry, angry about everything. Angry about nuclear bombs, angry about soup. "The system" certainly had a lot to answer for.

How astonished would Polly's parents have been had they returned at this point. Polly had found a boy, after all. Or, rather, a man, and no punk or hippie either but an American army captain. Their daughter would, of course, have explained that she had only just met the bloke. That he had nothing to do with her at all. But something in the eagerness of her manner, and the way she was blushing beneath the female gender symbols on her cheeks, would have warned them that this was to be no brief encounter.

And how astonished would Jack's parents have been to see their deeply conservative son hanging upon the lips of such a strange-looking girl. A radical girl, a hippie girl, a girl not so different from the students whom Jack Senior had taught in the sixties and whom Jack Junior had despised as traitorous apologists for Hanoi. How they would howl with laughter when, later, they heard from Harry the extraordinary news that their little soldier son had fallen for a subversive! A peacenik! Their Reagan-loving, Red-bashing, liberal-hating offspring, for whom it was and always would be hip to be square, had come under the spell of the enemy.

Because that is certainly what happened. Jack fell for Polly like a man with no parachute. Even at that first meeting he was already half besotted. He wanted their lunch to go on forever. He could not remember having ever been in the company of such an exuberantly free spirit. This girl was the opposite of everything he wanted in his life, and yet he loved it. She was rude, untidy, undisciplined, unfettered, and anarchic, and he loved it. How happy Polly made him feel, how liberating it was just talking to her. Of course Jack knew that he was taking a considerable risk sitting openly in a restaurant with her. She was quite definitely not a suitable dining companion for an army officer, and were he to be spotted it would mean a severe reprimand. But on that special day Jack did not care. In fact, he gloried in the risk he was taking. Polly was making him feel as free spirited as she was herself.

Polly's second course arrived: chips, baked beans, peas, and carrots. She had asked if they had anything vegetarian but this being the days before that type of option was common in British catering, the unpleasant youth in the silly hat had said the best he could do was to take the meat out of a meat and potato pie for her.

Polly squirted red sauce out of a large plastic tomato all over her food and seethed at the fascistic, Thatcherite injustice of it all.

"They might at least offer something that isn't dripping with blood. I think we should protest."

"I thought you just did," Jack replied. After all, Polly had announced loudly that she resented being forced to eat in a fucking charnel house. This had sounded like protest to Jack. The manager (who had enough to worry about what with having arrived at puberty only that morning) scuttled over and told Polly that she was not being forced to eat anywhere and that she was welcome to leave at any time, the sooner the better, in fact.

Polly told the manager that in fact she was being forced to eat in his establishment because multinational capitalism had ensured that the only food available on the roads of Britain was supplied by the owners of the dump in which they sat.

"And when I say food," Polly added, "I mean of course shit."

A pretty comprehensive protest, Jack thought. Certainly enough to be going on with. Polly, however, had other ideas, and, taking out the superglue with which she was wont to block up police padlocks and car doors, she glued the sauce bottles to the table.

"Well, that'll certainly show them," said Jack.

"Nonviolent direct action. Anarchy, mate. You have to do it," Polly assured him.

"Yeah. I'll bet they're really gonna rethink their policy on animal welfare once they find out you vandalized their ketchup."

"Protest is accumulative," Polly assured him.

"Protest is self-indulgent and pointless, pal," said Jack. "Believe me, I know. My parents tried it. They spent the sixties knocking their country over dinner and waving banners at a liberal president. What did they get for their trouble? Richard Nixon. Ha! That showed them. Now they've got Reagan! Jesus, are they pissed. I phone them every time he cuts welfare just to rub it in. They're a couple of sad, fucked-up anachronisms who don't have the sense to see that God is a Conservative and the Gospel is money. The only way you're ever going to change anybody or any institution is to hit 'em in the head or hit 'em in the pocketbook. If you want to hurt these people you take their money."

"Well, ye-es," said Polly, slightly confused.

Jack looked about him. "So, let's go."

"What?" Polly inquired, not yet catching on.

"When I say run," said Jack, "we run."

"You don't mean . . ." Polly began.

"Run!" said Jack.

[12]

If Jack had been trying to find a way to impress Polly he had hit the nail on the head. *This is the stuff!* Polly thought as they charged out of the restaurant and ran for Jack's car. She could scarcely believe that her despised enemy, a member of the U.S. military, could ever do anything so cool as to run out of a restaurant without paying. Never judge a book by its cover, she might have reflected, had she not been so breathless with excitement.

They tumbled into the car and as Jack hit the ignition the sound system leaped into life along with the engine. It was playing Bruce Springsteen, Jack's preferred driving companion, and by a happy chance the tape was cued up on "Born to Run." Suddenly Polly found herself bang in the middle of the Boss's runaway American dream and she shouted with delight as, with tires screeching and Bruce pumping, Jack pulled out of the car park and onto the road.

"This is brilliant!" Polly shouted as Jack kicked down the accelerator, hammered through the gears, cranked up the Boss, and left any pursuers to eat his dust.

About a mile along the road, which they seemed to cover in about fifteen seconds, Jack slammed on the brakes and executed a spectacular hairpin turn off the main road, which nearly threw Polly out of the car. Suddenly they found themselves bumping along what was little more than a dirt track.

"Think I'll give the main roads a miss for half an hour," he remarked casually. "That manager kid is bound to have called the cops by now. Wish I had my off-road jeep four-by-four. Then we could have some fun."

"Four-wheel-drive cars are destroying the countryside," said Polly.

"Yeah. So?" Jack inquired.

They soon arrived at a gate that led into a field and Jack was forced to stop. After that it was all rather spontaneous. They scarcely spoke, just grabbing each other with passionate fury and feeding on each other's mouths and faces, tearing at each other's clothes. Later on, Jack would remember thinking that Polly even kissed angrily or at least with the same kind of serious commitment that she seemed to put into everything else she did. Polly was not thinking anything at all. Her mind had been emptied by this sudden and completely unfamiliar surging physical desire. Nothing like it had ever happened to her before. She had often wondered over the past three or four years what true passion felt like and whether she would ever experience it herself. She would wonder no more.

Then had come the inevitable environmental frustrations. It just isn't easy to make love in cars. In his efforts to get to Polly Jack very soon found himself with his knee in the glove compartment and his stomach impaled upon the gear stick. It was most frustrating. Jack had not experienced anything like it since high school and his body had been suppler then. He was halfway to being on top of Polly but he could get no further, not without major organ removal.

"Fucking gear stick," Jack growled, speaking for the first time since they had fallen upon each other.

"It's your own fault for driving a TR7," said Polly, feeling rather self-conscious because Jack had one of her breasts in his hand. "Everyone knows a TR7 is a wanker's car."

"Well, it would need to be," Jack replied, extricating himself. "You certainly can't fuck in one."

It was no good. They would have to go elsewhere. Then, as if by magic, the sun burst through what had until then been a rather gray day. The field beyond the gate turned golden. A glorious meadow carpeted with long, swaying grass with butterflies hovering lazily above it. Had that field been candlelit, strewn with red velvet cushions, and with Barry White's greatest hits wafting softly from speakers hidden in the hedges, it could not have seemed more like a good place for sex.

"Come on," said Jack.

They climbed the gate and fell together into their five-acre bed.

Deflowered amongst the flowers, Polly thought to herself, being not quite out of her teenage poetry stage.

It was a disaster. Making love in a field is almost as difficult as doing it in a car, especially if it's been raining the night before and you have a problem with pollen and what looked like soft grass turns out to be some kind of organic barbed wire. It's probably just about possible if you've brought a ground sheet, a mattress, a blanket, some DDT, and a scythe. Otherwise, forget it. Pretty soon Jack's elbows and knees were in cowpats, Polly's knickers were in shreds, and something with two hundred legs and fifteen sets of teeth had crawled up his backside.

For the second time since they had begun their desperate groping Polly and Jack were forced to put their passion on hold. With Polly's virginity still pretty much intact, Jack suggested a hotel.

"OK," said Polly, getting up and putting what was left of her knickers back on. "But I haven't got much money, so I'll have to pay you back later for my half of the bill."

Jack laughed, feeling a tremendous wave of affection sweep over him for this strangely intense girl. At that point the sun, which had disappeared into some clouds, came out again behind Polly and all of a sudden she was bathed and silhouetted with an almost luminous golden glow. She looked like some kind of pure and lovely teen angel and Jack's conscience began to trouble him.

"Polly, how old are you?" he asked.

"Seventeen," said Polly defensively.

"Oh, Christ," said Jack.

"But I'm a lot more mature than you, mate," Polly added. "I know that it's dangerous to play with guns."

Seventeen. Jack had been hoping for at least nineteen, possibly twenty, although he knew that twenty would be the absolute limit.

"Polly. I'm thirty-two. I'm fifteen years older than you."

Polly shrugged.

"Are you a virgin?" Jack asked.

"What if I am?"

It was worse than Jack had thought.

"I can't do this to you," he said.

Suddenly it was not the sunlight that made Polly glow but righteous indignation. Her cheeks reddened and her eyes took on a fiery glint.

"Listen, you patronizing bastard," she said. "You aren't doing anything *to* me. I do things for myself, all right? If I choose to go to bed with you—or in this case to a field with you—if I choose to use your body for my pleasure, then that's my business. I am a woman and males do not have a say in my life. In fact, emotionally and politically I'm a lesbian. It just happens to be my misfortune that I fancy men, that's all."

Jack had never been overly receptive to radical feminism in the past, but he was warming to it. "OK," he said.

They got back into the car and drove to a nearby hotel. It was a large, redbrick, eighties' place, built on a roundabout in the middle of nowhere with toy-town turrets and pastel-colored Roman pillars in the foyer. Polly wanted to hate the place as a prime example of the reckless urbanization of the countryside, but she could not because in fact she found it all desperately romantic. This, considering that the hotel was really just a large car park with a leisure complex, conference center, and executive miniature golf course attached, Jack found very touching.

There was some trouble at the check-in desk, not because of Polly's age—she was, after all, perfectly legal and did not look particularly young. It was the T-shirt she was wearing that required careful negotiation, the objection being that it had a picture of a cruise missile on it that had been altered to make it resemble a penis. Polly explained that this was a comment on the masculine nature of war.

"I'm afraid that other guests might find it offensive," the receptionist explained.

"Oh, and I suppose nuclear arsenals aren't offensive?" Polly inquired.

"Nobody is attempting to bring a nuclear arsenal into the hotel," said the receptionist. "Perhaps the gentleman could lend you his coat?"

Jack could not do this because he did not wish to advertise the uniform he was wearing underneath. Polly was clearly a loose cannon and a troublemaker and Jack did not want the manager phoning his colonel and complaining about the type of girl American officers brought to the hotel. In the end a compromise was reached. Polly reluctantly agreed to keep her arms folded across her chest while she remained in the public parts of the hotel, thus covering the offending political statement.

"I thought this country was supposed to have freedom of speech. I don't think!" Polly muttered as Jack led her away.

And so began a relationship that very soon was to become an intense and all-consuming love affair. A love affair that, although in some ways desperately brief, would last a lifetime. Two people of different ages, different backgrounds, and, most important, utterly different principles and values were to be bound together from that ecstatic moment on.

Newton said that for every action there is an equal and an opposite reaction. Jack and Polly certainly lent substance to that observation.

A few days after Jack's first encounter with Polly he wrote to Harry, angrily anticipating the sibling ridicule he knew he must endure.

"*Oh yeah, ho, ho,*" he wrote. "*You think this somehow proves your piss-weak psychological theories, huh? You think that this girl is like Mom, am I right, Harry? Of course you do. You're so transparent. Well, forget it. In fact before you forget it, shove it up your ass, then forget it. This girl is not a bit like Mom, or Pa, or you. She's like me! Yeah, that's right, like me, because she's a fighter, the real thing, a two-fisted bruiser with poison for spit. OK, maybe what she fights for is a bunch of crap, in fact it is a bunch of crap. Quite frankly I hear less woolly thinking when sheep bleat. But so what? She's got guts and she fights. She doesn't sit on her ass smoking tea leaves like Mom. She doesn't think that stuffing envelopes for the Democrats once every four years makes her an activist. What is more, Harry old pal, she hasn't hidden away from life making dumb furniture that a factory could make better and at a tenth of the cost, like you, asshole! Polly is a soldier, she's out there, punching hard and kicking ass for what she believes in. Besides which, she's the sexiest thing I ever saw in my whole life, so screw you.*"

When Harry read the letter he was pleased. Despite its abrasive tone it was by far the most romantic letter Jack had ever written. In fact it was the only romantic letter he had ever written. The only time Harry could remember his brother being even half as excited was when he had been promoted to captain at a younger age than any of his West Point contemporaries. Jack had never been enthusiastic about anything except sports and the army. He had certainly never talked about being in love and yet now his entire soul seemed to be singing with it. Of course Harry was happy for Jack, but in the midst of that happiness he was also uneasy. It seemed to Harry that his brother now loved two things—soldiering and this English girl. It did not take all of Harry's intellectual powers to work out that these two things were not compatible. Harry could see that in a very short time the crunch would come and Jack would have to decide where his loyalties lay.

It was Newtonian physics again; for every action there is an equal and opposite reaction. Jack's current happiness was surely storing up an equal quantity of unhappiness for someone.

[13]

"Polly? Polly! Are you there? Are you there, Polly?" The long-lost but still familiar voice breathed out of Polly's answering machine. It was rich and low and seductive as it had always been.

"Are you there?" Jack said again into the telephone.

A little way along the street Peter was getting frustrated. He'd been surprised to see the telephone box occupied. It never had been before at that time of night. He felt angry. It was 2:15 in the morning. People had no business using public telephones at 2:15 in the morning. Particularly his own private, public telephone, a telephone with which Peter felt a special bond. Many times on that very phone Peter had heard the voice of the woman he loved. The cold mechanics within its receiver's scratched and greasy plastic shell had vibrated with her adored tones. That phone, his phone, had been the medium through which Polly's precious lips had caressed his senses.

"It's you, isn't it?" she would hiss. Hiss directly into his ear, so that he could almost imagine he felt her breath. "Fuck off! Fuck off! Just fuck off and leave me alone, you disgusting little prick!"

Peter didn't mind Polly's anger at all. Some relationships were like that, fiery and tempestuous. After all, he certainly gave as good as he got. Peter liked Polly's fury. It was passionate, exciting. So many nights he had stood listening to those blistering, heavenly tones. Looking at the photographs he'd laid out on top of the tattered telephone directories, sucking on his precious straw, and masturbating into the lining of his overcoat.

That telephone box was where Peter had had sex with Polly. It was his telephone box and now some bastard was using it.

Peter felt the knife in his pocket.

A switchblade he had bought in Amsterdam one night when he had not had the guts to go into one of the shops that had women in the windows. Peter liked to carry that knife about with him for his protection and also because he fantasized that one day he would find himself in a position to use it in defense of Polly. He imagined himself chancing upon her in the street; she would be surrounded by vicious thugs who would be taunting her, pulling at her clothes. She would be weeping with terror. He would kill them all before claiming his reward!

Peter fondled the switch-blade in his pocket.

Still Polly did not pick up the phone. In fact she did not move. She couldn't; she was too shocked. The only animation she could have managed at that point of supreme surprise would have been to fall over. She avoided this by gripping onto a chair back for support.

"It's Jack," she heard him say again. "Jack Kent."

She knew it was Jack Kent, for heaven's sake! She would never forget that voice if she lived to be two hundred and fifty years old. No matter what was to happen to her, be it premature senility, severe blows to the head, a full frontal lobotomy, she would still be able to bring that voice instantly to mind. Its timbre was resonant in her bones. Jack's voice was a part of her. But what was it doing broadcasting out of her answering machine in Stoke Newington at 2:15 in the morning? His was quite simply the last voice in the world that Polly had expected to hear. If the Queen had woken her up to ask her round to Buck House for a curry and a few beers it would have seemed a more natural occurrence than this.

Still receiving no reply, Jack's voice continued. "Weird, huh? Bet you're surprised . . . Me too. I'm surprised and I knew I was going to call! How surprising is that? I just got into town. It's only ten P.M. in New York, so it's not late at all. Don't be so parochial, we live in a global village now."

It was the same old Jack, still cool, still cracking gags.

Still vibrant with sensual promise.

"I can't believe I just heard your voice, even on a machine. It's just the same . . ." Jack's voice was even softer now. Even softer, even lower. "Are you there, Polly? Look, I know it's late . . . real late . . . but maybe not too late, huh?"

Too late for what? Surely he didn't mean . . . ? Polly could not begin to think what he meant. She could scarcely begin to think at all.

[14]

Jack kept talking. He knew she could hear him.

"I want to see you, Polly. Are you there, Polly? I think you're there. Pick up the phone, Polly. Please pick up the phone."

Across the street Jack could see that the man he had noticed earlier was walking slowly toward the phone box. In his hand was what looked like it might be the hilt of a knife, but there seemed to be no blade. The man walked right up to within a yard or so of the phonebox and then stood and stared. Perhaps he wanted to use the phone. Perhaps he wanted to use the phone box as a lavatory. Perhaps he did not know what he wanted. Whatever was going on, it did not take the instincts of a soldier to work out that this man meant Jack no good.

Their eyes met through the cloudy plastic of the window. Peter and Jack, two men from opposite sides of the world, connected by a woman whom they had both wronged, with whom by rights neither should have been having anything to do at all.

Jack kept his eyes fixed on Peter's. Matching him stare for stare. Meanwhile, he spoke again into the phone. Delivering his voice back into Polly's life.

"I think you're there, Polly. Are you there? Pick up the phone, Polly."

He imagined her standing in her flat, staring at the machine. Its red light blinked back at her.

"Are you there? Pick up the phone, Polly."

Suddenly Polly did as she was bidden and snatched up the phone, fearful that in her hesitation the voice would disappear again, back into the locked vault of her memory, where it had resided for so many years. Clunk. Whirr. Clunk. The answering machine announced its disengagement.

"Jack? Is it really you, Jack?"

Down in the street, outside the phonebox, there was a glint, a flash of orange streetlamp light reflected on shining metal. Peter had pressed the button in his switchblade, and its wicked blade had leaped out into the night, thrusting itself forward from within the hilt, from within Peter's clenched fist. It glowed orange in the night like a straight, frozen flame.

"Yes, Polly, it's me," said Jack. "Listen, can you hold the line for just one second?"

It was not what Polly had expected to hear, and it was not, of course, what Jack had expected to say. You do not, after all, return from the dead, wake someone up in the middle of the night, give them the shock of their life, and then put them on hold. Circumstances, however, had forced Jack's hand. At this supreme moment in his plans, in his life, fate had suddenly dealt Jack a wild card. A mugger had clearly blundered into his life and the situation would have to be dealt with.

Jack kicked open the door of the phone box. It was a good kick, firm and accurate. A confident kick, which connected with the frame of the door rather than the windows and sent the whole thing swinging outward at speed and into the man who stood outside. Peter had been in the process of reaching for the door at the time and the force hit him first in the hand and then in the face, surprising him considerably and making him drop his knife.

As Peter leaned down to pick up the knife the door swung closed and Jack kicked it again. This time the door hit the top of Peter's head and he went over into the gutter. Jack left the phone hanging, stepped outside, and with one final bit of confident footwork sent Peter's knife down a convenient drain.

"If you want to make a call you wait, OK?" said Jack to Peter. "I thought the British were supposed to be good at standing in line. If you disturb my call again you'll regret it."

With that, Jack returned to the box and picked up the phone.

"Sorry, Polly, some guy thought he owned the call box."

Peter decided not to wait. He got up and ran. He was unbalanced and inadequate in any number of ways but his instincts of self-preservation were entirely healthy. He hadn't wanted a fight anyway and he had not intended to use the knife, he had just wanted to scare the fellow off. Since that was now clearly out of the question Peter decided to get himself away and consider his position.

Perhaps he would not telephone Polly tonight after all. His hand stung and his head hurt and he felt in no shape to begin the delicate task of restarting their relationship. What is more, he had promised his mother faithfully that he had no current plans to call her. She had made him promise again only that night. He had been trying to sneak out of the house quietly, but she had heard him and had come running from her room in her nightie. Peter hated seeing his mother in her nightie; she seemed so much older and more shapeless.

"It's gone midnight, Peter. Where are you going? You're not going to phone that bitch, are you?"

"I'm going for a walk, and don't call her a bitch. She's all right."

"I'll call her what I like, lad, and as long as you live in my house you'll leave her alone."

Peter had shrugged and headed for the door but she'd grabbed him by the ear.

One day she would do that one too many times.

"Do you promise?"

"Yes, Mum, I promise."

In fact, Peter's promises to his mother were pretty worthless. He had also promised that he would not obtain Polly's new unlisted telephone number. Computer hacking was something that the law took more seriously than swearing at people over their intercoms. Peter's mother was worried that if Peter did it again he would be put away. He had done it again, though, and Polly's number had been burning holes in his thoughts for weeks now.

But he would not phone her tonight. The tough American in his phone box had spoiled it. He would just walk up the street, round the corner, and past the building in which Polly lived. Peter liked to stand there in the emptiness of the night and stare up at her window. Imagining her alone in her bed. Imagining himself beside her.

Polly was not in bed. She was standing, phone in hand, shaking with shock.

"It can't be you, Jack. That's insane," said Polly. "What, now? You want to visit now?"

"Yeah, I'm in town."

"In town!"

He had said it like it explained everything.

"This is insane."

"Don't keep saying it's insane, Polly. Why is it insane?"

There were so many reasons why it was insane that Polly

couldn't begin to answer that question adequately. It would have taken her all night, all week, the rest of her life.

"I'm coming around," said Jack.

"No! Where are you? How long will you be? How long is not long? Jack! Jack!"

But the line had gone dead.

Polly put down the receiver and slumped into her office chair, which was actually one of her kitchen chairs. Polly only had four upright chairs, one of which was kept permanently by her desk, except on the rare occasions when it was required for a dinner party. If Polly ever entertained more than three people at the same time someone had to bring their own chair.

Polly's insides were doing somersaults. What could be going on? Why had Jack come back? Where had he come from? What could he possibly want with her now?

Such were the larger questions that tormented Polly as she sat there, shaking, in the shadowy half-light of her room, but they would have to wait. There were practical considerations to be dealt with and she must pull herself together. First and foremost she was in her night attire, if night attire was not too grand a term to describe the slightly ratty, threadbare old man's shirt she was wearing. She must get dressed and quickly. No matter how weird the situation, Polly had standards. She did not receive visitors dressed only in a shirt.

Rushing to her knickers drawer she grabbed a vaguely current-looking pair and put them on. The jeans she had worn on the previous day were still concertinaed on the floor where she had stepped out of them a few hours earlier. She stepped back into them and began hurriedly to pull them up. Then she had second thoughts. With her jeans already lodged halfway up her legs, she waddled across her flat and, flinging open a closet, began pulling out dresses. She held one up to herself in the mirror and, finding it unsatisfactory, tried another. Then a third and a fourth. Finally she chose the shortest and most flattering of the selection. She told herself that it was simply the smartest and most practical choice, but actually it was the sexiest.

Polly was about to remove her nightshirt and put on the dress when the front door buzzer buzzed.

"Christ's buggery bollocks!"

Polly stepped back out of the jeans and rushed over to the front door of her little flat. She lived on the top floor of a large house, one of the thousands of houses that once were home to prosperous Mary Poppins families. Places built to house twelve people and that ended up providing for twelve households. "There's room in this conversion for four decent-sized flats or six small ones," the property developers of the early eighties would say. "So what do you reckon? Fourteen? Or is that pushing it?"

That particular speculative bubble had, of course, long since burst, and there were now a mere six buttons on the front of Polly's building. One of which led right up to the attic of the house, which was Polly's home.

Polly gingerly took up the receiver of the entry-phone intercom that hung on the wall beside her front door. Her hand was shaking. This was insane. Why had he come back? She was furious, of course, all the old emotions returning, the ancient wound exploding open, but she was thrilled as well. How could she not be? Never had she expected to hear his voice again, and yet here he was, only four floors below, standing at her own front door.

"Hello," she said, attempting a noncommittal, matter-of-fact tone and failing entirely. "Is that you?"

Suddenly she was half her age. A young girl again, young and nervous and excited.

"Is that really you?"

"Your light was on. It's never been on this late before."

Polly stepped back as if she had received a blow. She nearly fell. The receiver dropped from her hand and bashed against the wall, swinging on its curly cord.

"Can't you sleep?"

The hated voice, the hated and shocking voice drifted up from the dangling receiver.

"I thought you might want company. If you tell the police I came round my mum will say I was at home with her. Are you wearing any clothes, Polly? Have you got a bra on? What color are your knickers? I bet you aren't wearing any this late at night, are you?"

Polly's eyes were full of tears now. Through the watery mist she focused on the red panic button that stood out upon the wall behind the door. It was so located that should an intruder ever push open the door, forcing Polly backward into her flat, the button would then be in immediate reach. There was another one on the wall by her bed. Polly wanted to push those buttons, she wanted to alert the whole house to her persecution, to set alarm bells ringing there and in the local police station, but she knew that she must not do it. Her enemy was not at the gate, he was in the street and would no doubt soon scurry off as he always did. He was no physical threat. There was no justification in summoning a screaming squad car, and the police did not take kindly to having their services abused. One does not cry wolf with panic buttons. When you push them you need to be believed.

Blinking back her tears, Polly grabbed up the receiver.

"I'm calling the police. I am calling the fucking police right now! Fuck off! Please fuck off!"

"You use that word a lot, don't you, Polly?" said Peter. "Is that because you like it, Polly? Fucking? Is that what you like?"

[15]

Downstairs the Bug turned and scurried away. He had taken a big risk ringing her doorbell like that. He'd certainly not intended to do it. He knew it would probably mean a police visit, more social workers, his mum in tears. But seeing her light shining so late, knowing that she, like him, was still awake in the small hours of the morning, perhaps even thinking about him, that had been too much for him to resist. Now, however, he must retreat. If Polly did call the police and he were found on her street no denial from him or testimony from his mother would prevent his arrest.

Leaning against the wall beside her door Polly struggled to control her pounding heart and the tears that she could feel beginning to prickle up into her eyes. Her legs felt weak. Slowly she slid down the wall, her back cold against the plaster until she sat upon her haunches. Jack and the Bug? Within minutes of each other? What could be going on? What was happening?

Perhaps half a minute went by before the front door buzzer sounded again. She was waiting for it but it still made her jump. Like the phone, the buzzer seemed much louder than it did in the day. Even in Polly's emotional state she found herself wondering if it could be heard in the flat below. She hoped not. She was currently in dispute with the man downstairs. He was a milkman who rose every morning at four and put on his radio, a habit that had caused Polly to voice numerous complaints. She did not want to arm the man with counteraccusations of late-night comings and goings.

The buzzer buzzed again.

She would not answer it. It would be the Bug again. Polly knew his pattern well enough. He tended to attack (which was how Polly privately described the Bug's intrusions into her life), then attack once or twice more before disappearing, long before any policeman might deign to turn up. On the other hand, supposing it wasn't the Bug? Supposing it was him, Jack? Unlikely, of course. After all, it was only a minute or two since Jack had telephoned, but he'd said he wouldn't be long . . . If indeed it had been Jack at all . . . In her distraught state Polly found herself prey to the most paranoid of musings. Had the Bug found out about Jack? Was he somehow playing a terribly cruel trick on her? Had she merely imagined that the voice had been that of her former lover?

Buzz.

She had to answer it. So what if it was the Bug? She would call him a sad no-dick. What was more, if she did not feel justified in using her panic button she could certainly let off her rape alarm into the intercom. Sod the milkman, sod everyone else in the house if it woke them up. They weren't being stalked. She would shatter the Bug's eardrum. Polly went to her bedside table and took up the little alarm tube. Suitably armed, she returned to the intercom and picked up the receiver.

"Yes?" This time her voice was like steel. Fuck-off-and-die steel. Her thumb hovered over the rape-alarm button.

"Polly. It's me. It's Jack."

It was Jack. There could be no doubt. There was only one Jack. The relief! The blessed relief. But what about the Bug?

"Jack. Is there anyone else down there? A man?"

"What?"

"It's a perfectly simple question! Is there anyone else there, Jack? Thin, pale, mousy hair?"

Down in the street Jack glanced about him. He did not know what he had expected Polly to say to him, but it was not this. The reunion conversation was not shaping up the way he had expected. First he had been forced to put her on hold, now she was asking him about other men.

"There's no one in the street but me, Polly. Can I come up?"

Polly struggled to become mistress of her emotions and her thoughts. It must be coincidence. Jack and the Bug could not be connected. It just so happened that on this very strange and crowded night the two men who, in their different ways, had hijacked Polly's emotions more effectively than any other people in her life should clash. The Bug had simply chosen this night to revert to form, the same night that Jack, Jack of all people in the world, had decided to drop by.

"What is this about, Jack?" she said into the mouthpiece.

"Can I come up?" Jack's voice replied from four floors below.

Everything seemed to be happening at a breathtaking speed. "I'm in my nightie, Jack!"

Jack did not reply to this. He considered making some smart-alec comment but decided against it, opting to leave her protest hanging on the wire that connected them. The tactic worked. Polly realized that however inappropriate the time and the circumstances might be, she was never going to simply tell Jack to go away.

"I'm on the top floor."

Polly pressed the buzzer and let Jack back into her life.

[16]

Watching from a little way along the street, in the pitch-black shadows of a derelict shop doorway, Peter's inner turmoil was the equal of Polly's. He could not believe his anguished eyes. A man was entering Polly's flat, and at 2:20 in the morning! It could only be Polly he was visiting. Hers was the only light that burned in the whole building. What was worse, the man who Polly was allowing into her home at such an hour was the vicious brute who had attacked him and, what's more, attacked him with scarcely an ounce of provocation.

Peter could hardly begin to imagine what was going on. To his knowledge Polly had no current boyfriend. There had been a man a few months earlier but he didn't seem to visit anymore. Perhaps it was the bricks that Peter had thrown through the man's car window on three separate occasions that had put him off. Recently Polly had always been alone. But now she wasn't. Now she was entertaining a violent American in the middle of the night.

Peter slunk farther back into the shadows. He must concentrate, decide upon a course of action. He dug into the pocket of his coat for the bag of sweets he had brought with him as a comfort against the lonely boredom of the night. Sucking noisily, he tried to think.

Upstairs, behind the glowing curtain, Polly was again acutely aware of her appearance. She was still wearing nothing more than an old shirt and a pair of knickers and there was a gentleman caller upon her doorstep; it would not do. She rushed to her bed and grabbed the dress she'd chosen and also some lipstick from her hand-bag. Catching sight of herself in the mirror she could only groan at her pillow hair and the slight reddening around her eyes caused by her crying.

An unbiased observer might have thought that despite the strangeness of the situation and despite everything that had happened in the past, Polly still wanted to look attractive for Jack.

Knowing that she had only the time in which it takes a man to walk up four flights of stairs, Polly attempted to brush her hair, wipe her eyes, and pull off her nightshirt all at the same time. She soon realized that these activities were incompatible. Particularly if one is also attempting to apply lipstick and search the unsorted clean washing bag for an unladdered pair of tights.

"Calm. Stay calm," Polly said to herself as her stomach executed a particularly startling element of the Olympic gymnastic routine, which it had been performing ever since Polly had been awakened scarcely five minutes before.

Outside Polly's flat, in the well of the building, Jack was climbing the last flight of stairs.

So this is where she ended up, he was thinking.

There is always something rather depressing about the communal areas of multiple-household houses. The mounds of junk mail and local advertising freesheets behind the front door. The piles of letters addressed to long-since-departed occupants stacked on the rickety hall table. The bicycles obstructing the way, the unloved and unwashed stair carpet, the large and perplexing stain on the elderly wallpaper. The single framed print hanging on the wall on the first landing, the dead lightbulbs suspended pointlessly from their dusty wires.

Such an extraordinary visit, thought Jack, and such ordinary surroundings. It was enough to quite depress a man.

Arriving at Polly's door, Jack checked the number one more time against the information in his file and knocked. Inside Polly yelped and stubbed her toe against a chair.

It was too late to get dressed. Swearing quietly, she pulled her nightshirt back down (better an old shirt than topless, she reasoned) and snatched up her dressing gown from where she had left it on the floor. One glance told her that it was not acceptable. It was as old and stained and horrid as the stairwell outside. No eyes but hers should ever look upon it. Stuffing the offending gown under the bed, she ran to the cupboard from which she had taken her selection of dresses and, scrabbling inside amongst the Chinese puzzle of wire hangers, she located and pulled out another gown. It was a tiny fluffy one, a Christmas present, slightly see-through and trimmed with fake fur. She had never worn it and she certainly could not do so now. She would rather be stained and torn than completely ludicrous and slightly pervy.

There was another knock. Polly could prevaricate no longer. In desperation she flung on a plastic raincoat. It did not look good, but it covered more of her than her nightshirt did, and it would have to do.

Polly approached her front door and peered through the spy hole. She recognized Jack instantly; even the darkness and the magnified fisheye effect of the spy hole could not disguise that handsome face and classically firm American jaw.

Jack was back.

Polly took off the chain and opened the door.

There he stood, in the shadows of the upstairs landing.

Like a spy.

He had on one of those timeless American gabardine overcoats that could as easily be worn by Humphrey Bogart or Harrison Ford. A coat that is forever stylish; like Coke and Elvis, age does not wither them. Jack wore it well, the collar turned up as with all the best men of mystery, and the belt knotted at the waist. Very little light emanated from Polly's lamplit room, and Jack was illuminated only by the streetlight orange that glowed through the bare window of the landing. Peter Lorre seemed almost to be hovering at Jack's elbow. He did not actually say "Here's looking at you, kid," but he might as well have done.

"Jack? It really is you, isn't it?"

Polly was also in shadow, dimly backlit by the glow of her bedside lamp. The whole scene was classic *noir.*

"Hello, Polly. It's been a while."

For a moment it seemed as if she would embrace him. For a moment she might have done. Then the memory of his betrayal descended upon her and turned what had begun to look like a smile into a frown.

"Yes, yes, it's been a while," she said, stepping away from him, back into her room. "Why change the habit of half a lifetime? What are you doing here?"

"I came to visit with you."

He said it as if it was a reasonable thing to say. As if no further explanation was required.

"Visit?! Now?!"

"Yes."

"Don't be bloody stupid. We don't have anything to say to each other. We have nothing to do with each other. What is this about?"

"Nothing," he said. "It isn't about anything, it's a social call."

"Oh well, that's nice. Perhaps I'd better put the kettle on and crack open a packet of my finest custard creams. It's after two o'clock in the fucking morning!"

"I know what time it is. Who were you expecting?"

"What do you mean?"

Polly felt it was she who should be asking the questions.

"Who's the thin man, Polly? The guy you asked me about, the guy who was supposed to be in the street?"

Where could she start? She didn't even know Jack and now she was supposed to explain to him that she was in the process of being stalked by an obsessive. She was supposed to stand in her doorway in the small hours of the morning and talk to a virtual stranger about the worst thing that had ever happened to her.

Or perhaps the second worst thing, but then Jack knew all about that already.

"It's a man who's been bothering me, that's all. I don't think he'll call again."

"Bothering you? What do you mean, bothering you? Like is he your husband or something? Have I walked into a domestic here?"

This was ridiculous. Suddenly it was Polly who was having to explain herself. Only a few minutes before, she'd been asleep, and now she was filling this man in on her personal details.

"No, a stranger. They call them stalkers. He's a nuisance, that's all. He thinks he loves me and rings my bell occasionally. It's not a problem or a big deal. Forget it."

Polly always described her torment in a far lighter tone than she actually felt. Like many a victim before her, she found her pathetic vulnerability rather embarrassing. It made her feel weak and inadequate. After all, if it was her life that was being attacked rather than other people's, perhaps the problem lay with her? Perhaps it was her fault.

Jack was thinking about his recent violent encounter at the telephone box. Thin, pale, mousy hair. The description fitted. On the other hand, it would have fit a million men.

"Actually, there was a guy like that hanging around the call box," said Jack, "but he's not out there now and I don't think he'll be back. Would it be OK to come in?"

And with that Polly realized that even in this supreme moment of strangeness, the Bug was taking over. That was the absolutely worst aspect of the Bug's crash landing into her life. She just couldn't get the bastard off her mind. Whatever she was doing he was always there. She had not been able to fully appreciate a single thing in her life since the nightmare began. Parties, shows, work. Everything had been affected by his existence.

But this, this was different. This was bigger than the Bug, bigger than anything. Jack was back, and he wanted to come in.

"No, you can't bloody come in!"

As if she would let him in. As if she wanted anything to do with him.

"Please, Polly."

"No! I'm not going to just—"

"Please, Polly. Let me in. If you don't I'll just keep standing here on your landing. It'll be morning in a few hours. What will you tell the other people who live in the house?"

The same voice, the same charming, sexy voice.

"Why the hell would I let you in?"

Jack suggested that old times' sake was surely a good enough reason, and it was, of course. That and the fact that Polly absolutely longed to let him in.

"For old times' sake I ought to kick you in the balls."

"Well, in that case you'd better do it inside. We don't want to disturb the neighbors."

Polly looked at Jack and tried to pull herself together a little, assuming what she hoped was a cool, emotionally invulnerable expression. Interested, certainly, but detached, reserved. In control of her space and her emotions. Jack thought merely that she still had a nice smile. He smiled back at her, his old smile, still fresh as a young boy's. That smile was so familiar to Polly, so inseparable from her memories of Jack that she could almost have imagined that he had not used it since. That he had kept it carefully in some safe place so that it would remain new and sparkling until the day he brought it out again, just for her. But it wasn't true. Polly knew that Jack used that smile every day. Whenever he wanted anything.

Polly stood aside. What else could she do? Jack walked past her and into the small room. She closed the door behind him, put her rape alarm back on the bedside table, and there they were. Alone together again.

They stood staring at each other, neither of them really knowing what to say or do next. Then suddenly Polly found herself enveloped in Jack's arms. She did not know how it happened, whether she had crossed the floor to him or whether he had grabbed her, or whether they had simply blended together by instant osmosis. But it happened. For a moment at least they held each other and in Polly's heart a tiny spark leaped instantly into life, a spark that had long lain hidden amongst the dead ashes of the ferocious furnace that had once burned between them.

[17]

"**Oh, God!**" Polly shrieked.

"Oh, God. Oh, sweet Jesus! Oh, God!"

Strange how some people discover their religious side while orgasming. Polly never bothered God at all as a rule, in fact she was an agnostic, an atheist, even, if she was feeling brave. Yet while in the throes of carnal climax Polly could make the very heavens ring with her piety and devotion. In fact since that day, only a few weeks earlier, when Polly had discovered sex, the Almighty had scarcely had a moment's peace.

"Oh. Oh. Yes . . . yes, that's it, that's it! Oh God, oh God, oh please, harder, longer, longer, harder . . . oh yes, oh please . . . Please . . . Yes yes yes yes!"

And then finally it was over. A quite spectacular orgasm, fueled with love and lust and all the gay abandon of youth, had run its noisy course. Slowly the room returned to normal, the overhead light stopped swinging on its cord, the teacups on the bedside table ceased to rattle, and the plaster clung less desperately to the walls and ceiling. Jack rolled off Polly's quivering body and reached for his cigarettes.

"So, did you come?"

Jack could joke at a time like that. He was older, experienced.

Confident and witty. American in the way Americans are supposed to be. Sexily sardonic and capable of sparking a Zippo cigarette lighter into life using only one hand.

"Just fooling," he said. "I imagine that there are people in other parts of the country who know you came. Certainly the only people in this hotel who don't know you came are either deaf or dead."

"Sorry. Was I too noisy?"

"Not for me, I'm used to it. I used earplugs."

Polly laughed, but she was embarrassed. Most people feel a little awkward and exposed when it comes to the noises they make during sex and it's even worse when you're only seventeen.

Jack lit two cigarettes and gave one to Polly.

"Don't worry, I'll call reception and tell them you're a Christian fundamentalist seeking enlightenment, asking God to give it to you longer and harder."

Polly felt that Jack's joke had run its course. She might have been young, but she was a woman out of whom only so much piss could be taken.

"Look, I was enjoying myself, all right? And to do that I need to express myself. People should express themselves more. People are too uptight. If people recognized their true feelings a bit more and let them out occasionally there'd be a lot less anger and violence in the world."

"OK, OK. Fine. I'm glad to have been a part of your personal fulfillment program. There was me thinking we were having sex and it turns out you were making a contribution to world peace."

Polly and Jack smoked in silence for a few moments. Polly wasn't really angry. In fact she loved fighting with Jack. She loved everything about Jack with the exception of his "Death or Glory" tattoo. Never before in her short life had she experienced such emotions, such passion. Every atom of her physical self tingled with it. The tips of her toes were in love, the hair on her head was in love, the backs of her knees were in love. And such exciting love, dangerous and wrong. Illicit love, forbidden fruit.

Polly stretched out under the covers and felt the crisp clean hotel sheets against her body. What luxury. Only rarely did Polly experience such exotic delights as clean sheets, let alone fresh soap and towels. And a lavatory! Her own personal lavatory. With a door! Only a person who does not normally have the use of one can understand just how wonderful having a lavatory is. Polly would sit on it for half an hour and read the hotel brochures, never tiring of news and minibreaks for two in the Cotswolds, the Peaks, and the heart of England's glorious Lakeland. Jack said he sometimes felt that Polly only slept with him in order to use the toilet.

"That's not true, Jack," Polly assured him. "You're forgetting the little chocolate mints the maids leave on the pillows."

Jack got out of bed, crossed the room, drew back the curtain slightly, and looked out.

"Can't we have the curtains open occasionally?" Polly asked. "It feels so claustro'."

"No," Jack replied. "It makes me feel too exposed. I mean, if we were caught together . . ."

Why did he have to remind her about that? Just when she was so happy. He was always reminding her about that.

"I know. I know! You don't have to go on about it."

"Hey, baby, I do have to go on about it because that's how I stay careful. And I have to stay careful because if my colonel ever found out about us my career would be over, you hear that? Everything I've worked at since I was seventeen would be gone. You're only seventeen right now, Polly. You don't have a life to throw away yet, but I do. They'd court-martial me, you know that? They might even throw me in the hole."

Jack returned to bed. Some ash from Polly's cigarette fell onto the sheet. She tried to brush it off but only made it worse.

"Leave it," said Jack irritably. "We're paying."

"I hate that kind of attitude," Polly snapped. "We've paid so we can act irresponsibly. And I hate this sneaking about too, this constant tension."

"I do not have a choice but to sneak about. I have to be discreet, which is something, incidentally, you have made considerably more difficult by your decision to dye your hair puke color."

In her heart of hearts Polly had to admit that the orange and green highlight effect she had tried to create had not really worked.

"If you don't like sneaking about, baby," Jack continued, "go hang out with one of your own kind."

"You don't choose who you fall in love with, Jack, and don't call me baby."

Polly was starting to look a little teary. She didn't like it when he referred to their relationship in such a casual manner.

"Oh, come on, Polly, not the waterworks."

All her life Polly had cried easily. It was her Achilles' heel. She wasn't a crybaby; it was just that strong emotions made her eyes water. This was actually quite debilitating in a minor sort of way. It made her look a fool. It would happen in the middle of some particularly frustrating political argument. There she would be, banging her fist on the pub table, struggling to find words to express her deeply held conviction that Mrs. Thatcher was a warmongering fascist and suddenly her eyes would start getting wet. Instantly Polly would feel her image transforming itself from passionate feminist revolutionary to silly overemotional little woman.

"Well, there's no need to cry about it," Polly's dialectical opponents would sneer.

"I am not bloody crying," Polly would reply, tears springing from the corners of her eyes.

The tears were there now and Jack did not like emotionally charged situations. He liked to pretend that life was simple. Polly thought him repressed and out of touch with himself. Jack just felt he had better things to do with his time than get worked up about stuff. But the truth was that he was worked up, terribly worked up. Beneath his highly cool exterior he was anguished and distraught. Because Jack was in love with Polly and he knew that he would have to leave her.

"Jack," said Polly, "we need to talk about where we're going."

Jack did not want to talk about this at all. He never did want to talk about it, because deep inside he knew that they were not going anywhere.

"You know why people smoke after sex?" he said, dragging at his cigarette. "It's an etiquette thing. It means you don't have to talk."

"What?"

"People smoke after sex to avoid conversation. I mean, in general postcoital is a socially barren zone. Particularly that difficult first time. You've known somebody five minutes and suddenly you're removing your horribly diminished dick from inside of their body. What do you say?"

Sometimes Polly found Jack's crude, abrasive style sexy and exhilarating. Other times she just found it crude and abrasive.

"We didn't say anything after our first attempt, did we? Because we were hiding in a field trying to avoid large insects and the police."

"Yeah, well let me tell you, it saved us a lot of embarrassment.

Any diversion is welcome in such a situation. Even the cops. Think about it. You're naked with a stranger. What do you say?"

"A stranger?"

"Sure, a stranger. The first time you sleep with someone ten to one they're going to be a stranger. How many times do you have sex with someone for the first time whom you've known more than a few hours?"

"Well, there's not much point asking me, is there?"

"Yeah, well take my word for it, babe." Jack did not like to be reminded of Polly's lack of sexual experience. It made him feel even more responsible for her than he already did.

"The first time you screw a person all you've been thinking about since you met them is screwing them. Then suddenly it's over and you don't have that agenda anymore. What can a guy say? 'That was fun'? 'That was nice'? It's so weak, so dismissive, like the girl's body was a cupcake and you took a nibble. On the other hand, 'That was awesome' is too much. She knows you're bullshitting. 'Oh yeah, so awesome it lasted two whole minutes and you shouted out some other girl's name.'"

Jack took another long drag on his cigarette and developed his thesis.

"So people smoke. The human psyche is so pathetically insecure that we would rather die of lung cancer than confront an uncomfortable situation. I don't know what will happen now everybody's giving it up. Maybe they'll share a small tray of canapés."

"I thought 'How was it for you?' was considered the correct inquiry."

"Nobody ever asked that. That question is a myth. How could you ever ask, 'How was it for you?'? No answer would be good enough."

"Why not?"

"Well, just now, for instance, when we made love. How was it?"
Jack had caught Polly off her guard.

"Well, it was fine . . . great, in fact, really great."

"You see," said Jack, as though his point were proved. "Already I'm thinking 'fine'? 'great'? Why doesn't she just come right out and say 'pathetic'? That's what she means. Why doesn't she just say, 'Your dick is a cocktail sausage. I get more satisfaction when I ride my bicycle over a speed hump.' "

"Oh well, if we're taking puerile macho paranoia into account . . ."

"Got to, babe, it's what makes the world go around."

Polly took another cigarette and lit it from her previous one.

"Well, I'm definitely giving up soon. Tomorrow, in fact; certainly this month or by the end of the year."

They smoked in silence for a while. Outside, the sun was setting. When it was dark they would leave, Polly knew that. Jack rarely consented to spend a whole night with her. She got out of bed and began to search for her clothes.

Polly never ceased to be amazed at the way her clothes disappeared while she was making love. Particularly her bra and knickers. It was a side of sex that had come as a complete surprise to her. It wasn't as if she hid them or anything. She did not deliberately secrete them behind the washbasin in the bathroom or between the sheet and the mattress, or hang them from the molding. Nonetheless after lengthy searching it was in such places that they would be discovered. On this particular occasion she eventually found her knickers wedged inside the Corby trouserpress.

This was Jack's favorite part of Polly's dressing process. He loved her naked, of course, he worshiped her naked, but somehow near nakedness was even more endearing. There was something he found particularly moving about Polly wearing only her knickers.

Polly said that it was because like all men he was subconsciously afraid of vaginas and preferred to see them sanitized with a neat cotton cover, which Jack thought was quite literally the stupidest thing he had ever heard anybody say in his entire life.

The gathering gloom within the room was making Polly feel somber. When the sun was shining and Jack and she were making love she could forget the circumstances of their relationship. Forget that he was a killer and she was a traitor. Forget the police and the soldiers. The razor wire and the searchlights. Forget her life in the camp. Forget the Cold War. Then night would fall and Polly would remember that it was life with Jack that was the dream. Outside was the deadly reality.

"It would be so lovely to be normal," she said, rescuing her bra from inside the hotel kettle (the lid of which she'd have sworn had not been removed even once since they had entered the room). "To be able to walk down a street together, go to the pub."

"Don't even think about it." Jack shivered at the very thought.

"I was arrested again yesterday," said Polly. She and her comrades had been attempting to prevent the missile transporters from leaving the camp. In the event of war the strategic plan for the missiles was that they would be bused about to various parts of the country on mobile launchers, making them less of a target for the enemy. Every now and then the army practiced this deployment, using empty transporters. It was to one of these that Polly had been attached when the police arrived.

"Arrested?" said Jack casually. "You didn't say. How'd it go?"

Jack always tried to act as if things were not important.

"Not great. You know the good cop, bad cop thing? I think there must have been an administrative fuck-up. I got bad cop, bad cop. No fags, no cups of tea, just a lot of abuse."

"That's cops."

The police, who for a while had been friendly, had begun to tire of the Greenham women's disruption and vandalism and had started to get tough.

"I was thinking while they were both shouting at me that perhaps down the corridor someone else had got good cop, good cop. Constant tea, endless cigarettes, keep the coupons . . ."

The sun was nearly gone. Inside, the room was almost completely dark.

"Polly, are you sure you've never told anybody about us?"

"Jack, you always ask that."

Jack got out of bed and went to the toilet. He left the bathroom door open, which Polly hated. She liked to keep a little mystery in a relationship where possible. Having a toilet door was such a luxury for her that it seemed deeply decadent not even to bother using it.

"You've told nobody?"

Jack raised his voice above the tinkling and flushing. His tone was firmer, as well it might have been, since the whole course of his life depended on Polly's discretion. He returned to the room, as always utterly unselfconscious about his jiggling, dangling, bollock-hanging nakedness. This was a side of male bedroom manners that Polly would never get used to.

"Of course I haven't told anybody," said Polly. "I know the rules. I love you . . ."

Polly waited, as countless women had waited before her, for the echo of that phrase, and, like the vast majority of those women, she was eventually forced to ask for it.

"Well?"

"Well what?" said Jack, lighting another two cigarettes.

"Well, do you love me too?"

Jack rolled his eyes ceilingward. "Of course I love you, Polly, for Christ's sake."

"Well, say it properly, then."

"I just did!"

"No, you didn't. I made you. Say it nicely."

"OK, OK!"

Jack assumed an expression of quiet sincerity. "I love you, Polly. I really love you."

There was a pause.

"But really really? Do you really really love me? I mean really."

This is, of course, the reason why so many men don't like to get into the "I love you" conversation, because it is open-ended. Very quickly degenerating into the "How much do you love me?" conversation, the "I don't believe you mean it" conversation, and finally the dreaded "Yes, and I'm sure you said the same thing to that bitch you were going out with when I first met you" conversation.

"Yes, Polly. I really really love you," Jack said in a tone that suggested he would have said he loved baboon shit on toast if it would keep the peace.

"Good," said Polly. "Because if I thought you were lying I think I'd kill myself . . ."

The room was now almost pitch black save for the glowing ends of their cigarettes.

"Or you."

[18]

When Jack got back to the base that night he went straight to the bar and ordered beer with a bourbon chaser. The room was empty save for Captain Schultz, who was alone as usual, playing on the Space Invaders machine. Poor Schultz. He hated the army as much as Jack loved it, not that he would ever have admitted it to anybody, even himself. Schultz tried not to have strong opinions about anything, in order to avoid unpleasant arguments. He had joined the army because that was what the men (and some of the women) of his family had always done. The fact that he was entirely unsuited for military command, being incapable of making a decision, was irrelevant. There had never been any choice for Schultz.

Jack had known him at West Point, where Schultz had just scraped through with a combination of family connections and very hard work. Not too long afterward, while billeted at the U.S. base in Iceland, he had been made captain virtually by default. Schultz's superior had found the posting rather cold and had attempted to warm himself up by trying to seduce every young woman in Reykjavík. After one too many dishonorable discharges the man was dishonorably discharged and Schultz found himself achieving early command. Jack had found it an interesting circumstance that he, the most successful student in his year at military academy, and Schultz, the least successful, should be advancing at much the same pace. Jack's rise was due to his own excellence, Schultz's to the frailty of others, but they were destined to shadow each other throughout their whole careers.

That night in the bar Jack wanted someone to talk to. He was still thinking about the conversation he'd had with Polly and was in a rare communicative mood. He wished that Harry was there so that he could talk to him about the painful mixed emotions he was experiencing. But Harry was thousands of miles away in Ohio. There was only Schultz. Jack stood by the Space Invaders machine and watched Schultz lose all his defenders in a very short space of time.

"Jesus, Schultz," said Jack. "That must be the worst score anybody ever got on that machine."

"Oh no," Schultz replied, giving up the game. "I've had much worse."

"What the hell are you like with a gun?"

"As far as possible I try not to use one," Schultz said, sipping at his soda.

"Tell me something, Schultz," Jack inquired. "Did you ever really really want something you couldn't have?"

Schultz considered for a moment. "Sure I did, Kent. Why, only tonight in the refectory I absolutely set my mind on the profiteroles and then they told me they just sold the last portion. I hate that. They should cross it off the board. Why do you ask?"

"Forget it."

Jack finished his drink and returned to his neat little army cell.

"*Dear Harry,*" he wrote. "*What the hell is wrong with me? I'm in pain here and nobody hit me. When I started this thing with Polly I thought I could handle it. You know, I thought I could have some laughs, get my rocks off, and walk away when I felt like it. Except now I don't want to walk away. Even thinking about ending it makes me want to go and punch some-*"

one. This is ridiculous, Harry. I mean, what am I? Some kind of soppy dick like you that lets himself get stupid over a girl? Never in my life did I get stupid over a girl. Suddenly I'm risking my career for one! I'm sneaking out of the camp with my collar turned up and my hat pulled down just so I can be with her! I must be out of my mind. In fact, I am out of my mind, because she's in it! All day this woman is inside my head! I can't do my job, I'm a safety hazard. I'm trying to monitor the arrival of nuclear warheads and I'm daydreaming about being in bed with Polly! Did you feel this way about Debbie? Of course you did. You still do, you lucky fuck. You and Debbie were made for each other. You fit, like one of those horrible kissing chairs you make. You're allowed to love each other. Nobody ever said 'A furniture maker can't fall in love with a firewoman.' But me! Jesus, my colonel would probably prefer it if I told him I was sleeping with the corpse of Leonid Brezhnev."

[19]

Their embrace ended as suddenly as it had begun.

Polly broke away. "I shouldn't be hugging you, Jack. I shouldn't be hugging you at all."

So much of her longed to continue, but a larger part remembered the hurt that this man had caused her.

Jack stepped back too. He had not expected their embrace. It had confused him.

"Yeah, well, like I said, it's good to see you."

Polly wanted to look at Jack properly. She turned on the lamp on her desk. The extra light further illuminated her dowdy room and she regretted switching it on.

"I've often wondered what your stuff would be like," said Jack, looking around.

Things were not at their tidiest. As a matter of fact, they never were. Things had only once been at their tidiest in Polly's flat, for a single afternoon, shortly after Polly had moved in and her mother had come to inspect. In preparation for that visit Polly had tidied and cleared and cleared and tidied and polished and buffed and tidied again.

Her mother had thought the place was a mess.

She also thought that the plates should be in the pan cupboard, the pans should be where the mugs were, and the mugs should go on little hooks of which there were none, but nice ones could be gotten at Habitat. Polly's mother then set about effecting all of these changes with the exception of the mugs, because she did not have the hooks. The mugs she left on the draining board to await Polly's do-it-yourself efforts and there they had remained (sometimes clean, more often dirty) ever since.

Polly's little life seemed suddenly small and depressing. Poky would have been a good word for it, or dingy. She felt embarrassed, which was really rather unjust because if anyone in that room had reason to feel embarrassed it was Jack, and yet Polly knew that it was she who was going red.

Hurriedly she began to tidy up. Polly was a dropper of things and a leaver around of other things. She did not tidy up as she went along, she tidied up once every seven days on a strict routine and she was already nine days into the current cycle. There were knickers and tights on the floor, a dirty plate and various mugs by the bed, and magazines and books everywhere. Polly felt that at least the intimate clothing had to be hidden away; also anything that had mold growing on it, particularly if the two were one and the same thing.

As Jack watched Polly scurrying about, stooping to pick up her knickers and bras, he could not help but remember Polly as a young girl, searching for her underwear in hotel rooms and the backs of cars. Once she had not been able to find the elusive garment at all and they had risked going down to dinner, not only in fear of being seen together but also in the wicked knowledge that Polly was naked beneath her little denim skirt. What a wonderful meal that had been. Jack had kicked off his shoe beneath the table and as they ate his bare foot had lain between Polly's legs. In the long years since that glorious meal Jack had relived it in his memory a thousand times. He doubted that he had ever had a happier moment. Certainly not in a motel restaurant, anyway.

"Bet you didn't think things would look as shitty as this," Polly said, stuffing dirty clothes into the clean clothes drawer.

As he watched her moving about Jack knew that it was as he had feared. That he was still in love with her.

"No, I didn't. I thought it would be much more shitty than this."

Jack could see that virtually everything Polly owned was on view. Her furniture, her clothes, all of her stuff. It didn't seem to him that she had changed very much either. There were her souvenir mugs from the 1984 miners' strike. A poster advertising a concert at Wembly Stadium to celebrate the release of Nelson Mandela. One of those plastic flowers that dance when music comes on (but only if the battery hasn't been dead for five and a half years, which in this case it had). A poster of Daniel Ortega proclaiming "Nicaragua must survive," a poster of Garfield the cartoon cat proclaiming that he hated mornings. A front page of the *London Evening Standard* from the day Margaret Thatcher resigned. (Jack, like many Americans, could not understand how the Brits had ever let that one happen; anyone could see that she was the best thing they had had in years— it was like after the war, when they dropped Churchill.) Polly had lots of books. A couple of IKEA "first home" easy chairs, a rape alarm, a small TV. Thirty or forty loose CDs and forty or fifty empty CD boxes.

Everything was as Jack might have imagined it. The only thing that surprised him was how little Polly owned. You would have been lucky to get two thousand dollars for the entire contents of the room.

Not a lot for a woman of thirty-four. Or was it thirty-five? Not a very impressive accumulation for a whole half-lifetime.

Polly glanced up from her tidying. She knew what he was thinking. "Not very impressive, is it?"

Polly still could not quite believe how spectacularly she had managed to screw up her life. Just how unlucky could a girl get? And why did it have to be her?

No reason, of course. Some people are fortunate in life and love, some are not, and you can never tell how the chips will fall. At school nobody would have looked at Polly and thought, she'll end up one of the lonely ones. She'll be the one who screws things up. She had been bright and attractive in every way. She might easily have made a great success of her personal life had fate favored her, but it had not.

How cruel to reflect upon the wrong turns and unsought circumstances of an unlucky life. When Polly and her friends had sat laughing in the pub together at the age of seventeen it would not have been possible to look at them and say, "Second from the left with the rum and Coke, she's going to have problems." It would not have been possible to predict that Polly, who seemed so strong and assured, was very soon going to fall head over heels in love and then get devastatingly dumped. That she would then spend years drifting unsatisfactorily from brief affair to brief affair before suddenly toward the end of her twenties being seized by a sudden desperate fear of being alone. That Polly of all people would be the one to get caught up with a married man (separated, waiting for divorce) who would lie to her, cheat on her, and eventually leave Polly for the ex-wife whom he had previously left for Polly.

Every golden generation, every fresh-faced group of friends, must statistically contain those who will fall prey to the sad clichés of life. The things they never thought would or could happen to them. Divorce, alcoholism, illness, failure. Those were things that happened to one's parents' generation. To adults who no longer had their whole lives before them. It comes as a shock when the truth dawns that every young person is just an older person waiting to happen, and it happens a lot sooner than anyone ever thinks.

[20]

At the end of the summer, after Jack had left Polly, she decided to stay on at Greenham. Her parents did everything they could to persuade her to come home and go back to school but she was adamant. Her A-levels could wait, she explained, there was a planet to be saved. Polly told Mr. and Mrs. Slade that she had things to do, she had made great friends amongst her compatriots at the peace camp and was halfway through the construction of a ten-foot-high puppet of a She-God called Wooma, with which Polly and her friends intended to parade through Newbury. Of course, Polly did not tell her parents that she had spent the summer having a passionate fling with a man twice her age and that now he was gone her heart was utterly broken. She did not tell them that her whole being ached with sadness and that sometimes she thought she would actually go mad. She just told them about Wooma and that she was not coming home yet.

In fact, Polly never did go home. Instead she moved permanently into the camp, living in a caravan with an old granny called Madge. Madge had been widowed the previous spring and had decided that she wanted to do something useful with the rest of her life, so she had bought a little caravan and moved to Greenham to save the world. Madge was a good companion and Polly loved her, but she was obsessed with bowels, particularly Polly's. She would inquire earnestly about the state of Polly's stools, reminding her always to be sure to inspect what she had produced before shoveling on the soil. Madge never tired of assuring Polly that regular, punctual movements were the secret of longevity and constantly made bran muffins of such copious fibrousness that they could have prized open the buttocks of a concrete elephant.

Polly kept in touch with her parents via postcards and the occasional photograph. It was through the latter that Mr. and Mrs. Slade kept up with the changes in Polly's appearance, which was drifting from rather stylish anarcho-punk to depressing "who gives a fuck?" hippie grunge. Mrs. Slade wondered how Polly washed her hair now that it was all in great shaggy dreadlocks with beads sewn into them and the terrible answer was, of course, that she didn't. Mr. Slade worried that food might get stuck in Polly's new lip ring and rot there. He'd read somewhere that decaying meat was carcinogenic, then he remembered that Polly was a vegetarian and felt better. Neither of Polly's parents liked the tattoo she had had done on her shoulder, depicting the female gender symbol with a clenched fist in the center of it. Unfortunately the tattoo had been rather inexpertly applied by a stoned goth at the Glastonbury festival, and the fist looked like a penis, which was hardly a feminist symbol.

The Greenham camp was a bit like the Foreign Legion for Polly, a place to nurse a lost soul. She was relatively content there, apart, of course, from her aching heart and Madge going on at her all the time about her far too infrequent evacuations. Camp life was tolerable but, then again, if you consider yourself worthless and don't care whether you live or you die, which was how Polly felt, pretty much anything is tolerable.

Some aspects of Greenham life Polly never got used to. Even in her numbed state of mind all the singing and the holding hands could get a bit wearing. The peace women were so anxious not to emulate the aggressive posturing of the male of the species that sometimes they ended up just looking a bit wet. Sometimes at night, when the women were having their lentils, the British squaddies would pile back from the pub all pissed up and chanting, "Lesby, lesby, LesbiANS." When that happened Polly always longed to lob a ladleful of hot roughage at them and inform them that they were a bunch of brainless no-dicks, but that sort of behavior was not how things were done. The camp was there to stop aggression, after all, not to fuel it, so instead the huddled women would confront the baying young men with their impenetrable female energy, constructing a forcefield of love and calm through which the soldiers occasionally urinated.

Polly was not very good at this type of mystical feminism. She was more for the give-as-good-as-you-get school of protest. Madge often tried to explain that this was *exactly* the type of attitude that had started the arms race in the first place, but Polly remained restive and unconvinced.

Try as she might, she never could truly welcome her periods as an old friend. She simply could not regard the monthly stomach cramps as a small price to pay for the privilege of celebrating the timeless mystery of her menstrual cycle. Being as one with the rhythms of the moon was of very little comfort to Polly when she had a hot water bottle clamped to her stomach. It turned out that she wasn't very good at puppet-making either. The She-God Wooma's head had fallen off on its first outing, nearly killing a baby outside Boots in the Newbury shopping mall. Nor did Polly have any children's paintings to pin to the perimeter wires, or peace poems and haiku to send to the prime minister. Above all, apart from the mass protests and camp invasions in which Polly always played an enthusiastic part, life at Greenham could be very very boring. It was all right for the lesbians—they had something to do of a night—but for Polly the hours of darkness were long and lonely, and she would lie there shivering, listening to Madge snoring, trying not to think about Jack and wondering what she was doing with her life. Certainly she was saving the world, but was that enough?

After about a year Polly was ready for a break, and the miners' strike in 1984 gave the opportunity to move on. The whole of alternative society had been galvanized by the confrontation between Mrs. Thatcher and the miners. The prime minister seemed finally to have found an enemy worthy of her metal, and everybody wanted to be a part of what was confidently expected to be her defeat. Polly decided to leave Greenham for a while in order to carry a fund-raising bucket for the National Union of Mineworkers.

She went to stay with friends in Yorkshire, where she signed on the dole and offered her services at a miners' support group. There she took up with a middle-aged communist shop steward called Derek. He was a nice man but the relationship did not last long; despite both of their being politically on the far left, they were incompatible. This was, of course, inevitable, given that one of the hallmarks of the far left in those days was that almost everybody on it was politically incompatible with almost everybody else. The factionization was surreal. Groups would split and split again until individual members were in danger of being rendered schizophrenic. It made for an incredible array of radical newspapers. On the steps of every Student Union and on every picket line, one could buy *The Socialist This, The New Left That*, and *The International God Knows What* . . . Sadly, most of these papers were read exclusively by the people who printed and sold them.

And the only thing that all the disparate factions had in common was that they all hated each other. What is more they hated each other with a venom and a passion that they could never feel for the Tories. The Tories were just misguided products of an inherently corrupt system. Other Lefties were the anti-Christ.

Polly and Derek fell out over a point of sexual politics. He objected to her wishing to stand on the front line at the secondary pickets, which were becoming more and more violent as frustrations grew on both sides.

"Look, Poll," Derek said. "When me an't lads are stood standing at dock gates, tryin' t'stop foreign bastard scab coal comin' in, and Maggie's boot boys in blue are tryin' t'kick six types of shit out of us we do not need to be worrying about protectin' our womenfolk."

Derek, like most of the miners, still believed firmly that there was men's work and there was women's work. It was, in fact, to be the last year that men like Derek would believe such a thing, because within a very short time virtually every coal mine in Britain would be closed, the men would be out of work, and the women would become the principal earners in the home.

At the time, though, Derek definitely believed that women were the gentler sex. Faced with such positively Neanderthal sexism, Polly scarcely knew where to start.

"But . . . you . . . For God's sake . . . !" Polly could feel her eyes beginning to water with frustration.

"Well, there's no need t'cry about it, love," said Derek, and there their relationship ended.

The miners' strike finally collapsed in January 1985. Polly was alone and with no clear sense of purpose. Like Bono at about the same time, she still hadn't found what she was looking for. She thought about moving to London where yet another once-mighty union, this time the print workers', was preparing to dash itself against the walls of Castle Thatcher in a futile attempt to maintain their old working practices. In the end, however, she couldn't face it. Even the peace dirges of Greenham seemed preferable to endlessly chanting, "Maggie! Maggie! Maggie! Out! Out! Out!" and "Here we go, here we go, here we go," when clearly no one was going anywhere. So Polly returned to the camp to await the delivery of the cruise missiles.

That was what she told herself, anyway, but the fact that for the first month after her return she scrutinized every American face that came or left the camp suggested that Polly's heart had not yet healed. Madge could see that Polly was still troubled, but of course she thought the whole problem was lack of roughage.

But it would take more than a high-fiber diet to cure Polly's pain. Only time would do that, and time moved slowly at the Greenham camp that spring for Polly. She had not told Madge about Jack, or any of the women with whom she began again to share her life. They would not have understood. Polly did not understand it herself, except to know that love is blind. Everything Jack stood for Polly truly did despise, and she despised herself for having fallen in love with such a man. What was worse, she despised herself for not having the strength to forget him.

When the missiles finally did arrive, Polly was among that briefly celebrated group of women who managed to breach the perimeter fences and carry their protest onto the base itself. Polly's poor, horrified parents opened their newspaper one morning to discover that she and her comrades had reached the landing runway and had very nearly forced the huge U.S. Air Force transport planes to abort their landings. It was a great propaganda triumph, which in the opinion of the USAF very nearly caused a nuclear disaster. In court Polly pleaded guilty to criminal trespass but stated that she had acted in order to prevent the greater crime of millions of people being vaporized in nuclear explosions. The magistrate declined to accept global geopolitics as mitigating circumstances and Polly was bound over to keep the peace.

"Ha!" said Polly. "Keeping the peace is what I was doing anyway."

Which she thought was rather a clever thing to say.

[21]

Polly was not the only one still grieving for the past. Jack too found himself unable to step out from under the long shadow of their relationship. With Jack, however, the effect was more positive; the memory and continuing presence of Polly in Jack's heart was to prove a considerable influence on his life and career.

After leaving Greenham, Jack spent most of the rest of the eighties stationed in the lovely old German city of Wiesbaden, a part of the vast American military presence that had been camping in Europe since the end of the Second World War. Wiesbaden was the headquarters of the U.S. Army in Europe. Over the years the local German community had grown accustomed to the presence of hordes of young foreign men in their midst, and an uneasy relationship had grown up between the military and its host community. Of course, there were tensions and conflicts, but discipline was strict and scandals were rare. Rare but not unknown. One night in a bierkeller in Bad Nauheim, a town a few miles up the autobahn from Wiesbaden, there occurred an incident that the army subsequently quickly tried to forget.

Normally Jack would not have been in a bierkeller at all. He was not much of a pub man. Being extremely ambitious, he tended to reserve his spare time for study or sports. However, on this particular night Jack was ready to relax. He had been out on a week's field training, a week of camp food and camp beds, during which time he had been cold and wet for twenty-four hours a day. Jack was ready to spend an evening drinking the German winter out of his bones.

Being a little tired of Wiesbaden, he took the army bus to Bad Nauheim, where he very soon fell in with some fellow officers.

"Hey, Jack, come over here and have a beer, you enigmatic bastard," a captain known as Dipstick shouted as Jack entered the bar. Dipstick was so called because he was a mechanical engineer and also because he liked to talk about how much sex he was getting. He shared an off-base house in Bad Nauheim with another army captain called Rod. Dipstick and Rod were a real couple of good ol' boys and were already half full of beer. Between them sat a German girl called Helga. Helga was the sort of girl who liked soldiers and in particular getting drunk and having sex with them. Had Helga been a man she would have been called a good ol' boy too, just like Dipstick and Rod, but because she was a woman it was well known that she was a slut.

Helga had been seeing quite a lot of Dipstick in the weeks preceding the night in question, but on one occasion she had also slept with Rod. Originally, the evening had been planned by Dipstick and Rod as a threesome. They had brought Helga to the bar in the hope of persuading her to have sex with them both. Rod and Dipstick had every reason to think that Helga would be amenable to this idea, because they had laughed about the possibility together on a number of occasions. Helga had even boasted that it would take at least two of them to handle her properly. A threesome was just the type of dangerous game that Helga was likely to get herself into because beneath her bravado she was a lonely, insecure girl and what she craved most was attention. A psychologist might have made much of

Helga's exhibitionism and lack of any real sense of self-worth. Dip-stick and Rod just thought that she was a crazy, horny bitch.

Also at the table when Jack arrived were Brad and Karl, two young lieutenants who had been in Germany for only three months, and Captain Schultz, Jack's characterless, ineffective acquaintance from the Greenham base. Schultz had been dropping his wife off at her bridge club and had popped into the bar for a Coke and some food. True to form, Schultz was dithering over the bar menu, unable to decide between the roast pork sandwich and the Wiener schnitzel with sauerkraut.

Jack got some drinks and joined the group, which meant that there were now six men at the table and one woman.

"We're kind of guy-heavy here, babe," Dipstick remarked to Helga. "Could you call a friend?"

"OK, baby," said Helga and went off to make a call.

Sure enough, in a short while a girl called Mitti turned up. It was fun for the older men to watch Karl's and Brad's eyes pop out as Mitti joined their table. Her tiny waist and substantial bosom turned heads right across the bar. Mitti and Helga were both good-looking girls who were skilled at making the most of what they had, the fashions of the time being well suited to advertising one's wares. Both women wore short, ballooning ra-ra skirts and cowboy boots. Helga had on a denim jacket encrusted with glittering fake dia-monds and a picture of Los Angeles painted on the back and the words "Hot LA Nights" spelled out in twinkling studs and costume jewels. Under this she wore a pink shining spandex boob tube, from which her bosom seemed permanently in danger of escaping. Mitti wore a wet-look leather jacket, also jewel encrusted, with a collar that stood up round her ears and shoulders and jutted out about a foot and a half both ways, making it necessary for her to go through narrow doors sideways. Both Helga's and Mitti's hair was astonishing in a way that only mid-eighties hair could be; it was "power" hair, "me" hair, "fuck you" hair, and "will you fuck me?" hair all rolled into one. Two great tousled blond manes with platinum highlights. Gelled, sprayed, teased, streaked, glittered and glued, and no doubt sheltering enough CFCs to bash a hole in the ozone layer the size of Germany. These were young women with lovely skin, but they had covered their faces in makeup, tan foundation, laden lashes, and great bruises of purply blusher dusted across each cheekbone as if both women had been punched on the sides of their faces. They spoke through smoke-filled mouths, their glossy shining baby-pink lips edged with dark liner that made them look hard and vain.

Drinks were poured and then more drinks, and the conversation got dirtier. That old favorite, swearing in different languages, came up and caused roars of laughter as Helga regaled the soldiers with the various German words for a blow job.

Karl and Brad were loving it. It felt great being real soldiers, hanging out with the older guys, talking dirty with the Kraut tarts. Even Jack was enjoying himself; it was all harmless enough; the girls were witty in an obscene, streetwise sort of way, and Dipstick as always knew the latest gags from the States.

"Why does Gary Hart wear underpants?" he asked. "To keep his ankles warm!"

The Democratic primaries were under way back home, and Gary Hart, a promising, charismatic politician who had at one time been front-runner for the Democratic presidential nomination, was now in deep trouble over what were coming to be known as "bimbo eruptions." Hart had a reputation as a womanizer, a reputation that had been confirmed when he had been caught on a yacht canoodling with a bikini-clad girl who was in no way his wife. Most of the guys on the base were aghast that such a thing could be enough to fatally wound the man's professional aspirations.

"He'd get my vote," Dipstick assured the company. "What do we want in the White House? Faggots?"

The two young men roared their approval at this comment and slapped their thighs to show what regular guys they were. Schultz felt a little differently.

"Well, I don't know. I think we have a right to expect the very highest standards from those in public life," he said. "After all, if a man lies to his wife, how can we tell he's telling the truth to us?"

"Bullshit, Schultz," said Dipstick. "If a man says he doesn't lie to his wife then he's a liar anyway."

Jack realized that Mitti was looking at him intently. He returned her stare and smiled, thinking to himself that she was probably very attractive underneath all the hair and makeup. Mitti's lips fell open slightly in the orthodox manner of the *femme fatales* of *Dynasty.* Her lips and teeth glistened, and slowly the pink, wet, pointy tip of her tongue gently journeyed from one corner of her hard-looking but soft mouth to the other. Mitti was not a subtle girl. She could not have made her intentions more clear if she had sent Jack a note asking for sex. She liked the look of Jack. She had quickly realized that he was a cut above the other men at the table. He roared less loudly, he leered less obviously, and he was not forcing his legs against hers under the table.

Jack was surprised to find that he was interested too. It had been a long time since he had made love. He had not been entirely celibate since running out on Polly four years before, but he'd not been very active either. He still thought of Polly every day. He wanted her every day and no girl he had met since had remotely matched up to her. Certainly not this tawdry, brassy, blousey woman waggling her tongue at him across the table. She was everything that Polly had not been and vice versa. Yet there was something in Mitti's eyes, something behind the silver eyeshadow, the thick liner, the great caked mascaraed lashes, that Jack recognized. Perhaps it was honesty, or a sense of humor; it might well have been loneliness. Jack found himself returning Mitti's stare.

"This dump's getting kinda crowded," said Dipstick, a white mustache of beer froth on his upper lip. "How about we all go drink champagne at the American?"

The Hotel American was a favorite venue for one-night stands among the more discerning members of the Allied Armed Forces in the area. It was not sleazy, being rather well appointed and expensive, but neither did it object to partying. Its two suites boasted whirlpool baths in which three could sit comfortably and four even more so. This was a time when the almighty dollar was so strong that other currencies cowered before it; even the not unmuscular German mark doffed its cap respectfully in the face of the purchasing power of the U.S. buck. Americans overseas were far better off than they were at home, and suites at the Hotel American were well within the budgets of discerning U.S. officers.

Helga said she was happy to drink champagne any time, Rod was of course enthusiastic about the idea, and Brad and Karl could hardly believe their luck. Mitti just shrugged. She shrugged directly at Jack, a shrug that suggested that she would like the idea a whole lot better if he was in on it. All eyes turned to Jack. Nobody considered Schultz. Even the young officers ignored him; he was just that kind of invisible person.

Jack sucked at his beer and laughed. "So you guys are planning a party?" he said.

"Didn't you hear?" Dipstick replied. "Life's a party."

It was decision time. Jack wondered what he wanted. What he wanted, of course, was Polly but he couldn't have her, so perhaps he wanted Mitti. He was drunk and she was getting more attractive by the minute. Maybe he should go along with it. Have a few laughs.

He was so hard on himself most of the time; perhaps it would be fun. He looked at Mitti and her eyes were welcoming.

"Well, hey, no rush," said Dipstick. "We'll just all sit here getting old while you think about it."

Jack pulled himself together. He was dreaming. Orgies were not for him. It was a strange thing, but Polly, or at least the memory of Polly, had come to act as a sort of censor on Jack's life. He often found himself wondering what she would make of the things he said and the things he did. Of one thing he was sure: she would not think much of his cavorting at the Hotel American with drunken girls. It was almost as if having betrayed her utterly he was trying to make it up by not betraying her memory.

"No thanks. I'm going to get something to eat," Jack said, rising from the table.

"Hey, come on, Jack," Dipstick protested. "You can't break up the party."

"You don't need me, Dip." Jack laughed, and as he did so he caught Mitti's eye and the disappointment there. He could not help but smile at her and that was enough. Mitti got up too.

"I'm coming with you," she said boldly.

"*Nein, Mitti*," Helga said.

"Yeah, *nein*," Dipstick added.

Helga and Dipstick could both see the ratio of the sexes changing from six:two to five:one and neither of them liked it.

"C'mon, Jack. You and Mitti have gotta stay."

"Mitti can do what she likes, Dipstick, but if you think I want to see your white hairy ass in a spa bath you've been in the army too long," Jack said, putting on his coat.

"I don't think I'll bother either, guys," said Schultz. "I have an early appointment at the chiropodist tomorrow and I'd hate to be all bleary for it. Thanks, anyway."

Dipstick ignored Schultz.

"Who said anything about a spa bath, Jack?" he protested. "We're just going to get some booze."

"Yeah, sure, Dip. Absolutely," Jack replied, and, nodding his farewell to the table, he turned and headed for the door, but not before casting a questioning glance at Mitti. There followed a brief exchange between Mitti and Helga in German, the gist of which was Mitti asking Helga if Helga minded being left. Helga was not particularly delighted about it, but she was a grown-up girl and it was a well-established rule that in such pickup situations it was every woman for herself. Helga told Mitti that if she wanted to go with Jack then she should do it, but she was to be sure to phone her in the morning and give her a full report.

"You too," Mitti replied in English, "but not too early."

Jack was waiting at the door. Mitti grabbed her jacket and the two of them left. Outside Mitti put her arm through Jack's and they walked together through the snowy streets. She was shivering, her little ra-ra dress and wet-look leather jacket being little protection from the cold. Jack put his arm around her. Most places were shut, but after a while they found a small Moroccan restaurant in a basement called the Kasbah. The only other clientele were North Africans, economic immigrants, the subject of much resentment in the town.

That night, however, everything was smiles between the nervous black men and their unexpected guests, and Jack and Mitti sat down to couscous, lamb stew, and beer.

"So you really did want to eat," Mitti inquired.

"Sure, what else?"

They both knew what else. Mitti did not reply, but glanced coyly down at her food and then up again at Jack, which was reply enough. She did in fact have lovely eyes and without her ridiculous jacket she seemed much less hard and aggressive; even the huge hair appeared to be getting softer and less assertive.

They finished their meal and went to a small hotel where they made love. Even as they began, Jack wished that he had not. He liked Mitti; she was a nice girl and very pretty underneath the makeup, but the truth was that she was not his type. It was partly the smell. There was no part of Mitti's person that was not scented and treated with antiperspirant. She could have fucked for a year and not broken into a sweat. Every inch of her both reeked and tasted of chemicals; her scratchy, brittle hair, her sour-tasting neck, the soapy gloss on her lips, the all-over body spray on her breasts, even her crotch had been deodorized, her natural sexual scent bludgeoned into submission by some cloud of musky napalm. Merely undressing Mitti had given Jack a headache and a blocked-up nose. It was like trying to have sex on the cosmetic counter at Macy's. His throat hurt and he felt sick for a day afterward, like he had swallowed a bottle of aftershave.

Jack was a gentleman and he did his best, but they both knew that his heart wasn't in it.

After a while they gave up, got dressed, and Jack took Mitti home in a cab.

He kissed her good night and headed back to base feeling lonely and sad.

At about lunchtime the next day Mitti rang Helga to find out how her night had gone.

Helga said it had been fine, but she had sounded strange. After that Mitti did not see Helga for a week, by which time Helga had been to the police to report having been raped.

There were two stories of what happened to Helga after Jack and Mitti had left the bar that night.

Nobody disputed that Dipstick, Rod, Brad, Karl, and Helga

had all left the bierkeller in Bad Nauheim together, leaving Captain Schultz to his sauerkraut. Likewise, there was general agreement that the party had removed itself to the Hotel American where Dipstick had taken the best rooms available, a suite that boasted its own bar and a whirlpool bath. After this the stories begin to diverge. Helga admitted that they had all stripped off and squeezed into the hot bath together. Also she admitted, under police questioning, that she had then voluntarily had sex in the spa with Dipstick while the other men looked on. She also conceded that she had briefly masturbated certainly one other man, Rod, she thought, and possibly one of the others, too. After this Helga claimed that Rod had suggested that she now have sex with him and then also with the two younger officers. Helga said that at this point she had become nervous, as the men were beginning to get noisy and raucous. She declined Rod's request for sex, saying that she had now had enough, and attempted to leave the spa bath. After this she claimed that Rod and Brad had raped her in turn while Karl and Dipstick sat by and continued to drink.

The men, on the other hand, all swore under oath that Helga had consented to all the sexual acts that had happened that night. They swore that there had been no difference at all between Helga's attitude to having sex with Dipstick and then having sex with the other two men. They pointed out that Helga had not cried out and that afterward she had not left the hotel until the following morning, even accepting a cup of coffee from Karl. Everyone admitted to having been very drunk.

Helga could not explain why she had not cried out, except to say that she thought she might have been too scared. She was also not entirely sure why she had remained in the hotel for some hours after the incident, apart from the fact that she had felt weak and sick and upset. When asked why it had taken her five days to report the alleged attack, she said that she had prevaricated because she knew very well how the whole incident would look. The only thing of which Helga was absolutely certain was that the last two men who had had sex with her had known that she was no longer a willing participant.

The courts decided in favor of the men. The fact that Helga had had a previous sexual relationship with both Dipstick and Rod and the fact that she had gone voluntarily for sex at the hotel told heavily against her. Besides which, in the long run it came down to the word of four people against one.

Helga moved away from Bad Nauheim almost immediately following the court case. She wrote home once or twice and Mitti heard that she was living in Hamburg, but after that she seemed to disappear.

The careers of the four soldiers never recovered. Whatever the courts may have decided, such a sordid incident was too much for the army to ignore and they were marked men. One by one they returned to civilian life in the States, angry and bitter and having learned nothing from their experience. Quite the opposite, in fact. All four men came to believe absolutely that their treatment had been grossly unfair and that the woman Helga had set out viciously to destroy them for no better reason than feminine pique.

The case shocked and disturbed both the army and the local community. Jack, who was called as a witness to recall the course of events during the early part of the evening, found his emotions and his principles confused and divided. He engaged in a heated correspondence with his brother Harry on the issues raised by the awful affair. Harry felt that it was obvious that the four soldiers were in the wrong and that they had got off far too lightly. Jack could not see things so clearly. He remembered the sight of the young man Brad crying in the witness box, pleading that he had really thought that the sort of girl that Helga was did not care much about one man more or less.

"*And what about you, Jack?*" Harry wrote back furiously. "*Is that what you think? Does being a soldier make a guy so dumb that he can rape a woman by mistake?*"

No, Jack knew that he could never do that, but he wondered. He wondered what he would have been like as a man if he had never met Polly. Would he have been like Brad? Would he too have been capable of getting drunk and seeing a woman not as a whole and complex person, confused and in pain, but just as some kind of two-dimensional sexual animal? It was possible, of course it was possible. All men had a darker side; that was what made them capable of killing. Jack was a soldier and he knew that very well. To Jack what the Bad Nauheim case had shown was what that dark, uncivilized side of man was capable of when it gained the upper hand. It was a lesson he was not to forget.

Jack may have betrayed Polly's love but Polly's love had not betrayed him.

[22]

Polly finally left the peace camp with the gap that Jack had left in her heart and soul still not filled. She was unsettled and restless. She could not return to her old life, the one she had known years before; it had moved on without her. All her friends from that time were already in their second year at university. She saw them occasionally but she no longer had anything in common with them. She knew that deep down they felt sorry for her.

"But what are you going to do after all this?" they asked. "You can't just be a protester all your life."

"Yeah, well, maybe I can," Polly replied, but she knew that it sounded stupid.

Still looking for something and nothing she became a traveler, a member of one of the New Age convoys that roamed the country at the time. Polly liked living on the move. It gave her the impression that she was going somewhere. She started seeing a casual dope dealer called Ziggy who owned a Volkswagen camper. Polly was fond of Ziggy. He was thirty-six and painfully handsome with deep, piercing blue eyes. He had a Ph.D. in ergonomics and was an extremely bright and interesting conversationalist, when he was not stoned. Unfortunately, this was only for about fifteen minutes each morning. For the rest of the day Ziggy tended to merely giggle a lot.

It was fun for a while, rejecting hierarchy and property, but it couldn't last. Slowly but surely Polly began to long for a more structured life, a life where she could watch television without having to stare through the window at Dixons and go to the toilet without taking a spade. She was twenty-one, Mrs. Thatcher had just won yet another election, and Polly had not been entirely clean since Duran Duran had been at the top of the charts.

She left Ziggy, which hurt him badly.

"But why, Poll?" he asked. "I thought we had a scene going."

"It's the giggling, Ziggy. I just can't handle the giggling."

"I'll giggle less," he pleaded. "I'll start smoking hash instead of grass. It's a much mellower high."

But it was no use. Polly left the convoy and moved to London, where she virtually became a street person, spending two months standing on the never-ending picket outside the South African Embassy. It was while on the antiapartheid picket that Polly met an alternative comedian called Dave, whose opening line was "Good evening, ladies and gentlemen. Would you like to see my bollocks?" Dave was nice, but he was, in his own words, "Not into monogamy, right?" In truth, he saw his gigs as no more than a good way of pulling girls. There might have been a time when Polly would have turned a blind eye to such behavior, but these were the great days of AIDS paranoia so Polly took one last look at Dave's bollocks and moved on again.

It was around this time that Jack also moved on, leaving his regiment in Germany and returning to the U.S. to take up a post at the Pentagon. He, like Polly (and Bono), hadn't found what he was looking for either, but, unlike Polly, he had a good idea of what it was and where it might be found. What Jack was looking for was success, and, for a soldier without a war to fight, that meant going to

Washington. In Washington promotion prospects were, if not good, certainly better than on the Rhine.

It was a frustrating time for an ambitious soldier, although paradoxically the military had never been held higher in the nation's esteem. Reagan, who had never served in the forces himself, was a soldier's president. He believed in big defense budgets and plenty of parades. U.S. prestige could not have been greater, the Soviet Union was hemorrhaging in Afghanistan, and the corridors of power buzzed with news of the famed Star Wars initiative with which the Pentagon intended to militarize space. Public interest in the army was unprecedented, with gung ho movies like *Rambo* and *Top Gun* filling the cinemas. Things had improved considerably since the dark days of twenty years before when an adolescent Jack had refused to accompany his parents and his brother Harry to see *M*A*S*H* and *Catch-22*, a terrible, demoralizing time when America had been briefly ashamed of its fighting men.

Nonetheless, for all the celluloid mayhem, real soldiers do actually need real wars in order to be promoted. If the fellow above you does not get shot, then you have to wait twenty years for him to retire and the same goes for the fellow above him. Jack was thirty-six and getting frustrated.

"I'm middle-fucking-aged and still a captain!" he wrote to Harry. *"I was one of the youngest captains ever. You remember that? It was in the local paper and everything."*

Harry did indeed remember it. Their father and mother had been furious with embarrassment.

"Not only does he have to be a soldier," Jack Senior had lamented over his muesli and fat-free organic yogurt. "He has to be a successful soldier. Why didn't we just bring up a fascist and be done with it! I just hope that none of my students get to hear about this. Every day I bust my ass trying to civilize young people and now my own son is the youngest damn captain in the army!"

At the time Jack had been delighted at his father's discomfort, but as the years went by and he felt himself sinking into career doldrums Jack felt less inclined to crow.

"*The youngest captain, Harry!*" Jack wrote from Washington. "*That was what I was for a couple of years, and by hell did I rub Pa's face in it? Then for a while I was a youngish captain, now I'm just a reasonable age to be a captain. It won't be long before I'm an old captain. Then like thousands of other captains I'm going to have to decide whether to retire and strike out in civilian life, fifteen years behind all the other guys (with you and Dad laughing in my face), or stay on and face the possibility of a very sad career indeed. Jesus, when Napoléon was my age he'd conquered the world once and was thinking about making a comeback! When Alexander the Great was my age he was dead! I know I'm a good soldier, Harry, but there's no way of showing it. On parade I just look the same as all the other guys. You remember Schultz? The geek nerd I told you about before? He's in Washington too and he has equal seniority with me!! Equal!! I mean, he's a decent guy and all that, but Jesus! He has the strategic instincts of a lemming!*"

Harry was in no doubt what Jack should do. He told him to cut his losses and get out.

"*Never,*" Jack wrote back. "*The army is my life and I will never give it up, no matter how badly it treats me.*"

The truth was that Jack had already cut his losses. He had given up Polly in pursuit of military glory and whether he found that glory or not, he could never get back what he had lost.

As for Polly, she was in a much worse position than Jack. As the eighties turned into the nineties she was without a proper home, without possessions, without qualifications or security of any kind, and she was lonely.

She went to live in a squat in Acton, a sad house with boarded-up windows that had been repossessed by the council because they were widening the A40 to Oxford. It was occupied mainly by the warriors of Class War, a loose collective of malcontents made up principally of Oxbridge graduates who wanted to destroy the state, probably because unlike most of their friends they had failed to get high-ranking jobs at the BBC.

At twenty-five Polly knew that her life was twisting downward, out of control, but she did not know how to stop it. All her old friends were young professionals with incomes. Polly no longer saw them, but her mother, of course, kept her informed about their huge successes. Most of Polly's more recent friends were either stoned, in prison, or chained to lumps of concrete in tunnels underneath the roadworks on Twyford Down. The new decade had also brought with it the threat of war in the Middle East, which was most depressing for Polly, since if there was one meaningful thing she had tried to do over the previous eight years it was fight for peace.

By a strange twist of fate it was because of Saddam Hussein that Polly came to see Jack again, if only for a moment and only on the television, but it was a painful shock nonetheless. It was in January 1991 and Polly and friends were lying around their squat on their damp mattresses watching the military buildup in the Gulf on their tiny black and white portable television screen. John Major had just been speaking about the need to stand up to aggression and mad despots wherever they reared their heads.

"Ha!" said Polly earnestly. "If Kuwait dug potatoes instead of oil we wouldn't give a toss about them. We didn't mind about mad despots in Chile and Nicaragua, did we? And why? Because they were our mad despots, weren't they?"

Polly was just working herself up into a fair state of righteous anger when it happened. Suddenly, Jack was in the room. Standing in front of a tank, now a full colonel, and giving it as his opinion that Saddam's men were lions led by donkeys.

"We don't want to have to kill these soldiers," Jack said from within the tiny TV, "but let the butcher of Baghdad be under no illusions that we will kill them, and we will kill them quickly and efficiently."

Polly felt like she had been kicked. It was so unexpected and over so soon. While her companions continued to argue with the talking heads on television she retreated to the kitchen, all the anger and hurt welling up inside her once again.

And the love.

He still looked beautiful to her. Achingly so. Even in one of those awful Wehrmacht-style helmets that the Americans had taken to wearing at that time. He looked so commanding and so confident, so strong, forceful, and fit. All of a sudden Polly found that she did not just miss Jack, she was jealous of him. Jack knew what he wanted, he knew where he was going, he always had, and he was still on the winning side. Polly wiped the silverfish off the breadboard and started to cry.

[23]

Jack stared at Polly and smiled.

She was still lovely. Her home might be dowdy and her possessions rather run down and few, but she lit up that room like a search-
light, like a bright star. Jack swallowed hard. He had not expected
it, he really had not expected her still to be so very beautiful. As far
as Jack was concerned, the passage of time had completely failed to
dull her loveliness.

"I don't think you changed, Polly," he almost whispered. "You
didn't age a day."

"Bollocks, Jack."

Jack laughed. "Now there's a word I haven't heard in a long
time. But really, how did you do it? Is it some face cream made out
of dead whales, or do you have a portrait in your attic of some terrible dissipated old hag?"

"This *is* my attic, Jack. I live in it."

Now that Polly had got over the initial shock of Jack's arrival it
was beginning to dawn on her how strange the situation was.

"I don't know why I've let you in. I was asleep . . . The place is
a mess . . . Why have you come back?"

"Why do you think, Polly? Why do you think I've come?"

"How the hell would I know? I don't even know you."

"You know me, Polly."

"I know you're a bastard!"

Jack shrugged.

"It is nearly two-thirty in the bloody morning, Jack!"

"I do unusual work," said Jack, shrugging again. "Where I come from we keep strange hours."

He was just the same. Still arrogant, still forceful.

"Yes, well, back here on earth we tend to sleep in the middle of the night!"

"May I take off my coat? May I sit down?"

It was the small hours of the morning. He'd been gone for donkey's years and he wanted to take off his coat and sit down. Polly's mind reeled.

"No! This is absurd. I don't know why I let you in at all. I think you should go. If you want to see me you can come back in the morning."

"I'll be gone in the morning, Polly."

This was too much for Polly. It was hardly what might have been called a tactful thing to say, considering how they had parted the last time they'd been together.

"Yes, well, some things don't change, then, do they, you . . . You . . ."

Polly bit her lip and fell silent. Of course she was angry with him, angry with him for leaving her and angry with him for coming back in such a strange manner. But, for all that, she was so very glad that he had come back.

"It's just I'm only in Britain for a few hours, Polly. This was the only time I could come."

"Jack, it's been, it's been . . . I don't know how long it's been . . ."

"Sixteen years."

"I know how long it's been!"

As if she could forget. As if she didn't remember every moment of that summer and every day that had passed since.

"Sixteen years and two months, to be precise," said Jack, who seemed also to have been carefully marking the passage of time.

"Exactly! Exactly. Sixteen years and two months, during which time it appears that you have been more than capable of getting by without seeing me, and you want to visit me now!"

"Yes."

"And seeing as how it's only been sixteen years and two months, seeing as how it's only been the merest decade and a half since we last set eyes on each other, you have to visit immediately, not a moment to lose, at two-fifteen in the morning!"

"I told you. I'm only in town for one night."

"Well, why not drop by when you have a little more space in your diary! Heaven knows, we might even arrange a mutually convenient appointment."

"I'm never in Britain, Polly. This is the first time I've been here since we . . . since I . . . since then." His voice trailed off rather weakly.

They were both remembering the chill dawn when he had left.

"Why didn't you come back before?" asked Polly.

"I couldn't. I go where I'm told."

Weak. He knew it, and so did she.

"That is pathetic."

"Polly, I take orders."

"That's what they said at Nuremberg."

Jack bridled somewhat. He knew he was in the wrong but he was not the sort of person who found contrition easy and he certainly wasn't having Nuremberg thrown at him. All his life he had been deeply irritated at the way people, particularly people of a liberal persuasion, particularly his father and mother, had gotten into the habit of using the Nazis as some kind of ready benchmark for things of which they disapproved. If somebody wanted to cut welfare benefits they were a Nazi, if somebody wanted to raise the bus fares they were a Nazi, if they objected to graffiti they were a Nazi. It was just puerile. Jack was prepared to put up his hand to the fact that he may have acted like a swine but he had not murdered six million Jews.

"Oh, please, Polly. Is everybody still a fascist? Didn't you grow out of that yet?"

"Didn't you grow out of not having a personality?" Polly's withering contempt almost singed Jack's eyebrows. " 'I take orders,' " she snarled in a mock American accent. "What? And they ordered you never to write? Never to call? To disappear off the face of the planet and ignore every telephone in the U.S.A. for sixteen years!"

"They would not have approved."

"And if they ordered you to stick an umbrella up your arse and open it? Would you do that?"

"Yes, I would." Of course he would. What did she think he was? He was a soldier; did she think soldiers only did things they wanted to?

"Well, then, I hope they do. A fucking great Cinzano beach umbrella with a pointy end and a couple of twisted spokes."

Jack glanced at his watch. It was nearly 2:30. He had to be in Brussels for a lunchtime meeting the next day. That meant flying out at 10:30 at the latest.

Polly caught his look. "I'm sorry if I'm boring you!"

Jack hated that. Ever since Jack could remember, women had been offended with his checking his watch. As if his desire to know the time and keep his appointments was some kind of deathly insult to the power of their personalities.

"I like to know the time, that's all."

"It's two-fifteen in the fucking morning, Jack! We established that."

It wasn't, it was already 2:30 and Jack was on a schedule.

"Polly, believe me," he said. "I know I should have contacted you before. There hasn't been a day when I didn't think about you. Not a single day."

Polly did not know whether to believe him or not. It seemed unlikely, but if it was true it was a wonderful thing. That through all those years, especially those early ones when she had hurt so much at her loss, he had been thinking about her.

"They just never sent me back to Britain before, that's all," Jack continued.

"Even you get holidays."

What did she know? She didn't know anything. He got time off, certainly. Time when he was not required to spend the day planning the deaths of thousands of enemy soldiers. Time when he was at liberty to go fishing or take a drive along the coast. But men in his position did not get holidays, not real holidays, holidays from who and what they were. Jack was never just Jack, not for a single moment; he was General Jack Kent, one of the most senior figures in the defense systems of the United States. Twenty-four hours a day, three hundred and sixty-five days a year.

"I'm always on duty."

"Oh, for heaven's sake."

"I tell it like I see it."

"Yeah, well, so do I, and what I see is a coward and a shit."

"Hey, Polly . . . I'm not a coward."

He could always make her laugh. That effortlessly cool self-deprecating humor that only strong, confident people can pull off.

Polly almost weakened and laughed with him. For a moment a tiny smile twitched at the corners of her mouth. He saw it, and she knew he saw it, but she wasn't giving in that easily.

"So now, after nearly seventeen years your 'duty' brings you back to Britain for a night?"

"Yes. One night."

"And you couldn't warn me? You couldn't call from the airport?"

"No. I couldn't warn you. I'm sorry, but that's the way it is. All I could do was come and I did. I got into Brize Norton tonight and I came straight here."

It was a lie, of course, but Jack sort of felt that it was true. He had after all wanted to come straight to Polly. He had certainly come the moment his circumstances allowed him to, the moment he had made his presentation to the Cabinet and said farewell to the ambassador.

The lie worked. Polly stared into Jack's eyes. He had come straight to her. That was certainly something, something exciting she could not deny. Nor could she deny how handsome he had remained. More handsome than ever, even. She liked the gray at his temples and she preferred him without the early eighties' Burt Reynolds mustache. He seemed leaner somehow, tougher. He had certainly not gone old and soft over the years.

Then she remembered that she hated him. That he had dumped her without a word, without so much as a good-bye. He was a shit.

"This is absurd, Jack. I'm bloody dreaming. What are you saying? You came straight here! Why? Why did you come straight here? I was seventeen years old. It was nearly twenty years ago—"

"Sixteen years and two—"

"I know! I know how long it was! It was another life. We are total strangers now! I ought to throw you out."

Jack fell silent and looked at Polly. He said nothing, but his stare grew in intensity until Polly began to feel quite uncomfortable. It was as if Jack was preparing to unburden himself, to share his secrets with her. Then his spirit appeared to desert him, his shoulders sagged, his eyes dropped, and he sighed.

"You're right," he said. "This is dumb. Completely dumb. Insane. I should go."

Jack turned wearily toward the door, deflated and lost, a man whose poor, sad, hopeless dreams had been exposed as just that. It worked, of course.

"Don't be ridiculous! You can't just go!"

"I thought you wanted me to."

"No! That's not fair! You can't wait sixteen years and two months, wake me up in the middle of the night, barge in, and then barge out again."

Again a pause. "So you don't want me to go?"

"I don't know what I want."

Polly took up a packet of slightly milder than full-strength cigarettes from the kitchen table. As she bent over the gas stove to light one, the stiff plastic raincoat she was wearing stood out from her thighs and revealed a little more of her bare legs. She still had wonderful legs, fabulous legs. Jack had always loved Polly's legs, but then he had always loved everything about Polly. She turned back toward him, leaned against the stove, and inhaled deeply. Jack almost laughed, remembering the long evenings they had spent lying together after making love, watching the glowing ends of their cigarettes in the darkness, talking, disagreeing on every single thing under the sun except their desire to be together.

[24]

Peter's whole being reeled with hatred. He had watched from the shop doorway as the American man entered Polly's house and had stood for five minutes or so as if in a trance. The jealousy and sense of betrayal were so all-consuming that he had found himself unable to move. She was seeing other men! Sneaking them in in the middle of the night so that he wouldn't see them! Tricking him into thinking she was being good when in fact she was nothing but a lying, cheating slut. And as for him. As for that American bastard. Peter had no vocabulary in his head with which to encompass the scope of his loathing for that man. It sat in his consciousness as a sort of red blur.

However, once Peter had come round from his state of shock he knew absolutely that he must retrieve his knife at once. If ever he needed it he needed it now. He rushed back up the road to the phonebox, back to the drain down which the hated American had kicked his knife. Peter had seen that it had lodged on a jutting brick before he had run away. The question was, would it still be there?

Of course it was. How could it not be; it was Peter's precious knife and it would not be taken from him so easily. Kneeling in the gutter he could see it, lodged still, awaiting his retrieval. Peter went off to find a suitable tool with which to recover the knife and soon returned with an old wire coat hanger picked from the rubbish in a nearby Dumpster. Out of this he fashioned a long hook. He knew that the knife had a little hinged curve of metal attached to its innocent end by which a person might fasten the weapon to a belt. It was into this that Peter planned to place his hook. His challenge was to do this without dislodging the knife and causing it to fall farther out of reach. So he knelt down in the sodden gutter and set to his task, dangling his hook into one of the numerous gaping mouths that fed and watered subterranean London with rubbish, effluence, and rain.

"Bastard. Fucking bastard. I'll get you. I'll get you," mumbled Peter under his breath, and he was not referring to the knife.

[25]

"You still smoke?" Jack inquired.

"I'm giving up soon," Polly replied defensively, "in a week or two, this month, I hope. Certainly by the end of the year. Don't tell me you quit?"

Jack hadn't wanted to give up smoking, but he'd been forced to. He worked for the government; it was either give up or become a pathetic nonperson. Quite apart from anything else, smoking had got too tiring. The smoke exclusion zones around public buildings had been getting wider and wider since Clinton got in. In vain had he argued at the highest level that to make the Pentagon a no-smoking area was something of a sick joke. He and his colleagues had pointed out to their political masters that since the Pentagon was a building in which mass chemical and nuclear genocide was planned daily, it seemed almost tasteless to introduce a health code.

Polly was surprised. Jack had always been so gung ho about his smoking.

"You said you'd never give up. You said you'd rather die."

"Yeah, well, I didn't know then that the greatest country in the world would end up getting run by a bunch of killjoy liberal fucking pussies, did I?"

That was the other side of Jack, of course. Polly remembered it well. The unreconstructed reactionary. The bullying, bigoted, yobbo soldier with the sexual and political sensitivity of Genghis Khan's hordes on an angry and randy day. The strange thing was that she had always secretly found conservatism rather attractive. He was so honest and unashamed about being a right-wing bastard. As a deeply confused liberal herself, Polly found that kind of confidence rather compelling.

"Nice to know you haven't changed," she said. "The kinder, gentler America passed you by, then?"

"Oh yeah? Maybe we should start trying to be a little kinder and gentler to the guys who like to drink and smoke and read *Play-boy* magazine now and again! It's the hypocrisy I can't stand. They had their fun. Fifteen years ago those same star fucking Democrat assholes that are banning smokes were taking cocaine in their coffee. Now coffee carries a health warning."

"Yeah, well, you're lucky. I'd love to kick the fags," Polly replied. "Sometimes I buy one mgs, but then I just smoke them six or seven at a time."

Polly leaned against the table, placed her fingers over the little airholes in the filter that were supposed to dilute the tar, and inhaled deeply. Jack watched her chest rise as she did so and he longed to fall upon her as of old. She walked around the table to pick up an ashtray and again Jack could not help but notice how attractive her legs were. As good as ever, he thought; better, in fact. Now how could that be? He had it! They were shaved! Polly had shaved her legs, and recently, too. They were smooth and shiny, the skin bright in the light of the overhead lamp.

The old Polly, the young Polly, would on principle never have shaved her legs. She would have considered leg shaving to be a disgusting capitulation to sexist male stereotyping of the female form, a very short step from having four kilos of silicon pumped into her tits and appearing naked in *Hustler*. Not that Polly's legs had been particularly hirsute in the old days. No hairier than most girls', but then most girls actually do have quite hairy legs if they let it grow free, even seventeen-year-olds. At the time Jack had sort of liked it because he loved her. She had been so different from the plucked, waxed, and sanded-down cheerleading Barbies whom he had dated previously, but even then he had only sort of liked it. Jack was in many things a traditionalist. He liked his petrol leaded and his ladies smooth and there was no denying that Polly's shapely calf muscles were all the finer without the fuzzy edges.

Polly exhaled again. The smell of smoke had filled the room by now and Jack breathed it in greedily.

"I'd love to take up smoking again," he said, "but I just don't have the guts. I fought the Iraqis, but the American antismoking lobby scares the shit out of me. If you light up in New York some mom in California will sue you for murdering her unborn child. It's insane. Guys who operate nuclear missiles for a living are getting sacked for perpetrating secondary lung cancer."

Polly realized that they were having a conversation. It had happened so easily she hadn't even noticed. After sixteen years and two months of pain and resentment, there they were, just having a conversation.

"Well, since you're here, Jack, you'd better give me your coat."

Jack took off his coat and Polly gulped with surprise. Underneath the coat Jack was resplendent in the dress uniform of an American four-star general. Polly laughed. It seemed the only thing to do. Jack could not have looked more out of place if he'd been a *Baywatch* babe in a nunnery. His epaulettes glinted, his belt buckle sparkled, his buttons shone, his shoulder braid strutted grandly, and his medal ribbons competed for attention upon his splendid chest. Anybody who had known Jack a decade or so earlier when he had believed his career to be grinding to a halt would have gasped to see him now. In the cabinet room at Ten Downing Street Jack had looked superb. The creaky, threadbare, down-at-heel members of Her Majesty's Government had provided a more than fitting setting for this splendid warrior from the New World. But context is everything and in Polly's studio he looked like the conductor in a rather tasteless brass band.

"Jesus, Jack, what are you? John Wayne? Did you come back to Britain to invade it?"

It had not occurred to Jack until that point that he was dressed in a manner that some might consider unusual. In Jack's position he was expected to wear dress uniform all the time, and on the whole he rather enjoyed it. Now, however, he felt self-conscious. Like a person who has proudly put on a black tie to attend a very special function but still has to get to the event by bus. It feels great while you are attaching the bow tie and the cuff links. It'll feel great again when you're greedily plucking the first flute of Italian sparkling from a passing tray. The period in between, however, is not so good, when one is forced by circumstance to mix with the less exalted, the ordinarily dressed. At this point, frankly, one feels a bit of a prick.

"You never did like uniforms much, did you?" he said with the tiniest hint of ill grace.

"I think they're a bit sad, that's all. If you can't express your authority without strutting about like a fascist, then you can't have had much authority in the first place."

Again that childish fascist thing. Jack let it go.

"Yeah, well, I had to wear this stuff," he said instead. "It was required."

"What, for me?"

Jack would have to be honest. "No, not you. When I said I came straight here, what I meant was that I came straight here when I could. I had a meeting earlier, that's why I'm in Britain. Politicians like to see you in uniform. I think it makes them feel important. They're the only kind of people who ever get to play with real soldiers."

Jack had calculated that this last comment would appeal to Polly, but if it did she ignored it.

"Politicians? What politicians?"

"Mainly your prime minister."

Polly gulped again in astonishment. When the phone had woken her a little while ago she'd been dreaming, of what she couldn't remember, but being a dream it would no doubt have been fairly surreal, possibly containing marshmallow hippopotamuses in tutus and a great deal of falling. Since then her life had been a whirl of psycho-stalkers, old flames, and ancient enemies, and now casual references to visits with the highest in the land. Reality was proving far more bizarre than anything Polly's subconscious mind had been conjuring up. The pink hippos were beginning to seem rather mundane.

"The prime minister! The prime fucking minister! You've come here after seeing the prime minister!"

To Jack this wasn't such a big deal. He saw top people all the time. Certainly the prime minister of Britain was an important person, but there were any number of prime ministers dotted about the world, fifty at a minimum. They came and they went, sometimes before the news readers had even learned how to pronounce their names properly. Jack had met most of them one way or another and Polly's astonished reaction rather took him aback. He was about to say "Yeah, the PM. So what?" but then decided it would be rude. To her, he supposed, it was as if he'd turned up at an apartment in the Bronx and casually remarked that he'd just been visiting with the president and first lady.

"It wasn't just me, you know, one on one," he said, as if to downplay the grandeur of the situation. "There were the chiefs of staff . . . That's the top guys in your . . ."

"I know who the chiefs of staff are, Jack. Unless you'd forgotten, I once had the opportunity to study matters military at close quarters."

"Yeah." Jack laughed. "I guess you were a combatant too, weren't you? A soldier of the Cold War."

How many were there like her now? Ex-combatants of an ideological struggle that had simply faded away. All around the world were people hidden in flats and studios, eking out their lives, who had once been warriors. Who had once locked horns with superpowers. Soldiers, spies, resistance fighters, protesters. In her way Polly was such a one, another Cold War loser. For a time she had fought NATO with the same commitment that Jack had defended it. But it was over now and the battle that Polly had fought was fast fading in the memory of all but the people involved.

Jack remembered it, of course, and suddenly he longed with all his heart to return once again to that golden time, the summer of his and Polly's love. How he ached to see her naked once more. To be blinded afresh by her youth and beauty. A beauty that had been so pure and unencumbered by artifice. So naturally erotic, so effortlessly sexual. Jack longed to advance upon Polly then and there, as once he had, breathless and shaking with a dizzying, overwhelming passion, his entire being utterly and completely focused. No longer a whole and complex man but a desperate, straining sexual entity that knew no other time than the moment and no other purpose than to make love.

Polly caught the look in Jack's eyes as they journeyed downward and then up again over her body, lingering for a moment on her legs, bare to just above the knee and again on the triangle of flesh visible at her open collar.

"Look, if you're staying," she said, "I should get dressed."

"Why?" Jack replied.

[26]

Outside in the wet and empty street Peter knelt in the gutter, his fingers straining at the metal grid that covered the drain. His upper lip was crusted with blood from when the door of the telephone box had bashed his nose. The knees of his trousers were soaking up the filthy London water and the rain was falling on his head.

Peter noticed none of these things.

His whole being was concentrated on the black hilt and glinting steel blade that he could see lodged three feet or so below him. His precious knife, sitting precariously on the jutting brick within the wall of that water-bloated urban intestine. His precious weapon, teetering on the brink of the bowels of the city.

"Bastard. Bastard. Fucking bastard," he muttered through the soggy scabs of blood and the bitter-tasting rain.

[27]

Polly stared at Jack. What had he just said? Don't bother getting dressed?

His eyes had been awash with sensual longing and he had told her not to bother getting dressed. Now she scarcely knew what to think. Was he asking her to bed? That would be a bold move indeed. Had he burst back into her life in order to fuck her as quickly as possible? It was, after all, how it had happened the first time, in his TR7. They had been unable to keep their hands off each other. Looking at Jack as he looked at her Polly was shocked to discover that a substantial part of her was excited at the prospect of leaping instantly into bed with this man who had betrayed her. Her sensual self wanted to surrender instantly to whatever Jack wanted. Why not? She was a grown woman, she was entitled to take a bit of comfort as and when she pleased. Unfortunately for Polly's sensual self, her intellectual and emotional self recoiled at the idea, feeling angry and abused. Her political self felt even worse about it; outraged would not be too strong a word for how her political self felt. Did Jack think that he could have it all? That he could shatter her life into tiny little bits and then pick up a piece when the fancy took him?

"What do you mean?" said Polly, defiantly drawing herself up to her full height. A gesture that served merely to raise her plastic raincoat higher, thus revealing rather more of her legs than was already showing.

Jack had not meant what Polly was thinking, in fact. Of course, to make love there and then would be nice, ecstatic in fact. Like Polly, a part of Jack longed to pick up where they had left off so many years before and go to bed. His sensual self would have delighted in spending the remainder of the night making the crockery rattle and furniture jump round the room. But also like Polly, Jack's intellectual self was raising objections; sex was not what he had come for, or what he had expected. There were things he wanted to discuss, things he needed to know. Sex would get in the way and Jack did not have a limitless amount of time. He tried to correct any misunderstanding.

"When I said 'Why get dressed?' what I meant, of course, was why get dressed when you'd only have to get undressed again?"

Which of course did not correct any misunderstandings at all.

"What the hell do you mean by that?"

Jack tried again. "No, I don't mean . . . What I mean is I can't stay long . . . I don't want to inconvenience you."

"Which is why you dropped round at two in the morning."

Polly had always had a caustic side. Jack could remember having found it rather cute. At this point he couldn't quite remember why.

"I don't have long, that's all."

"Well, thank you so much for giving me a whole five minutes out of your busy schedule after seventeen years without a word and at two-thirty in the morning. I'm so grateful."

"Look!" said Jack, a little more firmly than he had intended. "I just don't have all that long. I'm sorry, but it's true. Anyway, why get dressed? You're probably better dressed now than you were when we met the first time."

Both Polly and Jack were straddling two different times. Principally they were in the here and now and it was late and their relationship was edgy to say the least. But also, for a moment, they were back there and then and it was glorious summer and love was flowering in the very shadow of Armageddon. The first time that their paths had crossed, before their encounter at the restaurant on the A34, when they had met and did not know even that they were meeting. At the gates of the camp, when out of the valley of death had ridden a handsome soldier mounted on a jeep who had found his way obstructed by a beautiful golden maiden, a symbol of peace.

"Yes, well, sartorial considerations tended to go out of the window in those days," Polly replied.

"Not that you had any windows," said Jack.

"No, I didn't, that's right. You can't put windows in a woodland bender."

Jack had not expected that he would feel things quite this violently, that his emotions would be so very much the same as they had been before.

"You were so beautiful, Polly," said Jack. "So wild. I can see you now as if it was only a heartbeat ago. Like some kind of . . ." He struggled for words. Jack had never been big on flowery prose, but he had a go: ". . . like some gorgeous woodland creature running along the side of the road, tanned legs in the long grass, the sun in your hair."

"Screaming at you to fuck off and die."

It was true. To her shame (and the embarrassment of Madge), Polly had often chose to ignore the nonaggressive principles of the peace camp and address the soldiers in most unpeaceful terms.

"We love you! We want to understand you!" Madge would shout.

"Fuck off! Fuck off! Fuck off!" Polly would add.

And in the evening around the fire the women would all agree that it was important to try not to give mixed signals.

"You were perfect, Polly," said Jack, his eyes half closed. "A vision. I remember the first moment I saw you exactly. I have it fixed in my mind like some kind of idyll . . . like an Impressionist painting."

"Jack, I was wearing a dustbin liner."

"You still like plastic, I see."

Polly remembered that she was wearing a raincoat and returned to the present with a bump.

"I don't have a dressing gown, I'm afraid."

In her punkier days Polly would not have thought twice about receiving guests in a nightie and a plastic raincoat, but times had changed. "I'm not used to entertaining under these circumstances. Sit down, Jack. I'd ask you to step through into the lounge, but I haven't got one."

"Hey, you never used to have a roof."

"Yeah, haven't I done well? I no longer sleep in the open."

Polly was embarrassed about everything. What she was wearing, her little flat, her stuff. Why couldn't he have given her some warning of his visit? Just so she could have got herself together? She would not have needed long. Just enough time to move house and acquire some beautiful and glamorous possessions. Shift her career up ten or fifteen gears and have a little minor repair work done on the cellulite that was beginning to appear on her upper thighs.

Instead Jack was seeing her life as it really was.

"Still rejecting capitalist materialism, I see."

Jack had never been the most tactful of people.

"No. These days capitalist materialism is rejecting me," Polly replied. "Getting its own back for the years I abused it. Sit down. You won't catch anything, you know."

There were two easy chairs for Jack to choose from, both, of course, already occupied with assorted stuff. Polly's theory was that when you live in one room everything is a wardrobe. Chairs, tables, plant pots, casserole dishes. Everything is a place in or on which to put other things. In fact as far as Polly was concerned her whole flat was one big wardrobe and she was just one of the things in it. Jack could never have lived like that. Being a military man who had spent most of his life ready to pack up and leave at a moment's notice, he knew that the key to comfort was organization.

One of Polly's chairs was clearly an impossible proposition in terms of sitting down. Jack could see that there was no point in even thinking about unloading the dazzling cornucopia of things it contained. There were jumpers, books, newspapers, magazines, a partially dissected Russian doll. Stuffed toys, a guitar, an old typewriter, videocassettes, a radio, a bicycle pump attached to a deflated inner tube, coffee mugs, and a roll of rush matting. Also wedged onto the chair was a Fair Trade South American string shopping bag containing three cans of baked beans and a packet of chocolate digestives. Polly was quite good about putting away groceries, but only quite. She always dealt with perishable items like milk and frozen peas the moment she got in from the shops, but dry and tinned goods she tended to leave in the shopping bag. After all, what was a South American string shopping bag if not a bag-shaped cupboard made of string?

On top of all of this was a strange, blue, plastic, traylike object that Jack recognized immediately from the back of a thousand Sunday color supplements. It was an abdominizer, a device for exercising the tummy. Polly had sent off for it two years previously. It had never been used, of course, and the unread instructions had long since been lost. The thing just drifted gently about Polly's home from year to year, settling for a while before moving on silently and unnoticed. It had been on its current perch beside the shopping bag for about a month and was probably vaguely thinking about moving on. Perhaps to the clean clothes drawer, where there was always plenty of room. Apart from gathering dust the abdominizer's only contribution to Polly's life was to cause her the occasional pang of guilt. Not, however, a pang sufficiently strong to cause her to lie down upon the thing and gently roll her shoulders upward by means of contracting her stomach muscles (while keeping her knees raised and her feet flat on the floor).

There was no way that Jack was ever going to be able to sit on that chair. There was more stuff wedged between its arms than could possibly ever logically or physically actually fit. Jack could see that if he were to empty it into the room he and Polly would have to stand outside.

On Polly's other chair was a big plastic sack of fertilizer. Jack found this item slightly surprising.

"Fertilizer, Polly?"

"I have a window box."

Since the fertilizer was clearly a simpler proposition to clear than the contents of the other chair Jack lifted it to the floor. Not an easy task. This was a sack of fertilizer, not a bag but a sack.

"Jesus. Some window box. What are you going to do? Grow a tree in it?"

"I run a tight budget. Things are cheaper in bulk."

Jack thumped the sack down on the floor. Polly winced, thinking of the milkman below.

In the flat below, the milkman stirred in his bed. He glanced at his radio alarm clock. 2:40.

"Ha," thought the milkman with sleepy satisfaction. The next time the upstairs woman asked him to turn down his morning radio, which he already had on so as you could barely hear it, he would be ready.

"Twatting great thumping and banging at two-thirty in the morning, love," he would say. "Nearly jumped out of my twatting skin. Couldn't get back to sleep for an hour after . . ."

That is what he would say, the milkman thought, as he drifted back to sleep.

"Sorry," Jack said. "Damn thing slipped out of my hands."

"Well, for Christ's sake be careful," said Polly. "I have to share this house with other people, you know."

"Yeah, well, like I said, sorry."

Jack looked down at the plastic sack and for some strange reason felt a momentary tremor of alarm. Something about that bag was wrong, or at least resonant of something wrong, but he couldn't imagine what. Suddenly he felt uneasy, slightly threatened as if the bag was a warning. He had the distinct feeling that he ought to be making some kind of connection, but it was eluding him. Fertilizer? What could possibly be bad or sinister about that? Yet he wondered.

"Chemical, too," Jack said, his tone betraying a slight hint of his unease.

"You have a problem with that?" Polly inquired.

"No, not at all."

Of course he didn't. What could possibly be wrong about fertilizer?

"Except," he added, "it's not quite the organic pastoral utopia you and the girls used to talk about, is it? I would have thought you would have favored natural fertilizer."

"Yeah, well, it's tough keeping an animal in a studio, Jack. I used to shit out of the window, of course, but the neighbors complained."

Jack sat down on the chair he'd cleared. As he did so his mobile phone rang. Polly jumped nearly out of her skin. For a moment she imagined that the Bug was back.

But that was just silly. He was hardly likely to have Jack's number.

[28]

"Excuse me," said Jack. "I have to take this."

Polly's look assured him that he was not welcome.

"Yeah?" said Jack.

It was Schultz, General Kent's number two. After all the years, Schultz's career was still shadowing Jack's. It was astonishing to Jack that such a man could become a general, but he seemed to have always been in the right place at the right time. And of course he never gave offense to anybody. Being incapable of making a decision, he had never ruffled any feathers, and that was an important part of promotion in a peacetime army. Schultz had appeared to simply float up the ranks in the wake of better men. For the sake of the soldiers in the field Jack prayed that Schultz never floated into a combat command.

"I hope I'm not disturbing you, General," Schultz said.

"Jesus, Schultz, of course you're fucking disturbing me. It's the middle of the night. I was asleep!" Jack snapped into his phone.

From a desk deep inside the American Embassy, General Schultz would have liked to point out that some people were lucky to be getting any sleep at all. But he didn't. He was far too scared of Jack. Instead he apologized and explained that he had been forced to call because their schedule for the following day had changed.

"It's the Brussels summit on the former Warsaw Pact nations," Schultz explained.

This was Jack's least favorite subject. The planned expansion of NATO up to the very borders of Russia. He thought it dangerous madness. Jack had risen high in the army but he expected to rise higher and he had no wish to do so only to inherit a crippled defense alliance for which he would then be held responsible. If, a year or two down the track, NATO found itself overstretched and unable to secure and control its own borders, it would be his, not some ex-president's, career that would end in ignominy.

"It's in-fucking-sane!" Jack barked into his phone. "We have a defense alliance that has kept Western democracy secure for over half a century and now on the whim of some fat fucking yuppie who just happens to be president we are inviting every basket case this side of the Urals to join. We can't possibly guarantee their security and we wouldn't want to even if we could. Half of them are going to end up dictatorships anyway!"

Polly sat down on her bed. It was all too strange to take in. There appeared to be a man using her room to conduct the business of the Western nuclear alliance. She was a peace woman, for heaven's sake!

In the American Embassy General Schultz was uncomfortable too, horrified that Jack should express such robust views over an easily tappable cellular phone. Jack's opinion was so alarmingly contrary to that of the president, who was, after all, their commander in chief.

"General Kent, as you are aware, the undersecretary of state feels—"

"The undersecretary of state is a triumph for the Pushy Ugly Women Lobby. She got her job because the president wants to show that in his America not only male assholes can achieve high office."

Polly harrumphed loudly from the bed. Now she was being forced to listen to laddish, sexist abuse. Jack made a silent sign toward her as if to say that he was sorry and that he wouldn't be long. Polly grimaced in reply.

Schultz was grimacing too. He was only trying to do his best.

"General, as you know, the undersecretary of state has accepted your proposal that the Russians attend the summit."

This was something. After all, it was the Russians and their worryingly unstable army whom Jack and this new NATO would be facing.

"But it seems," Schultz explained, "that the admiral of the Russian fleet needs to get back to the Black Sea by suppertime. I think he's scared they won't save any food for him. Or that his flagship will have sunk with the rust."

This was an attempt at a joke, but it fell flat.

"Funny, Schultz, I'm laughing here. I love to be woken up at two-forty-five in the morning by comedians."

In fact Jack did not think that the desperate plight of the ex-Soviet armed forces was remotely amusing. The fact that the world's second-largest nuclear force was now in the charge of cold, hungry, and embittered guardians who had been stripped of all status and pride struck terror into Jack's heart whenever he thought about it.

"I'm sorry," said Schultz over the phone. "It's been a long night. Just working out the seating for this thing is a minefield. Who gets priority, the Germans or the French?"

"The Germans, of course. The French will take offense wherever you seat them, so you might as well give them something to moan about."

"Well, anyway, the Russians want the meeting brought forward to noon Brussels time tomorrow," said Schultz. "That's eleven A.M. with us here in the U.K."

"Fucking Euros," Jack grumbled. "They think they can run a single currency; they can't even synchronize their watches."

"Our plane needs to leave Brize Norton by ten. Can I get them to send a car for eight?"

"I'll be here at the hotel waiting."

Jack put his phone away.

Polly was not happy. She did not like hearing herself denied in such a casual manner. If Jack was ashamed or embarrassed to be with her, then he should not have come. He had no right to sit there, on her chair, in her house, pretending that he was in a hotel. Old and bitter memories welled up inside her once more. Memories of a relationship denied, furtive and secret, conducted as if she had something of which to be ashamed. Memories of sneaking away from camp and skulking in bus shelters, waiting, sometimes for an hour, for Jack's car to appear. Memories of his making her swear over and over again that she had told no one of their affair. Of never being allowed to call Jack or even write to him directly. Of messages sent via the cold anonymity of a post office box. "Bus shelter. Six P.M."

For a time it had all seemed exciting and wicked, as if they were spies. But now it all looked merely deceitful and cowardly.

"Why did you pretend you were asleep, Jack? Why did you pretend you were still at your hotel?" Polly demanded. "Still the same gutless wonder? Still keeping me a secret? Still scared what the army will think?"

Jack did not want to quarrel. He had only one night and Schultz's call had just shortened it. There was so much he wanted to say. So much he wanted to know. He pushed NATO and its business from his mind and returned to the matter in hand.

"You live alone, don't you?" he said, ignoring Polly's irritation and stating the obvious.

"I do now."

"Now?"

"I was in something for quite a long time but the relationship had problems."

"What kind of problems?"

"Oh, nothing very much, just his wife and kids."

Jack looked hard at Polly. Now he thought about it she did look older, of course. No less lovely but definitely older. He was a good judge of faces and he did not think that Polly's life had been a particularly easy one.

"Tell me about him," Jack said gently.

Polly nearly did. She nearly sat down and blurted out the whole painful story of how, just when she had been getting herself back together again, she had allowed her life to be hijacked for a second time by an entirely inappropriate love affair. She nearly told him, but she didn't. Jack knew quite enough about her uncanny ability to choose the wrong men.

[29]

Polly left the squat in Acton in the late summer of 1991 and with a little money borrowed from her parents she took up her first entirely legal abode since leaving home eight years previously. A proper rented room in a shared house in Chiswick. From there she enrolled in a part-time A-level course at the local college of further education and set about picking up her life where she had left it before the summer of Jack's love.

It was a new decade, a new prime minister (if still a Conservative one), and a new beginning for Polly, who believed that she had finally really and truly got over Jack. Seeing him on the television had helped, a shock though it had been. Until then he had remained vigorously alive in her memory as her first, her most complete and special love. His sudden devastating departure had been the watershed of her young existence, marking the point at which she had lost a grip upon her life. Then all of a sudden he was on the TV and he was a stranger. A creature from another planet. An anonymous member of a hateful, sand-colored army of half a million men. He had nothing to do with her. It seemed extraordinary and unreal that he ever had.

The news broadcast had been repeated a number of times that evening, the same footage being shown again and again. Polly nearly told the story, she nearly pointed at the screen and stunned her friends by saying "See that bloke standing in front of the tank? I've had him," but she didn't. It was all too strange. Polly no longer really believed it herself.

During her A-level year Polly worked part-time as a waitress in an upmarket burger joint called New York New York (address, Chiswick High Street). The hours were unsociable but the tips were good and Polly shocked herself by discovering that with a judicious smile and a flirty manner she could make the tips even better. It did not take long for her to find out that shorter skirts meant more generous gratuities. She occasionally wondered what Madge and the girls from the camp would have made of that, but then she reasoned that if lads wanted to be wankers it seemed silly not to profit from it.

Feminism was changing anyway, at least that was what the style sections of the Sunday papers were saying. It was the year that saw the beginning of what was to become known as the new lad/new ladette trend, a period when it was pronounced all right to be a yob and behave badly. Of course in pubs and clubs up and down the country, life simply went on as usual. The lads carried on drinking beer and fighting, while the girls continued to discuss male member size loudly over bucketfuls of vodka and orange. To the metropolitan-style media, however, the new lad trend was a revelation. It appeared that boys and girls had become tired of the terrible social constrictions of political correctness and were now ready to be naughty again. With hindsight, the only lasting cultural impact of the whole business was that it became possible to have proper bra adverts again and that young women started to swear on Channel Four. At the time, though, it was all taken very seriously.

These were happy times for Polly. She liked having a proper home again, even if it was only a room plus shared everything else.

The two girls Polly lived with soon became friends, despite the usual problems of communal living. It seemed to Polly that Sasha always left the bathroom reeking of horrible perfume while Dorothy appeared to require every single saucepan in the house in order to boil one egg. For their part the other girls objected to Polly's apparent need to keep all of her underwear hanging over the bath even when it was dry. Also, inevitably, each of the three was convinced that she was the only person who ever cleaned the toilet or emptied the garbage or washed the tea towels, and there must also have been a thirsty ghost in the house because those teacups in the sink were certainly not any of hers. The phone, of course, was also a constant problem. None of the girls had wanted to bother with a timer, which would obviously be completely boring and fascistic; on the other hand, when the bills came none of them could believe that they had made a third of the calls.

There were only occasional real rows, but when these did happen they were proper, high-octane, full-volume, three-girl cat fights that they all secretly enjoyed. Anything could set one off: the carton of milk that one person had bought and the other two had drunk, the unreplaced washing powder, the hoovering, the boyfriend who vomited on the sofa and just put a cushion on it and left.

"Right, that's it!" they would scream at each other, "I'm sick of you bitches. I'm moving out!" But they didn't. They were having too much fun.

After A-levels Polly stayed on as a student and took a degree in sociology. Despite being rather depressingly classified as a mature student, she managed to have a pretty wild time in her first year. Illegal raves were the big thing at the time, the idea being to find somewhere vast, concrete, and fantastically unpleasant and stay there for fifteen hours. This, she thought, was the reason drugs suddenly got so big again. It was the only possible way to get through such a horrible night. Polly and the other girls took Ecstacy on a number of occasions, but soon got scared of it. There were so many stories going around about people who had only looked at a tab before becoming immediately paraplegic or dead.

The aftermath of a night on E was also rather painful. Polly was used to waking up with hangovers, but coming down in the cold gray light of dawn in the middle of a disused cattle market in Sussex presented a new low even for her. When she took a look around her at some of the dazed specimens upon whom she had bestowed huge kisses and protestations of undying affection on the previous night, she decided that booze was a safer drug.

It seemed to Polly that studying and raving was all students did anymore. She had been most disappointed to find how little political activism there was in the colleges. Fear of the future had long since beaten that out of the young. In the sixties and seventies it had been possible for students to rail and rant against society in the comfortable knowledge that they would shortly be joining it at a fairly elevated level. In the eighties, however, the world for graduates had become as uncertain as it was for everyone else, and few students felt they had the luxury to worry about other people.

After graduating Polly managed to get elected to Camden Council, with whom she also acquired a job working in the Equal Opportunities Office. It was here that she met and fell in love with another complete disaster.

The disaster's name was Campbell. Handsome, clever, highly qualified (a doctor), Campbell was also an extremely married man. He and Polly met during a weekend conference entitled "Race, Gender, Sexual Preference, and Local Government." Until tea on the second day Polly had found the conference only slightly more interesting than being dead, but Campbell changed all that. Like her, he was a Labour Councillor, but unlike her he was a leading

light in the local party, very much tipped to be selected as the par-
liamentary candidate to fight the next election. John Smith had died
and Tony Blair's leadership had ushered in a whole new generation
of slick, handsome, media-friendly professionals. Campbell was perfect for it, if a little old at forty.

Their affair was electric, one of those instant physical attractions
that cannot be denied. Polly and Campbell missed the final session
of the conference, "How Many Members of Senior Management
Have a Clitoris?" because they were having sex in a stationery closet.
After that they seemed to be incapable of meeting without having
sex. They took appalling risks, having it off in council offices, at
Campbell's surgery, behind the speaker's chair at the town hall, in
car parks, behind hedges, in front of hedges, on top of hedges, and
in the toilet of the Birmingham Pullman.

Polly worried about Campbell's wife, but Campbell of course assured her that he and Margaret had long since drifted apart. This,
sadly, would have come as surprising news to Margaret, who had absolutely no idea that anything was wrong.

If Margaret was ignorant of what was going on, then Polly was
not much wiser. Campbell was arrogant and weak and he spun a web
of desperate lies around himself and both women. When he and
Polly moved in together he told her that the three or four nights he
spent away each week were out of obligation to his children. He explained that although he and Margaret were now separate they were
still friends and had decided to maintain the family home until the
kids grew up. To Margaret he explained that he had taken up a part-
time teaching post at the University of Manchester Medical School
and hence would be away for half the week.

It could not last, of course. Campbell's lies got ever more desperate, particularly to Margaret. He told her that Telecom had still
not installed a telephone line in his Manchester flat; he told her that

for some reason his mobile could not get a signal where he was living. He told her not to phone the university as the cuts had so overstretched the secretarial staff that private calls were frowned upon.

And he told her, of course, he still loved her.

One Sunday morning Margaret turned up while Polly and Campbell were having breakfast together in the house they shared in Islington. Margaret had discovered the address from an electricity bill she had found in the laundry. It was probably the most excruciating encounter of Polly's life. She had stood there, a piece of toast frozen in her hand while the man who had said he loved her begged tearful forgiveness from the wife he claimed to have left.

Campbell left Polly that day. He had his kids and his political future to consider, and the initial all-consuming passion between him and Polly was dying out anyway. Margaret took him back, accepting his protestations that Polly had seduced him. She didn't want to take him back, she hated the idea, but she was a middle-aged housewife. She did not know what else she could do apart from have it off with the window cleaner in revenge, which she did.

Polly could no longer afford the house on her own and moved out. After a week or two of sleeping on floors she shifted into the Stoke Newington loft where Jack was to find her. Polly was alone once more, rejected and homeless, just when things had seemed to be shaping up. Polly simply could not believe what an idiot she had been. She did not even have the energy to hate Campbell. She was too annoyed with herself.

Her next all-consuming relationship was to be with Peter the Bug.

[30]

Jack reached into the bag he'd brought with him.

"I brought some Bailey's and some Coke. Is that still what you drink?"

"Young girls drink stuff like that, Jack. It's like eating sweets but with alcohol. We give it up when we discover gin."

Jack began to put his bottles away.

"Oh, all right, go on, then. I'll get some glasses." Polly's resistance had lasted all of ten seconds. "I haven't got anything to offer you, I'm afraid," she said.

Polly had stopped keeping booze in the house. She only drank it. Not that she was an alcoholic, but if there was alcohol around she would certainly have it. After all, how could a girl come home from the sort of job she did and ignore a nice big treble gin and tonic if it was standing on the sideboard? And once you've had one treble gin it seems slightly absurd not to have another. If there was a halfway decent late film on the telly or she'd rented a video, Polly could do half a bottle in an evening. She would pay for it, of course, with a saucepan by the bed all night and a slightly spacey nausea to follow, which sometimes lasted for two whole days. As Polly got older she had begun to find it safer to drink only in the pub.

Jack had also brought some bourbon for himself. Polly went

into her little kitchen and rinsed out two glasses, being careful to thumb off the lipstick on the rims. A girl did, after all, have standards.

Jack poured the drinks long, alarmingly so. Polly was not sure that she could handle a quarter of a pint of Bailey's.

"But you aren't married?" Jack inquired casually. "I mean, you've never been married?"

"No, I think marriage is an outmoded and fundamentally oppressive institution, a form of domestic fascism."

"Still sitting on the fence, then?"

Polly laughed despite herself.

"And you live alone?" Jack added.

"Yes, Jack, I live alone in Stoke Newington, which is, incidentally, a long way from the Pentagon. How the hell did you find me after all these years?"

Polly reminded herself that it should be her setting the conversational agenda, not him. Jack had no reason to be in her flat and certainly no right to be asking her about her personal life.

"Why are you here, Jack?"

"This guy, the married one. Did you ever tell him about us?"

"I said, why are you here?"

There were so many reasons why Jack was there. "I told you. To visit."

"Jack, that is not a good enough answer."

"You want me to go?"

He had her there and they both knew it. She did not want him to go, so she remained silent.

"Did you ever tell your boyfriends about us?" Jack continued.

"Why would you care?"

"I'm curious. You know . . . about what you thought of me after . . . if you thought of me at all. How you ended up describing me, to your friends and stuff . . . Did you tell them?"

"What possible business is it of yours whom I tell about any aspect of my disastrous life?"

"Well, none, I guess. I just wanted to know."

"I'll tell you," said Polly, "if you tell me how you found me."

Jack laughed. Finding people was no big deal to him. "That's easy. I'm an army general. I can get things found out."

"You mean you had me traced?"

"Sure I had you traced."

Now it was Polly's turn to laugh. "What? By secret intelligence or something? Spies?"

"Well, you know, it's not exactly James Bond. I mean nobody died or anything or used a pen that's also a flamethrower. I just had you traced. Any decent clerk can do it. You start with the last known address."

[31]

"A field, General?" the spook had said.

"That's right, Gottfried, that is the last address I have for her. A field in southern England called Greenham Common. We used to have a base there."

Gottfried was a captain in military intelligence. He had a keen brain and he spotted instantly that as addresses went this one was on the vague side. He did not say so, of course, it was not his place. Gottfried had the gentle, self-deprecating air of a good butler and like a good butler he missed very little. He inquired if perhaps this field had a house on it or even a hut.

"No," Jack replied. "When I knew Polly she lived in a bender, although I doubt that it's still there. I guess with carbon testing you might pick up traces of the fireplace, but I doubt that would help."

"A bender, General?" Gottfried asked.

"Yes, a bender, Gottfried. It's a shelter made of mud, sticks, leaves, and reeds."

"I understand, sir," and something about the slight quiver of Gottfried's eyebrow made Jack fear that what Gottfried understood was that Jack was out of his mind.

"Perhaps, General," Gottfried inquired gently, "if you just gave me the surname of the young lady in question we could discover her address from the British tax authorities. I feel certain that they would cooperate if we made the request via the Embassy."

"Coupla things," said Jack firmly. "First, do you want to make colonel?"

"Yes, General sir, I do," Gottfried replied.

"OK, then. You don't do this thing I'm asking via the Embassy, understand? You do this yourself. You don't delegate, you don't get somebody else to do the legwork, this is just you, OK?"

"As you wish, sir," Gottfried said.

If General Kent knew one thing about the Grosvenor Square Embassy it was that the CIA were all over it. It was their principal European station, their center of operations. Nothing happened in that building that they did not know about, and Jack did not want them knowing about Polly.

"Next thing," said Jack. "Her surname wouldn't help you, I'm afraid. It . . . it wasn't real."

"Am I to understand, sir, that the young lady in question operated under a pseudonym?" Gottfried inquired.

"Yes, she did," said Jack, reddening slightly. "Her surname at the time I knew her was 'Sacred Cycle of the Womb and Moon.'"

Jack had asked Polly her real name but she had refused on principle to tell him.

"I am who I decide to be, not who society dictates," she used to say, and Jack had thought it simply too stupid to argue; it had not seemed important at the time.

Gottfried betrayed not an ounce of the amusement he felt.

"I see, sir," said Gottfried. "So that would be Polly Sacred Cycle of the Womb and Moon?"

"Yes, it would."

The spy solemnly produced a notebook and jotted down the name, respectfully repeating it under his breath as he did so.

Jack shuddered at the memory of Polly's stupid name. Checking into hotels with a woman who insisted upon signing herself Polly Sacred Cycle of the Womb and Moon had to be one of his more excruciating memories. Eventually Jack persuaded her that it just drew attention to them and that they should pretend to be married anyway, but for a while it had been a major embarrassment for him.

At the time, Polly had been convinced that Jack was only embarrassed because he was so totally uptight and straight. She believed that if only he could center himself and shake out his chakras he would see that it was a lovely name. She found it practical as well as beautiful. For a person who was arrested on a regular basis a good pseudonym was essential and having such a long one absolutely infuriated the police. They used to try to get away with just writing "Polly Sacred," but she would insist on her full name being noted. It drove them mad, particularly on winter mornings when their fingers were cold.

"OK, that's all I got," said Jack. "I'm afraid it ain't a lot."

"I'm sure it will prove sufficient, General," Gottfried assured him.

"Good."

"So, then, just to recap, sir. A girl called Polly, Greenham peace lady. Seventeen years old in 1981. Find her and kill her."

"That's right . . . *No!* For Christ's sake! Jesus, I never said anything about killing her . . ."

"I'm sorry, sir, I just assumed—"

"Yeah, well don't. Just find her, OK? Get her address, hand it over to me, and then forget we ever had this conversation."

[32]

"**God help** the American taxpayer," Polly said with some feeling.

Jack acknowledged that it had been a questionable use of public funds, but what was the point of power if you couldn't abuse it?

"Fuck the American taxpayer. I've given them twenty-eight years of my life. Uncle Sam owes me."

"He doesn't owe you anything. You love being a soldier."

"Murderer, you used to say."

"That's right."

"It's because I'm a soldier that I lost you."

"You didn't lose me, Jack, you discarded me and I don't think it was because you were a soldier. I think it's because you were a gutless bastard. In fact, I think you still are, since you seem to think that calling or writing to an old flame would result in a court-martial for treason."

"I told you, Polly, I couldn't."

Polly didn't understand and she wasn't likely to. Of course he had lost her because he was a soldier. The army would not have accepted his and Polly's relationship in a million years. Jack had been faced with a straight choice and he had chosen his career. That did not mean he liked it, it did not mean that a part of him had not regretted the decision every single day since.

"Why did you have me traced, Jack? Why are you here?"

"I thought you already had your answer. I already told you how I found you."

"This is a subclause. Why did you find me?"

"Why do you think? To find out what I'd let go. To find out what you'd become."

"Jack, we knew each other for one summer in a totally different decade and you dropped me. That was it, end of rather stupid story. Now you turn up out of the blue talking about us like we were a Lionel Ritchie lyric. What is this about?"

"That summer was the best summer of my life, Polly. The best anything of my life."

"You just miss the Cold War, that's all."

"Well, hell, who doesn't?" Jack laughed. "And what's happening with you in the new world order, then? I noticed when I met him that you weren't the prime minister yet."

"I never wanted to be prime minister, Jack. I wanted there not to be any prime ministers. I wanted the nation-state with its hierarchies to be replaced by an organically functioning system of autonomous collectives."

"With you as prime minister."

"Not at all, although obviously some kind of nonoppressive, nonauthoritarian body of governance would be required."

"And anybody who didn't like your nonoppressive, nonauthoritarian governance could get shot."

"That wouldn't happen."

"Polly, it always happens when you fucking idealists get to defending your revolutions. You always start shooting people. By any means possible, as Lenin said. Stalin, Pol Pot, Mao. The most pious murderers in hell . . ."

Polly very nearly rose to it. Very nearly slammed her fist on the table and launched into the ancient and terminally tedious arguments of the left. Just in time, she hauled herself back from the brink.

"Jack, this is ridiculous! Are you out of your mind! I'm a completely different woman now, twice as old, for a start, and you turn up after nearly twenty years quoting Lenin and trying to continue the conversation we were having."

Jack smiled. She was just the same. The same passion, the same beauty.

"I don't know. I just thought it might have been kinda fun, you know, for old times' sake. Like the first time we talked."

"Fought."

"Yeah, fought. In that hellhole on the A34."

"Except then, of course, we ended up in . . ."

Polly did not finish the sentence. She did not need to. Her eyes gave the thought away. She did not need to say "bed" because there it was, right there, not ten feet from either of them. Her bed, unmade and inviting, the duvet tossed aside, the deep impression of Polly's head still there upon the pillow. A bed just climbed out of. A bed ready to be climbed back into.

"I've never been in one of those restaurants since," Polly said.

Jack fixed his stare on hers. She could feel herself going scarlet.

"That day changed me too, Polly. I'll never forget it."

"They're just so disgusting. I mean, how do you ruin tomato soup?"

"I didn't mean the restaurant, Polly, I meant . . ." Jack's tone spoke volumes, but Polly was trying not to listen. She stuck resolutely to her topic.

"Putting a stupid hat on a sixteen-year-old dropout does not constitute training a chef."

"Polly, how long can you stay angry at a bowl of soup?"

"No, but really. How do you mess up tomato soup? It was hot on the top and cold in the middle. With a skin on it! That has to be deliberate," said Polly, once again reliving the horror of that gruesome cuisine.

"Forget the soup," Jack pleaded. "Walk away. It's been sixteen years, you have to let it go now. We weren't bothered about eating, anyway. We went to that little hotel. Do you remember?"

Polly looked puzzled. "A hotel? Are you sure? I don't remember that."

Jack could not conceal his disappointment. "Oh, I thought you would—"

"Of course I fucking remember, you fucking idiot," Polly said as loudly as she dared without provoking the sleeping milkman downstairs. "I lost my fucking virginity, didn't I!"

Jack got it. "Oh, right," he said. "British sarcasm."

"Irony."

He hated that. That was a British trick, the sarcasm and irony trick. Earlier in the evening the senior British officer had tried to make the same distinction.

"Oh, yes," the pompous little khaki shit had said, having cracked some particularly weak sarcastic put-down or other. "You American chaps aren't big on irony, are you?"

Jack thought it was pathetic the way the British aggrandized their penchant for paltry sarcasm by styling it "irony." They thought it meant they had a more sophisticated sense of humor than the rest of the world, but it didn't. It just meant that they were a bunch of pompous smartasses.

"So you do remember," he said.

"Of course I bloody remember," Polly replied. "I remember every detail. The soup—"

"Forget the soup."

"The pie—"

"Forget the pie."

"I wrote to the restaurant, you know."

"Christ, hadn't you made enough fuss already?"

Not that Jack had minded at the time. Usually he hated any kind of scene. Under any normal circumstances the fuss that Polly had made on the first day they met would have ended their relationship right there. The funny thing was that he had loved it then and he loved it still. He remembered every detail. Polly announcing loudly that she resented being forced to eat in a fucking charnel house, supergluing the sauce bottles to the table. Even now he laughed at the memory of that wonderful, funny, sexy, sunny lunchtime.

"You sure showed them," he said.

"Nonviolent direct action. At least we didn't pay," Polly replied.

That was one of Polly's favorite memories of her whole life. That glorious runner. The suggestion, the decision, the execution, it had all happened in one mad moment. Suddenly the two of them, her and an American soldier, were charging for the door and out into the car park. It had been such fun, so exciting, piling into his car and screeching out onto the A34 before anyone in the restaurant had realized what had happened.

"I just couldn't believe that you, a soldier and everything, were prepared to run out without paying."

After sixteen years Jack decided it was time to own up.

"Actually I did pay, Polly. I left a five-pound note under my plate."

Polly could scarcely believe it. This was astonishing, horrible news.

"You paid! That's terrible! I thought you were so cool!"

"I was cool. It got you into my car, didn't it?"

That was true enough. Jack's astute deception all those years before had certainly got her into his car, certainly made her breathless and excited and ready for anything. Who could tell? Had that little trick not occurred to him then perhaps their relationship might never have happened. After all, if Jack had simply asked Polly to go with him to a field and then to a hotel, it is most unlikely that she would have gone. It had been the drama of that single moment that had carried her into his arms and changed both their lives forever.

"You bastard," said Polly. "If you hadn't—"

"Polly, life is full of ifs. If that receptionist hadn't decided to turn a blind eye to your pornographic T-shirt maybe we would have seen sense and walked away."

"There was nothing remotely offensive about my T-shirt!" said Polly, the passage of time having done nothing to blunt the memory of that confrontation. "That receptionist was just a stupid Nazi bitch."

"Polly, just because somebody did not approve of what was emblazoned on your T-shirt doesn't make them a National Socialist."

"Take the toys from the boys," said Polly. "What could be offensive about that?"

"Beats me," Jack replied, "unless it was the picture of that huge flying penis you had printed across your tits."

Polly never failed to rise to this one.

"Well, what were those bloody missiles but big blokes' willies? Nuclear dickheads, we used to call them."

"Yeah, we all loved that one on our side of the fence," Jack said with heavy sarcasm (or perhaps it was irony). " 'Tell us the one about missiles being penis replacements again,' we used to shout. We'd laugh all day."

"You're only making fun because actually you felt threatened."

"Terrified. Couldn't sleep. You know, Polly, maybe it's kind of late in the day to say this, but the idea of dissing things because of their so-called phallic shape. It's always struck me as kind of banal."

"Because it reveals an uncomfortable truth about yourself."

"No, because it's dumb. Things get shaped straight and thin for reasons of aerodynamics. Missiles and skyscrapers are shaped the way they are on the soundest principles of engineering, not as monuments to the dick. In fact, so is the dick. The dick is shaped like a dick because that is the most efficient shape for a dick to be. That's why it's dick shaped. I mean a dick shaped like a table would cause all sorts of practical spatial problems. Surely you can see that?"

"Jack, it's a point of satire, not civil engineering."

"Yes, but it's such lazy, unconvincing satire. It always annoys me so much the way you girls trot it out like you're saying something so astute and revealing. Like with cars; a guy gets a cool car and suddenly according to you and the other femmos it's his dick. Well, dicks don't look a bit like cars. No guy ever stood outside a Cadillac showroom and said, 'Oh, boy, I wish I had one of those. It looks exactly like my dick.' Jesus, if my dick looked like a Cadillac I'd go see a doctor. Personally, I drive a pickup truck. You ever see a dick with a trailer?"

"Jack, I'm not interested. This is your problem. I never—"

"You might as well say a trombone is a phallic symbol, or a stick of gum! Maybe when a guy shoves a piece of gum into his face what he's really saying is that he is a subconscious homosexual and has a secret desire to be chewing on a big old Cadillac!"

"Jack—"

"Phallic symbol, for Christ's sake. When they built the World Trade Center do you think they stood around saying 'Looks great and it'll be even better when they put the purple helmet on the top'?"

Polly used to love this type of conversation with Jack. They would shout and rant and swear at each other.

Then, of course, they made love.

"Jack, don't you think you're getting a little worked up over this? Protesting too much?"

"I hate that way of arguing! That is a woman's way of arguing! Say something outrageous and when the guy gets angry act like *he's* got the problem."

Polly wondered whether perhaps this might be the reason for Jack's visit.

"Is this some kind of therapy thing? Is that why you've come? Has some army analyst discovered you hate women and told you to go and confront your past?"

Now Jack really went off. "Are you kidding me? See an analyst? I'd rather stick my Cadillac in a blender. Analysts and therapists have destroyed the world. They're a cancer. I'd put the lot of them against a wall and shoot them. Every one. Them, their unconscious selves, their recovered personalities, and particularly, above all, their inner fucking children."

Polly had not expected Jack to have suddenly turned into a liberal in the years that had passed since their last meeting, but if anything he seemed to have got worse.

"You know what, Jack? It's lovely to see you and all that, but I'm rather tired, so—"

But Jack wasn't listening. He was on a subject that moved him deeply, to Polly's mind rather disturbingly so.

"Jesus, the entire twentieth century was corrupted by the theories of some Jew who thought women wanted to grow dicks and guys wanted to fuck their mothers! Where I come from that's fighting talk. We'd have killed that pervert the first day he opened his mouth. We'd have hung him from a tree, and you know what? We would have been called uncivilized."

There was something venomous about Jack's tone that Polly didn't like. He still had all his charm but it had taken on a steely edge.

"Jack, I'm not interested in your Neolithic opinions. I have no idea why I'm even having this conversation, I have to work tomorrow. Why are you here?"

"I told you! I wanted to see you—"

"So you've seen me! What now?"

What indeed? Jack hardly knew himself. He had thought he knew, but that was before they got talking. Jack had rehearsed all this in his mind so many times. Yet now he was not so sure, not so sure at all. He glanced at his watch. It was after three.

"Look, if I'm keeping you," Polly snapped, "you can go!"

"I'm not going, Polly. I want to be with you."

There was something about his tone that Polly did not like. Something commanding and possessive. Polly did not like men acting as if they had the right to intrude on her own private space. She had had enough of that with the Bug.

[33]

Peter watched as the taillights of the police car disappeared around the corner at the end of the road, the spiteful red dots dragging great bloody streaks along behind them in the glistening reflection of the wet road.

Twice now Peter had been forced to retreat into the shadows as passing cars had disturbed his desperate efforts to recover his knife. Once it had been a carful of yobbos, drunken revelers shouting into the night. Their car had hurtled into the road at speed. Peter had been on all fours and had had to roll out of the gutter onto the pavement. The souped-up white Sierra had screeched past, sending up an arc of spray, further soaking Peter's retreating body. Another second, a moment's hesitation, a slower reaction, and all Polly's problems with the Bug would have been over. But he survived, wetter, dirtier, and angrier. The Sierra sped on, its reckless driver unaware of how close he had been to killing a man.

Peter retrieved his coat hanger and returned to his task, but no sooner had he done so than a police car appeared, not screeching and hurtling but prowling. He sat on the curb and waited for it to pass. It seemed to take forever, slowing to a crawl as it drew parallel with him. He put his head in his hands and ignored it. The police officers inside the car repaid the compliment. A few years previously they might have investigated, but the night streets were now so full of people with nowhere to go that if the police looked into every sad-looking case they passed they would never get more than two hundred yards from their station.

When the coppers had gone and he had the street to himself again Peter knelt once more in the filthy gutter and resumed his delicate task. It was clear to him that if he dislodged the knife it would fall completely out of reach. He would have only one chance to touch it with his wire. Hook it, or knock it away forever.

"Peter! What on earth do you think you're doing!"

He spun around, dropping his piece of wire, which fell with a tiny clatter into the drain.

"Mum!"

"Get up out of the gutter!" Peter's mother said. "You're filthy and you're soaking. What're you doing? Are you drunk?"

Peter had been gone so long that his poor mother, unable to sleep, had come out searching for him. She had known where to look, of course. There was only one place he would have gone at that time of night. She felt so angry, even though she knew that he couldn't help it. It was all starting again. Just when she had hoped that perhaps he was getting over his madness it was all starting again.

"I dropped my knife, Mum."

"Good. You shouldn't have had it, anyway. You know they're illegal. What were you doing with it in the first place?"

"Just playing with it."

"Playing with a knife? On her street? A knife, Peter! What if you were caught?"

Sometimes Peter's mother just wanted to break down and weep. She really did not know how much more of it she could bear. If that woman thought she had it hard, she should try being his mother.

Peter refused to go home. His mother tried ordering him, reasoning with him, pleading with him, but he was adamant. She stepped forward into the flowing gutter and reached out to him. Her shoe filled instantly with filthy water. Peter merely drew away.

"Come home, Peter!" his mother pleaded one more time.

"I'll come home when I've got my knife back" was all he would say.

She gave up. There was nothing she could do. She cried all the way home, her tears mixing with rain, making her half blind.

Peter went back to the builder's Dumpster to root out another piece of wire.

[34]

Jack sat back in his seat and quaffed deeply at his whiskey.

"So come on. My question. Tell me what you do now." He had some information about Polly from the file that Gottfried had prepared, but not much. Jack had specifically asked his secret agent to confine himself to a couple of current photographs and Polly's address. He had not wanted even Gottfried to know any more about Polly than was absolutely necessary.

"I'm a councillor," Polly replied.

Jack's face showed that he was not impressed.

"What, you mean like an analyst? A therapist? You tell fucked-up people to blame their parents?"

"Not a personal counselor, Jack, a town councillor. I'm on the council."

Jack laughed. "The council! You're on the council! I thought all hierarchies were fascism."

Yet again Polly rose to the bait. "I was seventeen when I said that, for heaven's sake! Although they are, of course, but all structures are not necessarily hierarchical—"

Polly stopped herself. This was ridiculous. "I don't want to discuss politics with you!"

"OK, OK. Whatever you say, Polly."

A silence descended. Polly was getting impatient with Jack's enigmatic visit, but she did not want him to go and he did not seem anxious to explain himself, so there was very little she could do.

"So what do you do on your 'council' then?" Jack asked and Polly did not like his slightly patronizing tone.

"I'm with the office of equal opportunities."

Jack sniffed and his patronizing tone became slightly more marked.

"What? You mean it's your job to make sure there's a suitable quota of disabled black Chinese sodomites getting paid out of public funds?"

"Yes, that's exactly what I do," Polly snapped sarcastically. "You're incredibly intuitive, Jack. I had no idea you were such an expert on local government."

"We have people like you in the army," Jack said, and now it almost sounded as if he was sneering. "Checking out that we have enough women in combat training. Homosexuals, too, that's coming. A queer quota. Can you believe that?"

Polly inquired if this offended Jack, and he replied that it damn well did offend him.

"You think that makes me a fascist, right?" he added.

The atmosphere between them, having been definitely warming up, was now becoming chilly.

"Well, I certainly think it makes you a bit of a dickhead."

Jack went over to the kitchen table and grabbed the bottles.

"Have another drink, babe," he said, "and let me tell you something."

"Don't call me babe."

Polly was still sitting on the bed. Jack marched back across the room and sloshed more Bailey's into her half-full glass before refilling his own with bourbon. He had not intended to discuss this issue but he felt too strongly about it to let it go. Besides, this night of all nights Jack wanted Polly to understand something of his point of view.

"Christ, where do you people get off! Gays in the military. What does it have to do with you, anyway? You don't care about the army, you hate it, you wish it would turn into a network of crèches for single mothers! But you still think you can tell us how to run it—"

Polly raised her hand for him to stop.

"Hang on, hang on. Hang on! Me?" she said. "Don't lay your shit on me, mate. I'm a council worker from Camden."

"I'm talking about your kind, Polly. It doesn't matter where you come from or what job you do. Your kind are international."

"My kind!" Polly protested. "What the fuck do you mean, my kind?"

"Your kind, Polly, that's what the fuck I mean. Your kind."

Jack was sick and tired of them. These liberals, these feminists, these gay activists. The army wasn't a laboratory for social experimentation, it was the means by which the nation defended itself. He had tried to explain this point at the congressional hearings into sexual bias in the armed forces and what a waste of time that had been. It had been like Canute trying to turn back a tidal wave of bullshit. What an impotent fool he had felt, sitting there in front of that pious pulpit of political zealots and petrified fellow travelers. It was the scared ones Jack despised most. At least the true believers believed, insane utopians though they were, but the ones who knew he was right were beneath contempt. They just did not have the guts to risk offending the current sensibilities and so they nodded and sighed and stayed silent, mindful of their thin electoral majorities back home. It was McCarthyism in reverse. The liberals had become the witch-hunters: "Are you or have you ever been a homophobic?"

There was a terrifying new orthodoxy abroad and as far as Jack was concerned whether it was happening on Capitol Hill or in Camden Council it had to be confronted.

"We take communal showers in the army, you know that, Polly," Jack said bitterly. "You think about that. In the field we live in the same dugouts, wash in the same puddles. I don't want no queer grunt staring at my ass instead of the soap."

Polly did not want to discuss this, but like Jack she simply could not let it go. His attitude was just too disgusting. Every liberal instinct in her body screamed to reply.

"Gay men are not sexual predators, Jack."

"How the hell would you know? Straight guys are sexual predators!"

"Well, yes, you certainly showed me that!"

"Exactly," Jack said loudly, as if this proved his point.

"Keep your voice down! There's a milkman asleep downstairs."

On the floor below, the milkman was not asleep. Jack's voice had woken him up again and he was gleefully making a note of the time of the disturbance: *"Man's voice: shouting: 3:06 A.M.,"* he wrote. It wasn't that the milkman enjoyed being disturbed, but the upstairs woman had complained so often about his radio, even threatening to involve the landlord, that the current disturbance was manna from heaven. Let her try and complain now.

Little did the milkman imagine that within a few hours his notebook would be in the hands of the police.

Jack reduced the volume but his tone remained combative.

"If you think I'm a predator, well, let me tell you, honey, I ain't the worst by a long country mile. I'm the norm."

Jack was remembering Bad Nauheim and the night that the

German girl Helga had pushed her luck too far. Not all men were of the type involved in that terrible incident, but all men were men nonetheless.

"If you put any of the men in any unit I ever commanded in a showerful of women," Jack continued, "they are going to check them out for sure, and if they can they're going to try and get with them."

"Well, then, they need to rethink their—"

Jack had just sat back down in his seat, but his frustration made him leap up again and take a step toward Polly.

"Followed by heavy footsteps: 3:07 A.M.," the milkman wrote solemnly before rolling over and wrapping the pillow around his head.

Jack was standing over Polly now.

"I know you don't like it, Polly, but that's what young men do! They check out babes and they try to have sex with them and you can make up all the laws you like but that won't change."

Polly rose from the bed and squared up to Jack. There was no way this man was going to win his argument with intimidating body language.

"Yes, it can, Jack, it's called civilization. It's an ongoing process."

"Yeah, well, it's got a long way to go."

Polly checked herself. What was she doing? She did not want to have this discussion, she had work in the morning. In fact, it very nearly was the morning.

"Look, Jack. I really don't know what we're talking about!"

"We are talking about gays in the military."

"Well, I don't want to talk about gays in the military!"

"Well, I do! It's relevant!"

"Relevant to what?"

"Relevant to me! I want you to understand me."

The urgency of Jack's tone subdued Polly for a moment.

"You know what straight men can be like," he continued. "You feel I showed you that."

Oh yes, Polly certainly felt he had done that.

"So why not gays? What's so different about them, huh? Are you going to tell me that if you put a healthy young homosexual in a showerful of young men who are in the peak of physical condition he is not going to check out their dicks?"

Polly tried to stop herself replying. She did not wish to be having this conversation. On the other hand she had to reply. Jack simply could not be allowed to get away with this reactionary bullshit.

"Well, he might look, but—"

Jack leaped on the point. "And when he does he's going to get himself beaten to a pulp."

"That's not his problem—"

Jack laughed. "Excuse me? Getting beaten to a pulp is not his problem?"

"Well, I mean, obviously it is his problem if he's being beaten up."

"It's encouraging that you spotted that."

His attitude was unpleasant. Polly's point was not an easy one to make. Particularly if Jack was going to take cheap shots.

"But the problem originates with the people who are doing the beating!"

"Great, next time I get shot I'll take comfort from that. Hey, this is not my problem. The guy with the gun, he has the problem, he needs to get in touch with his caring side."

How many times in how many pubs had Polly had discussions like this one? The reactionary point of view was always so easy to put, the complex, radical argument always so easy to put down.

"Just because the world is full of Neanderthal morons doesn't mean we have to run it for their benefit and by their rules."

Jack searched his brain for a telling argument. Somehow it was important to him that Polly understood his point of view.

"Listen, Polly, when the guy who digs up the street checks out your butt you're pretty pissed, am I right?"

"Well, yes—"

"You're furious. You'd like to knock that guy off his scaffolding and drive a dump truck into his asshole cleavage. Well, men don't like having their butts checked out either, but unlike you they're actually going to do something about it, they're going to attack the guy who is checking them out and you cannot run an army with guys either sucking each other off or beating each other up."

Of course it sounded reasonable. Polly had spent her life listening to reactionary arguments and they always sounded reasonable. Which was why it was all the more important to counter them. Even at nearly 3:15 in the morning. Even with a mysterious ex-lover who had turned up out of the blue after more than sixteen years' absence. Polly had a policy. It was embarrassing at times and always boring, but her view was that casual racism, sexism, and homophobia always had to be confronted.

"People have to learn to restrain themselves," she said.

Jack had a rule too. It was that he would never suffer pious liberal bullshit in silence.

"Says you, babe, and you and your people can keep on wishing!"

Polly was shocked at how bitter Jack's tone had become.

"Me and my people?" she said. "What people, Jack? I don't have any people! What are you talking about? Why are you bringing me into this? None of this is any of my business."

Polly was not even sure that Jack heard her. He looked strange. There was a different look in his eye; she could see real anger there.

"You know what's coming next, don't you? Pacifists."

"What about pacifists?"

"In the fucking army! Why not? Some congresswoman is going to announce that pacifists have a right to join the army. In fact, the army should be encouraging them! Running a program to attract them! Because the constitutional rights of American pacifists are being denied by—"

Jack was becoming red in the face. For the first time he looked his age. A confused, middle-aged man with a chip on his shoulder.

"I'm not interested in your paranoid ravings, Jack. I want to know why—"

But Polly might as well have been talking to herself.

"Fucking Constitution! It's a sponge, it'll absorb anything anybody wants. It's like the damn Bible. Everybody can make it work for them. Well, the Constitution can only take so much. One day the Supreme Court is going to rule that the Constitution is unconstitutional and the United States will implode! It'll disappear up its ass."

"Good! I'm glad." Polly felt tired. She had to leave for work at seven-forty-five.

"Jack, I can't have this conversation with you now. I have to work tomorrow. Maybe we could meet some other—"

Jack lowered his tone. He spoke quietly and firmly. "I've told you, Polly, I only have tonight. I leave in the morning."

He stared at Polly as if that was all he needed to say, as if Polly could like it or lump it, neither of which she was prepared to do.

"Well, go, then! Go! I don't want you here. I didn't ask you to come."

Jack did not move at all. He just stood in the middle of the room, looking at her.

"I'm staying, Polly," he said, and for the first time Polly began to feel a little nervous. Something about Jack had changed. He was being so intense.

"OK, stay, stay if you want to, but . . . but you can't just drop in after sixteen years and talk about sexual politics and the Constitution, and . . . It's . . . it's stupid."

Jack looked tired too now. "You always used to want to talk about politics, Polly. What's changed? Is there nothing of value left for you people to fuck up?"

He seemed to say it more in sorrow than in anger. Nonetheless Polly wasn't having any of it.

"I have nothing to do with you or your hangups, Jack," said Polly calmly. "We knew each other briefly, years ago. We don't even live in the same country."

"Politics is international, you always used to tell me that," said Jack, and he smiled at the memory. "You read it to me out of that damn political cartoon book you had, *The Start-Up Guide to Being an Asshole* . . ."

"*Marxism for Beginners.*"

"That's the one."

Polly blushed at the memory of how naive she'd been. She had actually given Jack a copy of *Marxism for Beginners.* Not that she had ever been able to get through it herself, of course. Huge quotes from *Das Kapital* do not get clearer just because there's a little cartoon of Karl Marx in the corner of the page. It had been a gesture, a nod toward civilizing him. All Jack ever admitted to reading was the sports pages, and Polly had dreamed of politicizing him. Fantasizing about walking into the peace camp one day with Jack on her arm and saying to the girls, "I've got one! I've converted him." She had imagined herself the toast of the peace movement, having persuaded a genuine baby killer to see the light. Polly had been going to make the world's first vegetarian fighter pilot.

"Wasn't I the starry-eyed little fool?" she said.

"Well, did you ever read Churchill's *History of the Second World War*?" Jack replied. The book-giving had, after all, been a two-way thing.

"Be serious, Jack, it was about fifty volumes!"

"Oh, and Marx is easy reading, is it?"

Now they were both laughing. Neither of them had changed at all. They were still a million miles apart in every way but one.

"I wanted you to be a part of my world as much as you wanted me to be part of yours, Polly," said Jack. "You're not the only person who got disappointed. I believe that in my own way I loved you every bit as much as you loved me."

Jack was terrified to discover that he still did.

"You can't have done," said Polly quietly, avoiding Jack's eye, "or you wouldn't have left."

"That's not true, Polly. I had to leave. I'm a soldier. I'm not good at love, I admit that. I don't find it easy to live with. But whatever love there is inside me I felt for you, to its very limits and beyond."

[35]

While Jack and Polly were wrestling with their pasts in London, back in the States another drama of betrayal was being played out. A man and a woman were sitting alone together in the faded splendor of a dining room that had been beautifully decorated twenty years before. It was dinnertime in the eastern states and the couple had been sitting at their evening meal for an hour or so, but neither of them was hungry. Their food had gone cold before them. Hers remained entirely untouched; he had had a stab at his, but really all he had done was play nervously with the cold, congealed gravy.

"I'm sorry, Nibs," he said. "What more can I say? I don't want to do it but sometimes it just happens. I just can't help myself."

"Nibs" was the man's private name for his wife. It was what he always called her when they were alone, their little secret, a token of his affection. These days they were alone together less and less. Their professional lives had grown so complex that dining together had become a matter for diaries, and when his work took him away she could no longer go with him. Perhaps it was that, she thought. Perhaps her career had driven him into the arms of other, stupider, more available women. She wondered if he had special names for them. Perhaps he had called them Nibs also, for convenience and to avoid embarrassing mistakes. At the thought of this Nibs's eyes grew misty and briefly she took refuge in her napkin.

"I'm so sorry," he said again, "but it meant nothing, it was meaningless."

"What does she do?" Nibs inquired, attempting to make her voice sound calm.

"She works at the office. She's with the travel department. She books cars and flights and stuff," he replied.

"Fascinating," she said bitterly. "You must have so much to talk about."

"The point is, Nibs . . ."

"Don't call me Nibs," she snapped. "I don't feel like being your Nibs right now."

"The point is . . ."

His voice faltered. The point was that he was in trouble. That was the only reason he'd arranged the dinner, the only reason they were having the conversation. If he hadn't been in trouble he would never have told her about the girl, just as he hadn't told her about any of the other girls. Unfortunately, this current girl had not taken kindly to the brevity of their affair and had decided to hit back.

"She says she's going to accuse me of harassing her."

"Oh, for Christ's sake. Did you?"

"Not unless taking a girl to bed a couple of times is harassment."

Nibs bit her lip. Why had he done it? Why did he keep doing it? He thought she didn't know about the others but she'd heard the rumors. She knew about the jokes they told at his office. She'd caught the expressions of those dumb booby women when she accompanied him to business functions. She knew what they were thinking. "You may be a fancy lawyer, lady, but when your husband needs satisfying he comes to me."

"I have plenty of enemies," he said. "If this thing gets any kind of heat under it at all it could be very bad for me at work. I could lose my job."

"You fool!" Nibs snapped. "You damn stupid fool."

[36]

Jack swallowed half his drink down in one.

"Do you ever see any of the girls these days?"

"One or two," Polly replied, crossing one leg over the other as she sat. She could see Jack's eyes had been caught by the movement.

"You should organize a reunion," he said, smiling. "You'd have a blast. Go stand in a field somewhere, paint each other's faces, make some puppets. Eat mud sandwiches and dance to the subtle rhythms of your female cycles."

He was teasing her now. The anger had gone.

"Yes, and we could invite the American army along," Polly replied. "You could all drop your trousers and show us your arses. We used to love it when you did that. It was such a subtle gesture and so intellectually stimulating."

In fact it had been the British guards who did most of the arse-showing. The Americans were mainly technical advisers, a cut above that sort of oafishness, and were anyway on their strictest best behavior. Jack did not argue the point, though. He had always fully supported the British soldiers in their arse-showing and he would not deny them now.

"It was a clash of cultures. We were never going to get along."

"Except us."

"Yeah," said Jack, trying not to stare. "Except us."

They were so close. He in the easy chair, she perched on the bed. Two strides and they would be in each other's arms. The room crackled with the suppressed tension.

"Let's face it," said Polly. "You can put up with anything if the sex is good enough."

"Oh, yeah," Jack replied with great enthusiasm, his voice and his wandering eyes betraying his thoughts.

Polly was torn. Should she sleep with him? She felt confident that she could if she wanted to. Of course she could. She knew what men were like, they always wanted it. Scratch a man and you find a person who fancies a fuck. Sex had to be the reason that Jack had come back. It was obvious. He felt like a little nostalgic adventure. A little blast from the past. He had been sitting in the Pentagon one night thinking, "I wonder what happened to her?" and then he had thought, "I know. I'm a powerful man. I'll have her traced and the next time I'm in London I'll pop round and see if I can still fuck her." By rights Polly should be offended, she should throw him out. The feminist in her told her that if she screwed Jack she would be doing exactly what he wanted. Literally playing into his hands. But, then again, so what? She would be using him too. It wasn't as if she'd been exactly sexually satiated of late. Quite frankly, she could really do with a little passion herself. But could she trust her emotions? After what he had meant to her, after how he had behaved? Would she suddenly find herself hopelessly in love again or would she just want to kill him? Polly could not quite decide whether in the final analysis having sex with Jack would make her happier or sadder.

In her mind's eye the good memories were gaining the ascendancy.

"I nearly didn't go through with it, you know," she said. "That first time. When I saw that disgusting tattoo of yours. Kill everyone and everything horribly or whatever it said."

" 'Death or Glory,' " Jack corrected her. "I know you thought it was juvenile, Polly, but I'm in the army. It's our regimental motto."

"I used to work for Tesco's but I haven't got 'Great quality at prices you can afford' written across my arse."

Jack laughed and topped off his drink. He could certainly put the booze away, but then he had always been able to do that.

"I had a tattoo done too, you know, after you left," Polly said, pulling at the collar of her raincoat and nightie to reveal the blurred decoration that her parents had found so unpleasant. Jack inspected it.

"It's the female symbol with a penis in it," he said.

"It's not a penis, it's a clenched fist, for Christ's sake!" Polly snapped. "Why does everybody say that? It's so obviously a clenched fist."

Jack leaned in a little to inspect the design more closely. "Yeah, well, maybe."

Except, of course, he wasn't looking at the tattoo. By now he had shifted his gaze and was using his position of advantage to drink in Polly's partially exposed breasts. Polly had been aware when she pulled down her clothing to show her tattoo that she was displaying rather more of her bosom than was decorous, and she knew that Jack was looking at it now. Polly was rather vain about her breasts. She thought them perhaps her best feature. They were not particularly large or anything, but they were very shapely, cheeky almost. Age had not yet wearied them; they were well capable of standing up for themselves, so to speak.

Polly could feel Jack's breath upon her shoulder. It was hot and damp and seemed to be coming quicker now. He wasn't exactly panting, but he wasn't breathing easily either. Polly knew that she too was breathing more quickly and that her breasts were trembling slightly beneath Jack's gaze. She also knew what would happen to her body next. Spontaneously, involuntarily, her nipples began to harden under the nightshirt. It always happened when she felt aroused, and Jack, of course, knew that.

Even through the clothes Polly was wearing Jack could see the process beginning and it brought back such memories. How he longed to pull apart Polly's shirt and press his lips once again to those glorious dark pink buds.

But he didn't. He drew away and gulped again at his drink.

"Yeah, well, we both had some adjusting to do in those days," he said.

For a moment Polly did not know what he was talking about. She had lost the thread of the conversation they had been having. She readjusted her clothing, covering her shoulders, slightly confused. She knew that he had wanted to touch her, she knew that she would have let him do it too and she knew that he knew that; her body had given it away. But he hadn't touched her. Instead he was talking again. He had retreated across the room, clearly anxious to put distance between them. He was resisting his desires. Polly wondered why.

"Oh, yes, that's for sure," Jack continued. "We both had to make allowances in those days."

"What allowances did you have to make, then?" Polly inquired rather sharply. "I seem to recall that it was you who called the shots."

"Well, for instance, I cannot say I relished discovering your organic raw cotton sanitary napkins soaking in the bathroom basin."

The years had not blunted this point of contention. Once again the ancient row bubbled to the surface.

"That's because you fear menstruation!" she retorted. "You're scared of the ancient power and mystery of the vagina."

"No, Polly, it's because washing your sanitary towels in the bathroom is totally gross."

Polly still didn't understand this point of view. She found it as offensive as he had found her hygiene arrangements.

"What? Grosser than flushing great chunks of bleached cotton into our already filthy rivers?"

That was easy. Jack could answer that. "Yes," he said. "Much grosser."

"Are you seriously saying," said Polly, rising to the bait as she always did, "that you find the idea of a woman disposing of her body's by-products in a responsible manner using sustainable resources more gross than dumping used tampons into the water system? Grosser than the seas being clogged up with great reefs of them knitted together with old condoms? Grosser than fish feeding on toilet paper? Grosser than tap water being filtered through surgical dressings and colostomy bags?"

Jack had to admit that these questions were more difficult.

"Uhm . . . maybe about as gross," he replied.

"Jesus!" Polly snapped. "You're a soldier. I thought you were supposed to be used to the sight of blood."

How could Jack explain that as far as he was concerned there was a big difference between proper blood, manly blood, the blood that flowed from a wound, and blood left lying about the bathroom by menstruating feminists. He knew that this was not necessarily a laudable point of view, but it was how he felt.

"Look, Polly, we see things differently, OK? We always have. I'm sorry, but that's the way it is."

Polly smiled. Jack was embarrassed, which was something she had rarely seen.

"What is it they say?" she said softly. "Opposites attract."

And so they were back at the point at which they had been a

moment before. Looking at each other, the bed beckoning. The tender tension of love in the air. Jack's knuckles whitened on his glass. Polly wondered if it would shatter. She could see that he was struggling to control his desires. She did not know why he was struggling, but she decided that she hoped he would lose.

"You look great, Polly," said Jack, his heart thumping.

"Thanks." Polly met his gaze. "You too."

Jack did not reply. He could not think what to say. He knew what he ought to say. He had business to get through, that was why he had come. There were things about his past that only Polly knew, that only Polly could help him with. What Jack needed to do was ask the questions he had come to ask. But what he wanted to do was to make love.

"I'm glad you came back," said Polly.

[37]

Polly was smiling.

Polly was frowning.

She was yawning at the bus stop. Peter's mother knew those photographs almost as well as Peter did himself. Often when he was out she would find herself drawn to his room, where she would stand, surrounded by images of the woman whose existence had so infected her own. She knew what a terrible thing it was to be the mother of a child gone wrong, to be always looking back on life, searching for the moment when the change had come, when the damage had been done.

It seemed to Peter's mother that her whole life had been a preparation for this current despair. Every moment of her past had been rewritten by the present. Peter's boyhood, which had brought her such happiness, was now forever tainted by what he had become. Every smiling memory of a little boy in shorts and National Health Service glasses was the memory of a boy who had turned into a deceitful, sneaking pervert. Every innocent hour they had spent together was now revealed as an hour spent in the making of a monster. Could she have known? Could she have prevented it? Surely she could and yet Peter's mother could not see how. It was true that he had never had many friends but she had thought him happy enough. After all she was lonely too and so they had always had each other. Perhaps if his father had stayed . . . but that swine had gone before Peter had even been born. She could scarcely even remember him herself.

Seeing Peter that night, her own son, the flesh of her womb, squatting in a filthy gutter like a rat had torn at her heart. He was sinking back into madness, she could see that, and this time it would be deeper and more terrible than the last. Peter needed help, that was obvious, help that clearly she could not give him. She was the problem, she had made him in every sense. The help he needed lay outside their home, but to reach it Peter's mother knew that she would have to betray her son.

[38]

Once more Jack hauled himself back from the erotic adventure his whole being craved. It was not the time. He had things to do. The key to his future lay in his past and it was Polly who held it.

"Opposites may attract, Polly, but they're still opposites," he said, hiding behind his drink. "I guess we're lucky we didn't last too long, huh?"

This comment, rather brutal in the circumstances, brought Polly back to earth with a jolt.

"Oh yes, very lucky. You probably did us both a favor," she said bitterly. "When you had your final screw and then snuck off while I lay sleeping. You bastard."

Suddenly her eyes glistened. Polly's old enemy. Her tear ducts were responding as they always did when her emotions bubbled up. Although on this occasion some of the tears were for real. Jack was surprised to see Polly become so quickly upset, surprised to discover that the wound was still so raw, even after all the years. It made him feel ashamed. She had been the last person on earth he had ever wanted to hurt.

"It was my job, Polly."

"What? Fucking and leaving? Nice work if you can get it," she said, dabbing at her eyes with a tea towel.

Jack studied the carpet. "I had to leave. I get orders. It's a security thing."

"A security thing? Not to say good-bye? Oh yeah, of course, because World War Three would probably have started if you'd said good-bye."

What could Jack say? It had not been possible for him to say good-bye, that was all, but he knew that there was no point in saying so now.

"I mean, a note or a call to tell me our affair was over," Polly continued bitterly. "That might have been just the excuse the Russians had been waiting for to wipe out the free world."

All the intimacy that had existed between them a moment before had now evaporated. Polly was suddenly cold.

"I'm sorry," Jack pleaded, "I couldn't."

"You were too fucking gutless to face up to the fact that you were betraying the trust of a seventeen-year-old girl, and, what's more, over sixteen years later you're still too fucking gutless to admit it. 'It's my job.' Pathetic!"

She was right, of course. He'd been too scared to say good-bye. Scared of seeing her hurt, scared of a scene, but most of all scared that had he woken her and seen once again that adorable, trusting, innocent love light in her eyes he would not have been able to go through with it. He loved her too much to risk saying good-bye.

Polly, of course, had known nothing of Jack's tortured emotions. To her his departure had come like a cruel thunderbolt. She had no more expected the relationship to end than she had expected it to begin. She never dreamed that Jack had in fact tried to leave her many times during the latter part of their time together. In fact, from the moment he realized that he was in love with her he had been trying to find a way out.

"*What can I do, Harry?*" Jack wrote in anguish to his brother from the camp. *"How do I find the courage to end this? How do I find a way to leave?"*

In vain did Harry advise that if the army was forcing Jack to break his own heart and also the heart of an innocent, idealistic girl then maybe it was the army that he should be leaving and not the girl. Jack balled up Harry's letter in fury. Harry was a furniture maker, he did not understand the soul of a fighting man, he did not understand the all-encompassing power of truly vaunting ambition. Harry had never dreamed of being a leader of men.

"What do you know, you flake? Nothing," Jack wrote back. *"Try to understand that your weak sensibilities mean nothing to me. Try to understand that I would break the heart of every girl in the world. That I would tear out my own and feed it to a dog in the street if just once I could get the chance to lead an American army into a battle. Any army into battle. You think that's sick, I know. You think somehow Mom got inseminated by the devil, but it is what it is. I'm a soldier, first, last, and only."*

"Bullshit, Jack!" was Harry's reply. *"You call me a flake! You're the damn flake! You want to lead an army? You want to fight the world? You can't even find the courage to hurt one seventeen-year-old girl."* Except in the end, of course, Jack did find the courage.

[39]

She sat waiting for him, as she always did, hiding in the darkness afforded by the bus shelter. Her heart thumped with excitement, her ears strained at the approach of every car. She was used to waiting for an hour or more for him to appear and as autumn approached it was often chilly. Polly didn't mind. She knew that when he did arrive she would be instantly warmed by the furnace of their desire. What was more, tonight was to be a rare delight; they were actually to sleep together, sleep in the true sense of the word, be present for each other's dreams. Usually this was not possible, but occasionally Jack had a pass and those were the best times, times when they had the whole long night in each other's arms.

As Jack's car approached, Polly knew he would be moody. He always was of late, glum and preoccupied. She didn't mind that either. It was his job, no doubt. Who wouldn't be glum if they were an agent of mass murder? And he always got over it quickly. Polly soon made him smile, sometimes just a glance from her would make his face light up. She never imagined that he was glum because he was trying to say good-bye.

"*I couldn't do it,*" Jack wrote to Harry after one such night. "*I tried, just like I tried the other times. I told myself again that this would be the night I would leave her but again it wasn't. 'Good-bye' is such a small word. Why can't I say it? Every time I try it comes out as 'I love you.' Because whenever I look into her eyes I just want to stay looking into them forever."*

When Harry read this he tried to phone, he sent a telex, he even thought about getting on a plane. He wanted to shout "Don't do it, you fool! Don't throw love away, it's too rare a thing. Sometimes it only comes once in a lifetime." But it was no good. By the time Harry got Jack's letter Jack had already left Polly in the only way he felt he could. Abruptly and absolutely. Without a word.

It had been a wonderful night. Completely and exclusively passionate to the exclusion of all else, even conversation. Sometimes on their evenings together they would have some supper and talk, but on that last occasion they scarcely said a word. Jack drove them to the little country hotel he had chosen, they checked in, went straight to their room, and began to make love. Time and again they made love, fervently, desperately.

Polly's joy was all in the glory of the moment, but Jack was storing up memories, trying to make love to her enough to last a lifetime. Because he knew that he had to leave her that night. He knew as he lay there beside her afterward, listening to her gentle breathing as she slowly succumbed to sleep, that this was his last chance. He was certain that his resistance could last no longer. Another day or two in the sunlight of her love and he would be lost forever. As would his career and the life he held dear. Jack was perfectly sure then, as he had been ever since, that if he had not left her that week, that very night, he would never have left her. It was cowardly, of course, but if he had looked back even once, he would have stayed. That was something he had not been prepared to allow.

So, instead of saying good-bye Jack had waited until Polly slept and then had crept silently from their bed, gathered up his clothes, and snuck out into the hotel corridor. There he had dressed in the darkness, gone downstairs, paid the bill with the night porter, and left.

"What could I have done?" Jack replied when Harry berated him for being the cowardly shit that he was. *"I had to leave. She was a seventeen-year-old anarchist! A radical pacifist. A foul-mouthed swamp creature with a ring through one of her nipples!"*

This detail surprised even Harry, who was quite an alternative sort of person himself. This was back in the days when nipple rings were not something that nice girls had.

"I'm a thirty-two-year-old soldier with a crew cut, Harry!" Jack pleaded more for himself than his brother's benefit. *"Talk about star-crossed lovers! Jesus, Captain Jack Kent and Polly Sacred Cycle of the Moon and Womb make Romeo and Juliet look like an arranged marriage! Pamela Anderson and the Ayatollah Khomeini would have made a more natural-looking couple. We had no future, Harry, can't you see that?"*

In truth Jack did not really care if Harry saw it or not, it was Polly he hoped would somehow understand. She hadn't, of course, and she never would.

She could still remember every detail of that shocking awakening. She could still see herself, a distraught young woman standing alone in a cold, empty room clutching a piece of paper with a single word on it: "Good-bye."

She remembered the brown carpet, the orange coverlet, the floral pattern nylon pillow slips. She could still see the sheet of lace underneath the sheet of glass on top of the mahogany-style MFI dressing-table unit. The stained-glass-effect transfers on the windows, the ancient, scentless potpourri on the windowsill. The clock radio flashing the time at 88 past 88. Her little summer dress and leather jacket crumpled up on the floor where she had left them when she was happy. Her Doc Marten boots lying at the foot of the bed, her bra in the wastepaper basket, her knickers lodged behind a framed print of a fox hunt that hung upon the wall.

And nothing of Jack, no trace of him, remained. Polly might always have been alone in that room. Jack had even plumped his pillow before leaving. The habits of a thousand bed inspections died hard.

Polly dressed herself in a daze and went downstairs to reception.

"Excuse me," she said, her face burning with embarrassment, "but the man I was with . . . the American. Have you seen him?"

The woman inside the little reception hatch had had the face of Oliver Cromwell and the same glowering air of violent righteousness.

"The gentleman's gone." Her voice sounded as if it had been mixed with iron filings. She folded her arms menacingly, as if daring Polly to contaminate her house further. Even the woman's hair was hard and unforgiving, having been set into an impenetrable helmet of red-tinted Thatcheresque waves that would have kept their shape in a hurricane.

"He left hours ago. Didn't he say good-bye, then?"

Throughout the intervening years Polly would never forget the withering contempt of that woman's tone.

No, he had not said good-bye. Polly stood before the hatch as if bolted down, not knowing what to say or do, not able even to think. Tears started in her eyes, further blotching the black smudged makeup that surrounded them. The hotel lady misunderstood her emotions.

"Well, he paid my bill, love," she said.

Polly knew what the woman meant immediately. The woman thought Polly was a prostitute and that her client had done a runner.

This was indeed exactly what the woman had thought. What else would she think? When a smart-looking chap with money turns up late and signs in some grubby slip of a girl as his wife? A girl with bare legs, black eye shadow, and purple lipstick? When they go straight to bed without so much as ordering a toasted sandwich or spending money at the bar. When they keep the whole house up for hours with their disgusting grunting and when the noise finally subsides, after the man's clearly had his fill, he sneaks off in the small hours leaving his "wife" to get her breath back.

"Unless there's anything else?" the woman said, clearly anxious to rid the sanctified air of her house of Polly's noxious presence. Polly turned to leave. She could not speak to the woman; she had been struck dumb. The enormity of what was happening to her was too much to take in. Adored, then dumped, now despised. Ecstatic, then distraught, now only numb, all within a few short hours. Polly was only seventeen.

"He's paid for your breakfast, by the way," the woman said as Polly headed for the door. "You can have it if you want, but there's no more eggs and you'll have to be fast because I want to set lunch."

Never had an invitation to eat been offered with less enthusiasm. The woman could not have sounded more unwelcoming if she'd said that she would be serving turds instead of sausages.

[40]

"**I should** have had it, though," Polly told Jack, "because when I got out of the hotel I realized I didn't even know where I was and I only had about seventy-five pence on me and I hadn't even had a cup of tea. It took an entire day of buses and hitching to get back to camp and when I did they'd finished supper. It didn't matter, of course. I couldn't have eaten anyway. You'd torn my insides out."

Jack had no answer. There were no tears in his eyes, of course. There never had been, and Polly doubted that there ever would be such a thing, but nonetheless deep inside him he cried. Thinking about that unhappy morning had always been difficult for him, and at last hearing Polly's side of the story made it more difficult still.

His own day had been scarcely happier. By the time Polly had awoken he was long gone, pointing his TR7 for the coast. Jack had planned it, as he planned everything, meticulously. Everything he owned was in the car. He would not be returning to Greenham. He had arranged for his leave to begin that morning and when his leave ended he was to go to Wiesbaden in Germany. There he would re-join the regiment that he had left on being posted to Britain. Jack had already done three years at the base and it had not been difficult for him to persuade his superiors that he had earned the right to re-turn to some proper soldiering.

"I thought about leaving some money for you," Jack said in a quiet voice. "You know, to get back to camp and all, but you were such a feminist and all, I thought it . . . it . . ."

"Might make me look like a bit of a tart?" Polly demanded. "Yeah, well, no need to worry about that. That was already sorted."

They relapsed into silence for a moment before Polly continued to unburden herself.

"I rang the camp, of course," Polly said. "I didn't betray you even then, not that they would have believed a mad peace bitch anyway, but I was still careful for your sake. I pretended I was a cab driver who'd overcharged you. They told me not to worry about it. They said you'd gone. They said you'd left the country! Can you imagine how that felt?"

Of course he could, although he knew that she would never believe him. The truth was that he knew how she felt because he'd felt it too. As evening fell that day and he'd leaned on the rail of the car ferry, watching England disappear over the horizon, Jack had felt more desolate than he had ever felt. It had been no comfort at all that he had been the architect of his own unhappiness, or that he knew that it was the only thing he could do.

"You left that day!" The bitterness of Polly's tone wrenched Jack back from his momentary reverie. "You left Britain the same fucking day you left me!"

"Yeah?" Jack said. For a moment he was unsure why she was dwelling on this point.

"Which must have meant that you'd already made your preparations," Polly explained. "That you'd known you were leaving. That when you made love to me on that last night you knew what you were going to do. Your fucking bags must have been already packed, you bastard!"

"It hurt me too!"

"Good. I wish it had killed you!"

Polly did not believe Jack. She did not think he could have felt remotely what she'd felt. He would never have done what he did. She had been so completely in love with him. She'd trusted in him so absolutely and he'd left her all alone. For weeks afterward she had been quite literally sick with the pain. Unable to keep food down, she'd scarcely eaten for months. She lost two and a half stone, which left her dangerously underweight, and eventually she had had to see a doctor. At seventeen Polly discovered that it is not just the heart that aches when love is lost, but the whole body. Particularly the guts; that's where a person's nervous system really makes itself felt.

"It's not pretty," said Polly. "It's not romantic. It wouldn't look so good on the Valentine's cards. A stomach with an arrow through it."

Jack thought about saying he was sorry again but decided against it.

"So did you stay there long?" he asked instead. "After?"

"I stayed there until after you people delivered the missiles; three years, in fact, with a gap for the miners' strike."

Jack was amazed. "Three years? In that camp? In that toilet? You spent *three years* singing songs through a fence! You stayed there till you were twenty? I thought you were there for the summer. That's what you said. What about your . . . what were they called? . . . your A-levels?"

"I didn't take them, not then, and I never went to university either."

Jack whistled in disbelief, scarcely able to believe it. In his view, Polly had wasted the three best years of her life.

Polly knew what he was thinking. "I was waiting for you, Jack! I loved you."

"Three years! That's not love, that's psychosis. That's an illness."

He was right there, it had been an illness.

"I thought I saw you a thousand times. It was pathetic. There I'd be, screaming abuse at these people, and all the time I was hoping they were you so that I could tell you I loved you."

"Jesus, Polly, nobody takes three years to get over being dumped."

"It took me a lot longer than that, not that I'd have admitted it at the time. I believed in what we were doing. That camp was my home. But always, at the back of my mind, especially when there were new faces, new Americans on the other side of the wire, I'd think to myself, Maybe this time he's come back? Surely not everything he said was lies."

"You were so young, Polly. I thought you'd forget me in a week."

"I think young people are the most vulnerable in love. They haven't learned their lessons yet. You certainly taught me mine."

"I'm sorry," said Jack quietly.

"Is that why you've come back? To say sorry?"

"Sure, if it will help, if that's what you want to hear."

The old wound was aching badly for them both.

"I don't want——" Suddenly Polly was shouting. She stopped herself. Even in this highly charged emotional moment she knew she must not forget the milkman. She dropped her voice to a harsh whisper. "I don't want to hear anything! I don't want anything from you. I was asleep an hour ago. Why have you come back, Jack?"

Again the question he did not want to answer.

"Well . . . why not? Like you said, we never officially split up, technically you're still my girlfriend . . ." Jack laughed rather woodenly. "You always used to say that you weren't into conventional relationships."

"A relationship with a sixteen-year pause in it is not unconventional, it's over."

"I thought you'd be pleased to see me."

Why he thought that she could not imagine. Except that she *was* pleased to see him. Despite everything, she was very pleased. Looking at Jack it struck her that he looked tired, almost careworn.

"Are you hungry?" she asked. "Do you want something to eat?"

"Not really, no," Jack replied.

"That's good, because I don't have any food. Well, I do have food, sort of, just not real food. Frozen meals, serves two. That sort of thing."

"Serves two?" Jack's interest picked up.

"No. I told you there isn't anybody."

Jack looked hard at Polly, and for some reason she felt that some sort of explanation was required.

"They say 'serves two,' but they mean one, in fact not even quite one, really. You have to pad them out with toast and chocolate biscuits. They put 'serves two' on it so you don't feel so pathetic when you buy them in the shop . . . So you can pretend you're not alone."

It sounded so sad. Polly admitting that she was alone. Not positively and self-sufficiently alone, but alone because she had no one with whom to share her life. Lonely alone. The revelation hung heavily in the air between them. Polly smiled reassuringly and tried to make light of it.

"It fools the shopkeeper every time you buy one. Frozen meal for two, madam? Oh, yes, certainly. I'll be sharing this with my enormous, passionate, and deeply sensitive lover. We always like to share eight and a half square inches of microwaved lasagne after an all-night shagging session."

"How the hell does a beautiful woman like you come to be on her own?" Jack was genuinely surprised.

"Men are nervous of single women in their thirties. They think she's either got a child already, or that halfway through the second date she's going to glance at her biological clock and say, 'My God, is that the time? Quick, fertilize me before it's too late.' "

"You don't have to be alone. You're just being lazy. Not making any effort."

Who did he think he was? Her mother? He'd be telling her she had lovely hair and a super personality next.

"Not making any effort! What do you suggest I do? Stand naked on the pavement with my tongue hanging out and a large sign saying 'Get it here'? I go to pubs, parties. I even joined a dating agency."

Polly said this last defiantly. It had taken her a lot of courage to join a dating agency. It was another of those things that only a short while ago she would never in a million years have imagined happening to her. She knew what Jack would think. The same thing that everybody thought. How sad. How surprising. How pathetic. Never thought *she* would be so desperate. For months after Polly had approached "Millennium Match" she had kept the fact as a dark and shameful secret, never telling a soul. Then one day she had decided to come out. Come out as a lonely person. A lonely person who was trying to do something about it. Since then Polly had made a point of telling people at the first chance she got.

In shops. "Two kilos of carrots, please, a grapefruit, oh, and by the way, I've joined a dating agency."

At work. "Right, so before we address the issue of gender discrimination in nursery teaching, is everybody aware that I've joined a dating agency?"

The idea had been that Polly would overcome her embarrassment and shame by confronting it head on. That her proud honesty would educate people to see her decision for what it was, a legitimate effort to cope with the social challenges of an increasingly fragmented society. It hadn't worked yet, but she was perservering.

"A dating agency," said Jack in the same tone her mother had used. "That's insane. You're a babe."

"You don't have to have three heads, garlic between your teeth, and a season ticket to *Riverdance* to be lonely, Jack. All you need is to be alone. To have met all the people that your circumstances are likely to bring you into contact with and not be in a relationship with any of them."

Polly knew that she wasn't unattractive, she wasn't socially inept; she was just alone. And, to her surprise, the men the agency had introduced her to were much the same. Just alone, like her. The problem was that this fact hung over every new meeting like a cloud of slightly noxious gas. Polly would sit there toying with her food thinking, not bad looking, good manners . . . but he's alone. *Why* is he alone? Finding herself unable to dismiss the unworthy suspicion that unlike herself, this man was not merely an innocent victim of fickle fate but somebody who was alone for a reason.

Of course, Polly was sufficiently realistic to know that the object of her doubt was almost certainly thinking the same thing about her. Even the lonely stigmatized the lonely. The very people who knew best that you do not need to be a psychopath or a gargoyle to be lonely were the most wary of other lonely people. Like outcasts everywhere, they learned to despise their own kind.

"Polly," said Jack. "It's insane that you went to an agency. The world is full of eager single guys your age."

"I'm the same age now that you were when we were together, Jack. You think about that. When you were an eager single guy of my age you weren't seeking out lonely insecure women of your age, you were seducing a seventeen-year-old girl."

Well, she had him there, smoking gun and all, no doubt about that. He drained his glass and poured himself another large one.

"Jesus, Jack, I hope you're not driving."

He was, but he was going to risk it. Jack's courage and resolve were deserting him. The revelation that Polly was so lonely had been a shock. For years he had thought that he was the lonely one. He had always imagined Polly settled and happy in some gloriously perfect relationship. Living with a university lecturer, perhaps, or a Labour MP. Of course, his spy had revealed that she lived alone, but not that she was lonely.

Oh, how he would have loved to cure her of her loneliness. To whisk her away right there and then and make her happy forever. He couldn't, though, for exactly the same reasons that he had left in the first place. He had had his chance and he had chosen his path.

"I like to drink," he said. "It helps with moral decisions."

"Moral decisions? What moral decisions?"

Jack did not wish to say. "Nothing," he said.

"What moral decisions?" Polly insisted. Morality was a topic that Jack had never been interested in discussing in the past.

"Well, hey, every breath a person takes is a moral decision, isn't it?"

"Is it?"

"I think it is."

Polly could not imagine what Jack meant.

"Well, it's 'to be or not to be,' isn't it?" he explained. "I mean, that has to be the question."

"I don't really see why."

Polly would have been surprised to know that Jack had been thinking a lot about morality of late.

"I don't see why you don't see why," he said, "considering what a morally minded person you always set yourself up to be."

"I never set myself up to be anything."

"Every moment we decide to remain alive we are making a moral choice. Because our existence has repercussions, like a pebble in a very polluted pond. Everything we eat, everything we drink, everything we wear, is in one way or another a product of exploitation."

Polly knew that, of course, but she was most impressed that it had occurred to Jack.

"You don't have to be a sex tourist to abuse children in the Third World," Jack continued. "All you have to do is buy a carpet or a sports shirt. Or open a bank account. Or fill your car with gas."

"Well, yes, of course," said Polly, "and it's the duty of every consumer to confront and minimize that exploitation . . ."

Jack laughed. It was a laugh with a sneer at the back of its mind. "Confront and minimize? That's for wimps. It seems to me that the only truly moral thing a person could do in these sad circumstances is kill himself."

[41]

Got it! The knife was finally hooked.

Slowly, gently, with infinite care, Peter reeled in his prize, inch by inch hoisting the wire retriever back up through the grid, watching his beloved blade ascend.

Then he had it. It was in his hand once again where it belonged. He sat on the wet curb and studied it, carefully closing its blade and cradling it in his hands as if it were a tiny pet. Then he tried the catch. It worked perfectly; the blade sprang out of the hilt as if it were alive, snapping into place with the usual satisfying click. Peter's little pet was clearly none the worse for its time in the underworld.

Another car came round the corner, but Peter did not bother to move this time. He remained where he was, kneeling in the gutter. Now that he had his knife back he felt invulnerable.

[42]

In the chilly atmosphere of the formal but faded grandeur of her dining room, Nibs held her knife also. It was a cheese knife, but she was gripping it just as hard as the Bug gripped his.

The full story of her husband's most recent philandering, or as much of it as he had felt forced to tell her, had made grim listening. The dessert had been delivered and she had pushed hers away untasted; he'd eaten his, of course—he could always pig down pudding—and now the cheese had arrived. Nibs took a little English red Leicester but she couldn't eat it. They were both drinking quite hard and a third bottle of wine had been opened, but neither of them felt at all drunk.

"So I suppose you want me to stand by you," said Nibs.

"I want you to forgive me."

Nibs was not in a forgiving mood. Her fate was sealed. She knew that, but she was not under any obligation to be magnanimous about it. She was doomed to become one of the "women who stand by her man." They were a common type these days; you saw the famous ones on the television all the time. Politicians' wives, pop stars' wives—sad, trembling, red-eyed victims whom the press had hounded from their hiding places, baited onto their doorsteps, and forced by circumstance to lie through their teeth before a baying mob. The clichés never varied.

"My husband and I have talked things over and decided to put this incident behind us . . . We remain very much in love . . . Miss so-and-so is no longer a part of my husband's life," etc., etc.

All this actually meant was that the poor woman had nowhere to go, her position, her possessions, her children, her life in general, all being tied up with the mumbling apologist to whom she was married. He had taken her youth and her potential and now she had no obvious life options of her own. Nowhere to go except her doorstep, to assure the world that she was standing by her husband.

Nibs knew that she too would stand by her man. It was true that she was an accomplished professional woman in her own right. She would not be entirely lost on her own. Nonetheless, after twenty-five years and with children still in their teens, her life was inexorably tied up with her husband's. Her career had always been just a little bit secondary to his; his business had become her business too, she'd worked hard for it. His status was hers. Like many a woman before her, Nibs was caught between a rock and hard place and the hard place was her husband's dick. She did not like being betrayed, but on the other hand she did not wish to have to rebuild her life from scratch just because she was married to a man who couldn't keep it to himself.

"I'll stand by you," she said, "but I'm not going to lie for you."

"I wouldn't ask that," he replied.

But they both knew that in the end if she had to she would.

[43]

It occurred to Polly that although they had been talking for nearly an hour she still knew almost nothing about Jack's life. She realized with a tinge of resentment that she seemed to have been giving most of the information.

"So how about you?" she asked. "Are you in a relationship?"

"No, I'm married."

It was a joke, the sort of sexist little put-down in which Jack specialized. Normally Polly despised men who put their wives down behind their backs. She heard that stuff a lot. Scarcely a month went by without some married man or other telling her what a mistake he'd made with his life and how all he wanted was to be able to give his love to someone who would appreciate it. Experience had taught Polly to react to that sort of thing with nothing but feelings of sisterly solidarity.

This time, however, she scarcely noticed Jack's blokey humor. The knowledge that he was married had taken her completely by surprise. There was no reason for it to have done so, of course. Jack was an establishment man in an establishment job, he was almost bound to be married. She felt deflated. She knew she had no right to feel that way, but nonetheless she did. The truth was that deep deep down, without acknowledging it even to herself, Polly had been toying with the exquisitely exciting possibility that Jack might have come back for her. From the first moment she had heard his voice over the answering machine something in her most private self had hoped that he had come back to stay. It was nonsense, of course, a ridiculous notion, and she knew that now for sure. He was married, he had a life. All he had come back for was some easy sex. Perhaps not even that, perhaps he had been motivated by nothing more than curiosity.

"Oh yeah, I'm married all right," Jack mused into his bourbon. "But whatever we had died a long time ago."

"I'm sorry," Polly said, although she wasn't particularly.

Jack performed his favorite shrug. "There's nothing to be sorry about. Literally nothing. I can't remember the last time we made love. She has a diaphragm that ought to have been an exhibit in a museum of gynecology. The spermicidal cream is years past its fuck-by date."

"So why haven't you left her?"

"I don't have the guts." Which was a silly thing to say to Polly.

"You had the guts before."

"That was different."

"How was it different?" Polly asked angrily.

"We were together three months, Polly! We weren't married! Did you ever try to leave someone you've been with for years? It's like trying to get off the *Time Life* mailing list. I torment myself. Would she kill herself? Who would get custody of the credit cards?"

"Oh, come on, Jack!"

Polly may not have seen Jack for a long time, but she knew him well enough not to buy this type of bullshit. If Jack wanted something he was not going to let any finer emotions or sensibilities stand in his way. He never had.

"OK, OK," Jack conceded. "The truth is I can't leave her because I can't risk damaging my career. I'm near the top now, Polly. I mean real near. I'm tipped to be the man. Unfortunately the army is about a hundred years behind the rest of the world on social matters. They like you to be married and they like you to stay married."

Polly could hardly believe that it still mattered, that being a divorcé could still be a bar to promotion.

"Oh yes, it can be, Polly, in the army it can. More so now than a few years ago, the pendulum's swinging back. Can you believe it? I had to leave you for my career and now I can't leave my wife for the same reason. If I wasn't such a big success I might almost think that I'd fucked up my life."

Jack had met Courtney shortly after his arrival in Washington to take up his posting at the Pentagon. They were introduced by Jack's bumbling old friend Schultz. The meeting took place at a Republican Party fund-raiser, and it had been a rare moment of intuition on Schultz's part because Jack and Courtney became instant friends. They were as similar to each other in outlook as Jack and Polly had been opposites. Courtney, like Jack, was a sincere patriot and a conservative, but also like him she was no bubba-style redneck. The daughter of a congressman, Courtney was accomplished, cultured, and beautiful, and although still only twenty-six, she was already respected in her chosen field of company law. She and Jack made a splendid couple, he the tough, handsome soldier, she "the gorgeous girl most likely." Between them they looked like the stars of a Reagan campaign ad.

Harry had been suspicious from the moment Jack had introduced him to his new girlfriend. Courtney was perfectly nice and Harry could see that she certainly loved Jack, in an uptight, chilly, preppy sort of way, but Harry did not think that Jack loved Courtney. To Harry, Jack looked like a man going through the motions.

For a while Harry kept his silence, presuming that the affair would blow over, but when Jack wrote to tell him that he had asked Courtney to be his wife and that she had done him the honor of accepting, Harry could deny his fears no longer.

"*This isn't a marriage proposal, Jack, it's a career move!*" Harry thundered in his reply. "*It's too damn convenient to be true. If you asked the IBM mainframe to come up with the perfect bride for you it would have come up with Courtney. But real life isn't like that. You know that better than anyone because you loved Polly. Love is rarely convenient. Courtney isn't for you, Jack. You aren't in love with her, you just think you look so good together that you ought to be in love.*"

It was combative stuff but Harry was sure that his instincts were right. He still had Jack's letters from the final summer that Jack had spent at the Greenham camp. Then Jack really had been in love, with all its attendant joy and pain. Now it seemed to Harry that his brother was merely acquiring a lifestyle appropriate to his status and position.

"*Have you thought about Courtney?*" Harry wrote. "*I thought you officers were supposed to be gentlemen. That girl trusts you, she loves you; don't you think she has a right to know that you're still in love with another woman?*"

This last point was Harry's secret weapon. He was aware that Jack wouldn't take it lightly and he didn't. Fortunately for the two brothers, they were half a continent apart; otherwise there might even have been blows. Jack furiously denied Harry's accusations. He loved Courtney, she was a terrific person. Of course he knew that he did not feel quite the same for her as he had once felt for Polly. His knees didn't buckle at the thought of Courtney, his insides didn't ache, but surely that was a good thing? His love for Polly had been stupid and obstructive, more an obsession than a proper adult emotion. Jack certainly had no wish to go through his married life poleaxed with love and lust every time his wife walked into the room. It would be far too time-consuming. He had things to do, a career to forge.

"You think there's only one way of being in love?" he wrote back to Harry. *"You think it always has to be like you and Debbie? Instant fucking devotion? You think I have to be some kind of wet puppy dog drip like you? Jesus, I hope not. Let me tell you now. If ever me and Courtney start acting like you and Debbie did, take my gun and shoot me!"*

Jack had a point and Harry knew it. When he had first started dating his wife, Debbie, it certainly had been a bit gruesome. They were both very young and their powerful mutual attraction had manifested itself in a public gooeyness that should have remained private. They kissed at the dinner table, giggled together in corners, and occasionally even talked baby talk in front of friends. It was inexcusable behavior, but they just could not help themselves. There is no love like young love and theirs truly had been love at first sight. What's more, it was a love that had lasted. Harry and Debbie had become that rare thing, high-school sweethearts who seemed to have made a good and permanent marriage.

"Yeah, well, not every marriage starts with snookey fucking ookums, pal!" Jack wrote furiously. *"Courtney and I are adults and we love each other like adults and we're going to get married like adults, so fuck you!"*

Jack signed off, but there was a P.S.

"By the way, do you want to be the best man?"

It was a magnificent wedding attended by senators and congressmen, senior army and air force personnel. There was a message from President Bush and his wife Barbara, who knew Courtney's parents, and the cream of Washington society were in attendance. Even Jack's father made an effort, ditching his habitual fringed suede jacket and hiring a tuxedo for the occasion.

"Don't worry, son," he said. "I'll kiss ass to your Nazi pals."

The only tiny upset on the big day was the late arrival of Jack's old pal Colonel Schultz. Almost inevitably Schultz had gone to the wrong church and had let his staff car go before realizing his mistake. He and Mrs. Schultz arrived in a taxi just as the bride and her father pulled up in their limo.

At the reception Old Glory hung upon every wall, an eight-foot-high ice sculpture of the American Eagle glowered from within a sea of flowers, and impeccable waiters served California champagne. The band struck up Springsteen's "Born in the USA" and Jack and Courtney led off the dancing, looking stunning, he in his dress uniform, she in a cloud of white silk, and the whole room erupted into cheers and spontaneous applause. Such a very good-looking couple, so assured, so strong, so confident. Even Harry, standing at the back of the crowd with his arm around his beloved Debbie, believed in that moment that Jack had made the right choice for his life. He still could not help wondering what the English girl whom Jack had betrayed would have made of such a scene had she witnessed it, but in the glamor and romance of the moment Harry dismissed the thought. It had all been so long ago. His brother claimed to have forgotten his first great love and she no doubt had long since forgotten Jack.

The band moved on to Huey Lewis and the News's anthem to eighties' cool, "Hip to Be Square." Harry and Debbie joined the bejeweled and uncoordinated mob on the dance floor.

Jack and Courtney's marriage started off fine and for a year or so they were happy. They liked each other and found each other attractive enough to ensure a respectable if unspectacular sex life. The sad truth was, though, that Jack's heart was never truly in it. Harry had been right, and by the second anniversary that fact was becoming difficult to disguise. Jack had two loves in his life and neither of them was his wife. One was the army and the other, despite all Jack's denials, was Polly.

The breakdown of affection was hard on Courtney. She truly had believed herself in love and her wedding day had been the happiest day of her life. Unlike her husband, Courtney had not experienced real love before. Her career had always taken precedence over romantic entanglements and so inexperience fooled her into imagining that what she felt for Jack was the real thing. Therefore when Jack's attitude and manner began to grow colder she was deeply hurt. Nothing had changed as far as she was concerned, and yet it seemed that they were no longer happy.

Jack knew that he was hurting Courtney but he did not know how to stop. His cruelty to her was neither verbal nor physical, but simply that he had married her in the absence of love.

Jack wanted to write to Harry about it but he could not. Harry's life had changed too and he did not have room in it for Jack's problems. His beloved wife Debbie had left him. She had fallen for another man, a fellow firefighter, and one day she had told Harry that she was leaving. Debbie explained that even the most perfect love affairs sometimes have sell-by dates and she had reached hers. In vain did Harry protest that those sell-by dates are usually meaningless, that the food is just as good for months afterward—years, in the case of canned food. You just have to have the courage to not take the easy way out and throw it away but keep it until you had need of it. Debbie felt that the metaphor was overstretched. The simple fact was that she had become besotted by a big, tough, brave guy and that she no longer loved the man she had married almost as a girl, the man who spent all day making chairs and tables.

"How long has it been going on?" Harry asked.

"It doesn't matter how long," Debbie replied, unable even to look at the man whom she had loved so well and for so long.

And Harry knew that it had been going on for some time. His love had been betrayed.

Soon Jack and Courtney's marriage was also over in everything but name. He led his life and she led hers, which, during Jack's seven months in Kuwait and briefly Iraq, began to include the occasional love affair. There was no question of divorce. Courtney was a traditionalist, besides which Jack's career had finally begun to hit the fast track. After the Gulf War he was promoted rapidly and began to mix more in political circles. The Democrats were not going to stay in power forever and the Republicans were on the lookout for likely lads who might help to break their hold on power, particularly handsome war veterans. Courtney was highly ambitious, and her marriage to Jack became what Harry had suspected it was all along: a mutually supportive marketing exercise.

One thing Courtney was grateful for was that despite her occasional indiscretions, Jack appeared never to have affairs. She and he had occasional sex and that seemed to be enough for him. The only thing that Jack wanted to get inside was the uniform of the commander of the army.

"We're friends, sure enough," Courtney confided in her mother, "but I don't really think he has passion for anything but leadership."

It was not true, of course. Jack still had passion for one other thing besides ambition, although he had imagined that passion was long buried. He still craved Polly and now, as Jack stood once again before her, Polly knew it. She could see it in his eyes as he stared at her across her room.

"So your wife doesn't love you and now you're here. In the middle of the night," Polly said. "What's the idea? Suddenly fancied a little blast from the past?"

There. She'd said it. The thing she'd been wanting to ask from the beginning. Had he come here to try to fuck her?

Jack stared into his glass, nervously rotating it in his hand. The question was banging around his head. Had he come back to try to fuck her? The truth was, of course, that he hadn't, but by Christ he fancied it all the same.

"Well?" Polly asked again. "You're miles from home. Your wife doesn't understand you. Did you suddenly remember me and get a little horny, Jack?"

That he could answer. "Not suddenly, Polly. Always."

And he meant it. Not one day had gone by since the terrible night he'd left her when Jack had not wanted to see Polly again. To taste again the delights of sex with the only girl he had ever loved.

Polly could see that he meant it, too. It was written in his eyes. Deep inside her something was laid to rest. He had loved her after all.

"Oh, Jack." She stepped forward. She knew that she shouldn't. As a strong woman and a feminist she should spurn his selfish desires. She knew that he had only come back for a night. That he would leave again in the morning as he had done before, but she didn't care. If anyone had a right to a bit of comfort by General Jack Kent it was her. Let the devil take tomorrow; she was opting for one less lonely night.

"Do you know, I have never told my wife about us." Jack was still fighting it, still holding back.

"I don't want to talk about your wife."

"I thought you did."

"Well, I don't."

Polly shifted her weight slightly from one bare foot to the other; it was a tiny move, but sexual. A loosening of the body. Jack glanced up. She still stood that same way that she used to, relaxed, a little lazy on the hips. He felt his whole resolve dissolving.

"Yeah, well, anyway, I never told her. I never told anyone."

"As if anyone would care now?" said Polly. "As if it matters in the slightest after all these years. Unless you're embarrassed or something. Is that it? Are you scared that one day someone else but me might find out that you're a craven shit?"

"Maybe it's just that I don't want to share you, even in my memories."

Polly's emotions were on a knife edge. They could not have been more mixed if she'd run them through the washing machine. It is true that her desire for him had begun to overcome the anger she felt about his ancient betrayal. However, it did not take much to bring sixteen years of resentment back into focus.

"That's nice," she said. "Especially considering all you left either of us with is memories."

Jack looked so crestfallen that she felt sorry for him. Something she would not have imagined possible only an hour before.

"OK, OK," she put in quickly. "It was a long time ago. Different decade, different world order. It happened, that's all. I suppose you're not the only guy in history who did the dirty on a girl. And anyway. You did come back . . ."

Polly's stance relaxed further and the room positively hummed with Jack's longing. Her left hip dropped a little lower, pushing the knee forward. Her mouth fell slightly open. She rested her hands upon her thighs and was reminded that she was still dressed in a rather unflattering plastic raincoat.

"Think I'll take off this raincoat," she said. "My nightie's probably slightly less stupid."

Polly let the raincoat slip off as if it had been a negligee and stood before Jack dressed only in a shirt, the top couple of buttons of which were already undone. She was breathing more quickly now and her bosom was again rising and falling defiantly. Her hair, which Polly had thought a mess, might also have been described as gloriously tousled, ravishingly unkempt.

She was so beautiful, Jack could hardly bear it, yet still he hesitated.

"It's been a long time, Jack," said Polly, which was clearly a nice way of saying "Come to bed." She took a step or two toward him.

Jack could not help but catch a momentary glimpse of Polly's thighs as the movement of her legs parted her shirt at its hem. He was inches from the soft, pale splendor of Polly's most private self, and he could scarcely bear it. This had been no part of his plans.

Polly bent down and took the glass from Jack's hand. In so doing her nightshirt fell forward and Jack was almost painfully aware of her breasts as they hung before him inside the gaping shirt. He looked. How could he resist? He stared. For a moment he could actually see between her breasts and through to her stomach beyond and the top of her knickers, which were crimson against her skin.

"I've missed you too," Polly whispered softly, her mouth not nine inches from his ear. "I've been lonely."

"It's an international epidemic."

Polly put Jack's glass down on the little table beside his chair. Or rather on top of the pile of magazines, books, and coffee mugs already on top of the little table by his chair. Then she took Jack's hands and drew him to his feet. Jack could now feel the warmth of Polly's breath, the warmth of her body. Her hair smelled exactly the same as it had always done. He could see that her nipples had hardened again beneath the thin cloth of her nightshirt. She had always had such responsive nipples, he remembered. They were up and down all night, leaping into life at the slightest provocation, an infallible barometer of the state of her arousal. The current provocation was scarcely slight. They were both consumed with a taut, vibrant desire and the points of Polly's breasts seemed almost to be straining to reach him.

"You're such a beautiful girl, Polly. Still just the same."

"Nearly the same," Polly replied. "It's all still here, just a little closer to the ground."

It did not seem so to Jack. She appeared to him as beautiful as the day they had first met. As the day he had left. Polly reached up to him and took his face in her hands.

"Hello, old friend," she said, and drew his lips toward hers.

And then they kissed. This time Polly did not break away as she had done when Jack first arrived. It was a kiss that spanned sixteen years, a kiss so charged and full of memory and emotion that it was a wonder that the mouths of two people could contain it all.

Now their arms were about each other, mouths working with a desperate urgency. Even through the thickness of his uniform Jack could feel the soft splendor of Polly's body against his. If he chose he knew that he could be upon it in an instant. He had only to throw off his clothes and that divine skin would be against his, those adored breasts crushed against his chest. He clasped her even tighter to him.

"Is that a gun in your pocket?" Polly whispered playfully into Jack's ear. "Or are you pleased to see me?"

Jack loosened his grip, slightly embarrassed. "Actually it's a gun in my pocket."

Stepping back for a moment Jack reached under his jacket and took a pistol from his trousers.

"Sorry about that," he said and laid it down on the table beside his glass. Then he made as if to resume their embrace, but Polly raised a hand to stop him. She could hardly believe her eyes.

"A gun!" she gasped. "You're carrying a gun! You're armed!"

"Sure," Jack replied casually. "I'm a soldier. It's what I take to work."

"I'm a council worker but I don't have a file full of pointless forms and a leaky pen stuffed into my knickers! I can't believe you've brought a gun into my home."

Where Jack came from, of course, everybody had a gun in their home. People didn't even think about it. In fact if you didn't have one you were weird. Obviously Jack knew that things were different in Britain, but it still did not seem like a big deal to him.

"I'm sorry, Polly, but I need it."

"You need a gun in Stoke Newington in the middle of the night?"

"Yes, I do," Jack replied. "I'm a target."

This was not the type of conversation that Polly would have chosen to conduct in the middle of making love, but she could not just let it go.

"You do know you're breaking the law, don't you?" she said. "I mean, this is Britain, not Dodge City! You can't just wander around with a gun in your pocket."

But it seemed that Jack could.

"I'm one of America's most senior soldiers. Quite a lot of people about the place would like me to be dead. It's a diplomatic thing. We have an informal understanding with Special Branch."

Polly still could not accept it. "You come to my house dressed like Oliver North, you have informal understandings with the Special Branch, you carry a gun! I hate people like you. I've spent my life protesting about people like you!"

Jack shrugged and smiled his smile.

"So how is it . . ." Polly continued, "how the fuck is it . . . that you're the only man I've ever loved . . . ?"

"Bad luck, I guess," said Jack. Then he drew her back into his arms.

For a moment Polly thought about resisting. She thought about informing Jack that she was not a tap who could be turned on and off, that she did not consort with gunmen. But then he held her and she held him. Their lips met again with even greater passion, it seemed, than they had done a minute or two before. Again Jack could feel Polly's divine form crushed against him, could feel her hands pulling at the belt of his jacket. Now he really had to see her naked once more. He stood back a little, not so far as to stop Polly from undoing his belt but far enough for him to raise his hands to the buttons of Polly's nightshirt. Whatever his original plans might or might not have been, he simply had to see her naked again. He would die if he did not. He knew that it was wrong. He had promised himself that what was about to happen was the one thing that would not happen but he didn't care. He had been mad to imagine that he could control it. He loved her and he wanted her. Nothing had changed.

Now his hands were at the middle buttons of her nightshirt, his eyes straining, waiting to feast themselves on what lay beneath. His face, usually so mature and assured, was suddenly like a boy's, eager and scared. Polly, too, could hardly restrain herself. She'd opened his jacket and her hands had stolen to the fastening of his trousers. She neither knew nor cared what had brought Jack back to her door; she was happy to give away the past and ignore the future. Her entire life was crammed into the immediate living moment. Jack's fingers brushed against her skin as her shirt fell open and he felt her shiver gently at his touch. He shivered also, and by no means gently. Polly's hands tugged at his zipper. His whole body felt as if it would explode. He moved his hands from one button down to the next, allowing his fingers to explore the greater freedom that the opening of Polly's shirt now afforded. Her breasts felt smooth and firm, the skin springy and subtle. He wondered if he could ever let go now that he had them in his hands again.

"You got rid of the nipple ring, then?" he whispered.

"Yeah, everybody started wearing them."

Polly had a hold of Jack too, her hand deep in his trousers, gripping the straining erection through his shorts. Now Jack's hands were at Polly's waist, the final button of her shirt undone, his fingers slipping under the elastic of her knickers. Another moment and all would be revealed.

Then Polly's phone rang.

[44]

Peter had remained in the gutter for some time, kneeling in the dirty running stream, imagining himself somehow cleansed and sanctified by the waters of the night. Water has ever had a strong hold on the spiritual side of men's minds and it was no less the case for Peter, even though his spirit was warped and his mind ill. The rain upon his face and the stream lapping at his knees seemed somehow to lend a new courage and nobility to his resolve. In his unformed fantasies he imagined himself reborn and baptized, a martyr and a saint. He spread his arms, Christ-like, as he knelt. Like Christ he was an outcast, a man alone, and, like Christ, he knew a greater love.

But that love had been betrayed.

Peter had resolved upon murder. It just remained to decide who was to die. Would he kill the American? Would he kill Polly? Perhaps he would kill them both, and then himself. But if he killed himself how would his mother cope? Perhaps he would have to kill her too.

He got up, soaked to the skin but warm and happy. He had a purpose, a goal. He could see an end to his emptiness and longing.

Fumbling in his pocket for a coin, he made his way back to the phonebox.

[45]

Jack and Polly sprang apart. The ringing of the phone came as a shock, totally unexpected; they had been utterly lost in their mutual undressing.

"Who the hell is that?" said Jack, grabbing at his trousers to prevent them from falling down.

"How would I know? I'm not a clairvoyant," Polly replied, closing her nightshirt. But she did know.

"It's nearly four in the morning, Polly. Who's going to ring at such an hour?"

It seemed almost as if Jack was more anxious than she was.

"You tell me. You did."

After the sixth ring the answering machine kicked in and delivered Polly's familiar message. Of course Polly knew what was coming next. It would be the Bug. He was out there and he was trying to get in. A great wave of despair swept over her, so strong and so desolate that her knees nearly gave way and caused her to fall. Would she never have any peace from this man? This thing? Was he going to spoil every joyful moment for the rest of her life?

"You fucking whore," said the machine. "Is he in you right now? Is his fat Yankee dick inside you? Yes, he is. I know he is."

There was a pause. The line crackled. Polly and Jack did not speak. Jack was too surprised and she was too upset. Then the hated voice of the Bug began again.

"He's got AIDS, you know. He has. All Americans have, and now he's given it to you, or else you've given it to him, which is all either of you deserves, sweating and grunting like filthy pigs in your sty . . ."

Polly could no longer contain herself; it was all too much. She began to sob. Great, heartfelt, gulping sobs, dredged from the pit of her stomach. Why her? Why now? Why had she caught the Bug? Was she cursed? She made her way to the bed weeping as she went and sat down, burying her face in her hands, all the pent-up emotion of the evening spilling over into despair. For one joyful moment she had forgotten everything, both past and present pain, but it had been an illusion, she could see that now. She was just not meant for happiness. Even if she did sleep with Jack he would still be gone in the morning and she would be alone. Alone, that is, except for the Bug, who had infected her life and for which there was no cure.

Jack could only look on, his heart hurting for her in her distress. It was unbearable to see her this way. She seemed so helpless, her body shaking with her sobs, her chest, still half naked through the gaping shirt, shuddering jerkily with sorrow.

"What's he doing to you now, slut?" Peter's voice filled the room. "Has he come? Has he spunked his stuff into you yet? Maybe he's beating you up? You'd like that, wouldn't you, Polly? It's all tarts like you deser—"

Jack wanted very much to meet this unpleasant pest. He crossed the room and picked up the phone.

"Where are you speaking from, pal?" he asked in a friendly, matter-of-fact tone as if addressing an acquaintance. "We could talk about all this stuff face to face."

"I got my knife back, pal. And I'm going to kill you with it."

"OK, that's fine. That's good. Where are we going to do this thing?" Jack could have been arranging for a couch to be delivered. "I can meet you anywhere. We could get it over with right now if you like. Tonight. Just tell me where to go."

Down in the box in the street Peter could see that his money was running out. He had only one more coin and he hadn't yet fixed upon his plan.

"You can go to hell, mate," he said, and slammed down the phone.

Back in Polly's flat Jack hung up.

"Pleasant fellow. I think I met him earlier," Jack remarked casually to the top of Polly's head, her face still being lost in her hands. "I guess he's your stalker, right?"

Polly was regaining some control. "Yes," she said in a snotty, teary voice. "I'm sorry. Usually I try not to let it affect me, but it's been going on so long. He's always like that, disgusting, horrible . . ."

"Let me see if I can catch him," said Jack, and he might have been talking about the postman.

Jack took up his coat, slipped his gun back into his pocket, and hurried out of the flat, leaving Polly in a state of shock. Jack figured that there was a good chance that the man had been phoning from the call box where Jack had seen him skulking before. It was certainly worth giving it a go, because life would be a great deal easier for Jack if he could catch the sad bastard that night.

Peter had been making his way back from the call box on the other side of the road when he heard the door of Polly's house opening. Quickly he retreated into the shadow of a doorway. For all his bravado on the phone he realized how dangerous the American man was. Peter watched as his former assailant emerged from Polly's house and ran up the path. Peter considered leaping with his knife from the darkness as Jack ran past but the memory of their last encounter was too fresh, the taste of his own blood still in his mouth. Peter would have had to cross the road to get to the American and by the time he did that the man might have pulled out a knife of his own. Peter reasoned that he could take no chances. If he lost the fight he would never be able to take his revenge on Polly for betraying him.

Jack ran past and round the corner toward the phone box. Peter had intended to remain in his hiding place, but then he saw something extraordinary.

Jack had left the door to Polly's house open.

[46]

It was too good a chance to miss. Peter had not been inside Polly's house since the very beginning of their relationship, and now the door was open and Polly was alone. Peter darted out from the shadows and scuttled across the road and up the path of her house. He hesitated for only a moment before pushing open the door and going in.

Once inside the hallway he paused and breathed deeply, taking a moment to absorb the atmosphere. This was her private place, her home, her "sanctum," she had called it in court. He was risking a prison sentence just being there, but it was worth it. It was exquisite to be a part of her private world. He almost thought that he could smell Polly.

He began to climb the silent stairway, torn between the need to hurry and the desire to luxuriate fully in the moment. As he ascended he dragged one hand gently along the banister, imagining her hand upon the same polished wood, each morning and night.

In his other hand Peter held the knife.

A few moments later he stepped into the orange semidarkness of the top landing. Only one door led off it, which Peter knew to be Polly's. A light shone through the crack beneath it. She was inside, and she was alone. This, then, was it. The supreme moment. Peter did not know what would happen next. He had made no plan. His great opportunity had sprung itself upon him too quickly for that, but there was one thing he did know: if anyone was going to spend the night alone with Polly it was him.

He knocked on the door.

Inside the flat Polly stirred herself. She was grateful that Jack had returned so quickly; she had so hated being left alone. She got up from the bed, buttoned up her nightshirt, and went to the door. Contrary to her usual habit she did not glance through the spyhole before beginning to undo the chain.

The phonebox had been empty. Jack had not expected anything else; hunters rarely find their quarry presented to them on a plate. There had been no point in trying to search the street either. There were so many shadowy doorways, basement stairs, gates, and walls that it would have taken the rest of the night to investigate them all. Jack had longed for a set of infrared night-sights, but of course, he reflected, you never have the right tool when you need it. He walked back to the house deep in thought. Turning the corner into Polly's road, Jack noticed suddenly that the door to her house was wide open. He broke into a breathless sprint.

Polly turned the dead bolt and before reaching for the latch dabbed at her eyes with the hem of her nightshirt. She dreaded to think what sort of state her face must be in. Her eyes stung and she wondered if they were red and puffy, but there was nothing to be done. She opened the door.

Peter had seen Polly's shadow in the crack of light beneath the door, he had even fancied that he'd heard her breathing as the door chain rattled—but he was too late. He could hear noisy footsteps bounding up the stairs behind him. His enemy had returned. Quickly he stepped back out of the gloomy light and crushed himself into the darkness of the landing, pressing himself hard against the wall.

The door of Polly's flat opened. The American reached the top of the stairs and rushed in without breaking his stride. He did not see Peter in the darkness and Peter did not leap out to attack him as he had half intended to do. It was all too quick, too confusing. Killing was not an easy business. The door closed.

Peter stood for a moment, dumbfounded, scarcely able to contain his thoughts. She had been there. The door had been open. He had missed his chance to kill the man and possess Polly, have her for his own. On the other hand, he was inside the house. He had penetrated her environment and they did not know it. They thought themselves safe. He must work out his next move. Peter retreated down the stairs and sat down on the threadbare carpet to think.

[47]

Inside the attic flat Polly kissed Jack, grateful to him for trying to fight the Bug and glad not to be alone. Jack returned her kisses while trying to catch his breath, tasting the salty tears around her lips. She felt so small and helpless. Jack longed to protect her, to possess her. At that moment, he and Peter were experiencing very similar emotions. Jack steeled himself against such thoughts, against Polly's magic.

"I didn't get him," he said. "He'd gone."

"You'll never get him," Polly replied. "He's invulnerable. I've been trying for so long."

Jack put his lips to Polly's ear. "Did you ever think about killing him?" he whispered.

What a question. Of course she'd thought about killing him. Victims of stalkers often find themselves thinking about nothing else. Polly had wished that sick bastard dead a thousand times.

"No, I don't mean wishing him dead, Polly," Jack said. "I mean actually getting him dead. Killing him. For real."

"Don't joke," Polly replied. "You don't know what it's like. If you knew what it was like to be a victim, how awful it is, you wouldn't joke."

Gently Jack sat Polly down upon the bed and fetched her drink. "I'm not joking," he said. "I'll kill him for you."

"Oh, Jack, if only." She was near to tears again.

"Polly." Jack spoke firmly now. "I'll kill him for you. I just need to know who he is and where he lives."

Polly's head swam. It was such a lovely thought. Such a truly lovely thought. To have the Bug dead. Squashed. Gone forever. Not warned off, not threatened with arrest, not made to give a solemn undertaking to stay away, but dead. Completely and utterly ceasing to exist. It was a beautiful dream. But that was what it was, a dream. You couldn't just kill people.

Jack knew what she was thinking. "I'm a soldier," he said. "Killing people is what I do. It's not such a big deal."

"When soldiers kill people it's legal?"

"Since when did you ever care about the law? Certainly not when I knew you. There is a higher law, that's what you used to say. Or maybe you think it's OK that I kill strangers whose only crime is that they come from a different country. Persecuting the weak and intimidating women is fine as long as it's legal."

"I'm not talking about justice," Polly said. "I'm talking about the law, that's all. You'd get caught."

Jack smiled that charming, confident smile. "Hey, I'm out of here tomorrow. I'm gone. I'm on an army transport to Brussels and then home to the States. You think if I bump off some sad lowlife, no-life nut in Stoke Newington, somebody's going to say, 'Hey, I bet a general in the United States army did this.' Never in a trillion years."

"Stop talking like that."

"I was in Special Forces, Polly. Believe me, I know how to hit a guy discreetly. I can do it on my way to the airfield and still get breakfast."

Polly was silent now. She wanted to tell him to stop again but the words would not come.

"I mean, the guy's connected to you," Jack continued, "but he's not connected to me, right? Of course you're connected to me, Polly, but only you and I know that, don't we? That's true, isn't it, Polly?"

By a stroke of great good fortune Jack had stumbled upon a way of finding out exactly what he most wanted to know.

"I mean, if I'm going to do this thing I need to be sure that there's nothing to connect me with you. Is there anything?"

Polly spoke as if in a trance. "I only told the whole story once, to a guy called Ziggy, in a VW camper near Stonehenge, but he was stoned and didn't hear me."

"Anybody else?"

"A few people, you know, over the years. Every now and then I get drunk and say that I once fucked a soldier at Greenham, but I never go into details. I don't like to remember, Jack."

Polly was speaking, but it seemed like she was listening to someone else. She could hear herself reassuring Jack. "There is no way on earth anyone could connect me with you, Jack."

They stared at each other for a moment. Jack was grinning.

"Well, there you are, then," he said breezily. "Where do I find him?"

He wasn't joking, she could see that. She was in a dream, but it was rapidly becoming reality. Polly drew herself back from the brink. It was time to put an end to this dangerous fantasy.

"You can't kill him. I don't want you to kill him. I don't want you even to talk about it. No matter how much I hated someone I would never ever want to kill them."

Jack just kept grinning, his handsome eyes sparkling and his voice light. "People die all the time. It's no big deal."

"Shut up."

"Just try to think of this guy as an exploiter of the planet. You remember what I was saying before? About how every breath we take we're doing damage to others? Consuming the world's resources, abusing the world's peasants. Why not let me reduce the abuse?"

"Shut up!"

"This man is an evil, useless, pointless waste of food and air. Let me take him out. We'll all breathe easier. You'll be doing the world a favor."

Jack was still smiling; it was such a friendly smile. "Tell me where he lives."

"No!" said Polly, deeply shocked at the sincerity of Jack's tone. He really did mean it. He really did believe that murdering people could be justified just because you didn't like them. She was horrified at the thought. No matter what a person's crimes, the death penalty was never justified. No one had the right to take a life. The fact that she was the victim did not change that fact.

"Shut up, Jack! I mean it. Stop talking like that, it's horrible."

Jack shrugged and went to fix more drinks. "OK, OK," he said. "If you don't have the courage to defend yourself. If your precious principles have so weakened you that you don't have the guts to make your own personal decision about what's right. Lenin knew what to do, didn't he? If you have something you believe in you defend it by any means necessary. Don't you believe in your right to happiness, Polly?"

"Of course I believe in it!"

"Then have the courage to defend it."

Jack poured Polly another huge Bailey's and Coke and she gulped it down hungrily.

"Polly, I have to do something to help. This guy is truly a terrible thing. We can't just let him go on abusing you."

Even in her distress Polly thought about asking at what point Jack had suddenly become so concerned about her well-being, but she didn't. For the first time someone was genuinely trying to help her with the problem that had been destroying her life.

"Come on," said Jack. "Maybe I wouldn't even have to kill him. I could just scare him a little. It'd be very easy to scare him."

"It wouldn't do any good. He's too mad."

"Polly, believe me. I know how to scare people and I know how to hurt them. When I do it they're scared and they stay hurt . . . Come on. You have a right to defend your life. Not in the law, maybe, but under any concept of natural justice. Tell me where he lives."

Polly did not believe in violence of any sort.

She absolutely did not believe in violence.

That fact was a mainstay of her life.

On the other hand . . .

She had suffered at this man's hands for so very long. If anybody deserved to be punished it was him . . . And if it worked? If the Bug could be scared off, not killed but scared off, forever? The prospect of liberation rose like a new dawn before Polly's eyes.

Jack could see that she was weakening. "Where does he live, Polly?" he asked once more in his friendly, gentle tone.

Polly made her decision. She would act in her own defense. She would empower herself and defend her life. She would give Jack the Bug's address and she was glad. Why the hell should she suffer any more if she had the means to fight back? She had never done anything wrong and she did not deserve to be persecuted. That bastard deserved everything he got. Polly was fed up with being a victim. Let the other guy be the victim for a change.

The Bug's details were written on the court papers. Papers Polly had always studiously avoided studying for fear of becoming further connected to her persecutor. She retrieved them from the file, which she kept under a pile of dirty clothes, some books, and a pair of running shoes, and handed them over to Jack.

"Do anything you like," she said firmly, "but please don't kill him."

[48]

The milkman's radio alarm went off, wrenching the milkman from his slumbers. He was surprised to discover that he had nodded off again after all. He had not imagined that he would do so what with all the talking and walking that was going on upstairs. However, the milkman resolved not to let the fact that he had been back to sleep diminish his righteous anger. He still had his notebook cataloging the disturbances of the night and he decided that he would add a couple of instances more, since he was sure that the noises must have continued while he slept.

Upstairs they heard the music too.

"What the fuck?" Jack inquired.

"It's the milkman," Polly explained. "He gets up at four, the radio will stop at four twenty-five, then his door will bang."

Three floors down in the stairwell Peter also heard the music. He imagined that it must come from Polly's room. Were they dancing? Or maybe they were doing "it" to music? Either way, Peter's jealousy and resentment were amply fed. What should he do? How could he douse the fire of hatred that was burning inside him? Peter had never thought of himself as having a murderous disposition, but that American certainly deserved to die. Peter put his hand to his injured

243

nose and nearly yelped in pain. He wondered if it was broken; it was certainly swollen. Now he had made it bleed again, a steady flow of drops falling onto his trousers. Peter spread his knees and allowed the blood to drip between his legs and stain the stair carpet. Her stair carpet; she would be walking over his blood. Then Peter positioned the blade of the knife under his bleeding nose and watched the metal turn red.

Upstairs in Polly's flat Jack was a little anxious. The milkman's alarm call, unusually early though it was, had reminded Jack that the night would not last forever. Dawn was to be at seven-fourteen that morning and Jack wanted to be away long before then. He had found out the things he needed to know. He was reasonably certain that his history with Polly was a private one, and he knew the whereabouts of Polly's stalker.

One thing Jack was certain about: this man Peter would have to die. Whether Polly liked it or not, Peter was a dead man.

"I have to leave quite soon," Jack said, taking another slug of his drink.

It was like cold water. Somehow Polly had stopped thinking about Jack's leaving.

"I want you to stay," she said.

"I can't, not for much longer."

Polly felt desperate. All those familiar emotions were back, all those painful old feelings, the ones it had taken so many years to get over. Why had he returned if only to tease her and then leave her again? Now she must suffer the pain of rejection a second time and live with a newly broken heart.

"I got promoted recently," said Jack.

Polly did not know what to say to this. It was such a non sequitur. Did he think she was still interested in making polite conversation?

"I've been promoted quite a lot over the last few years, actually. I've done very well."

What was he talking about? Was he still fighting himself? Perhaps he really did want to stay. Perhaps he really wanted to make love. Perhaps this chattering was just a way of avoiding making a decision.

"Congratulations," said Polly. "You certainly never let anything stand in your way, did you?"

Everything Jack said reminded Polly of his desertion.

"You do not make four-star general just by avoiding ruinous love affairs. Nor by working hard or being talented. You have to get lucky. Very lucky." Jack paused for a moment and then said, "Sex."

"What?" Polly asked.

"That's what got me where I am today."

"I don't know what you're talking about."

"Sex is what made me, Polly. What brought me to my current elevated status."

"I'm not interested, Jack," said Polly wearily.

"I need to tell you what brought me here today," Jack insisted.

Polly sat back. It was pointless to resist. Whatever Jack wanted to do or say he would do or say in his own good time. She tried to concentrate as he spoke.

Jack began. By the end of the Gulf War, he said, he'd been a full colonel, one of the most successful soldiers of his generation, but despite this his prospects for future advancement had not looked particularly good. Traditionally, war was the way to get promoted in the army and despite Saddam's honorable efforts real wars, proper wars, were becoming less and less likely. There was, according to George

Bush, a new world order. The Soviet Union had collapsed, taking with it the Warsaw Pact, thus depriving the Western allies of their best available enemy. The Chinese, who had always been next in line to fight, were embracing capitalism and waging war on the stock market. McDonald's was opening up in Beijing, and the U.S. was importing gangsters from Moscow. The West had won. For career soldiers like Jack it was a depressing time. All those weapons and nobody to kill. It just wasn't fair.

Of course there were the various UN, humanitarian, and peace-keeping missions around the world, but that wasn't soldiering, and it certainly wasn't the way to make a four-star general. As Jack and the guys moaned to each other over bourbon in the mess, it was a very tough call to set your career alight dropping powdered milk on dead African people. Or digging up football fields full of skulls in Bosnia.

Jack had seen the way the wind was blowing when Bush wimped out of going all the way to Baghdad.

"We should'a had Saddam's ass hanging on the Pentagon flag-pole," he and his comrades had assured each other through mouthfuls of beer and chili fries. "But Old Man Bush listened to Pussy Powell. What kind of soldier was he? Too scared to risk his men. For Christ's sake, what is happening to the world? We have an army that thinks it has a right not to get killed! Powell was probably worried his men would sue."

In Polly's flat Jack was pacing up and down telling his story, almost ignoring her. She wondered what on earth he could be getting at. Whatever it was, she wasn't interested.

"Pussy Powell?" she asked.

"Lots of men left the service," Jack continued. "But I couldn't. I didn't know any life other than soldiering. I had nowhere else to go. Besides, I'd sacrificed too much to give it up."

They looked at each other. Polly might have spoken but Jack continued.

"Then something strange happened. Just when everybody thought they'd never get promoted again, sex came along. Sex is what saved the entire U.S. military career structure from stagnation. Sex replaced war. Funny, huh? Kind of what you guys always wanted in a way. Make love not war and all that bullshit."

"What are you talking about, Jack?"

Polly had resigned herself to the evening's going round in circles forever.

"Remember Tailgate?" he continued. "Bunch of navy flyers couldn't hold their brew and started waving their dicks at some lady sailors?"

Polly did recall it. The scandal had been big enough to be reported in the British media. There had been an appalling display of drunken brutality at a U.S. naval conference.

"As I recall, it was all a little more serious than dick waving," Polly remarked.

"Jesus, did the shit hit the fan. They court-martialed everybody! 'Sir! Yes, sir! I waved my dick, sir!' Dishonourable discharge! 'Sir. Yes, sir! I waved my dick too!' Out goes another one. A hundred and fifty thousand dollars' worth of training—gone! The brass thought they could calm things down by throwing a few minnows to the sharks. They couldn't. The shit flew upward. 'Yes, I failed to ensure that dicks were not waved.' 'Yes, I allowed a dick-waving culture to develop . . .' You want to know how many admirals were eventually implicated?"

Polly did not. She was not even slightly interested.

"Thirty-two, Polly! That's a historical fact. Thirty-two admirals. Our attack readiness was compromised. Navy morale was shot to ribbons. Comfort was given to our enemies. And all because we live in a world that thinks it can legislate against guys acting like assholes."

Polly could scarcely believe it, but even at this point in the evening Jack still seemed to be anxious to compare their political points of view, and yet again, despite herself, she could not help but oblige.

"You can legislate against rape and intimidation and harassment."

"Jesus!" Jack snapped. "These guys were sailors! The navy never should'a let those women anywhere near them. There was a time when being a disgusting fucked-up maniac was a military career requirement!"

"Change hurts sometimes," Polly snapped back.

"Oh yes, it does, Polly, it sure does. Change hurts all right. I've seen men cry. I've seen marines cry because they've just discovered that when they pinched some secretary's ass at the Christmas party they were in fact making a career decision."

Perhaps Jack had been right earlier when he'd spoken to Polly of "her kind." She could certainly empathize with this situation and her sympathies were not with the weeping marine. At her work Polly was called upon to deal with similar situations all the time and she knew all about the sort of activities that guys called "just bum-pinching."

"Well, perhaps your friends shouldn't go round pinching people's bums, then," she said.

Jack threw his arms into the air in frustration, spilling his whiskey as he did so.

"Hey! We all know that now, honey! Oh, we sure do know that now! Our learning curve has been real steep! Problem was, nobody told some of these guys till they were in court! Nobody told that poor tearful marine that the way he had *always* acted, the way his daddy and his granddaddy had acted, was suddenly criminal behavior. Nobody ever warned that twenty-year-service marine that it wouldn't be any Soviet commando that'd take him out in the end but some little girl with a grudge."

"Yes, well, maybe that marine should give some thought to all the little girls who've done the crying over the years."

"Well, maybe he should," Jack conceded, although he did so rather aggressively. "And he's certainly going to have plenty of time to reflect on it, because suddenly there's been an awful lot of vacancies in the military. I didn't get these four stars defending democracy, I got them for keeping my dick in my pants."

"So no female rookies raped on your watch, then?"

"I never was much of a party animal, Polly. In a way I owe that to you."

Jack was thinking of the poor German girl Helga and that bleak night in Bad Nauheim in the early eighties. He knew what men were capable of when they were drunk and in packs. Particularly soldiers. He had been with the UN in Bosnia, had seen what gangs of men could do when no civilizing factor restrained them.

"You may not believe it, but you changed me," Jack explained. "All that stuff you told me all those years ago. It genuinely affected my outlook, made me see the other point of view. I truly believe that you influenced me for the good, Polly. I believe I've been a better soldier because of you."

The irony of this was nearly too much for Polly.

"And over the years," Jack continued, "I've always asked myself what you would say about stuff. It was almost as if you were still there with me and I didn't want to make you angry."

It was true. Jack could not be sure, but perhaps his unfinished love for that passionate, idealistic seventeen-year-old girl he had once known had refined him and caused him to avoid the mistakes made by other soldiers. He wasn't thinking about terrible incidents like the brutalization of Helga—mercifully such events were rare— but the smaller invisible pitfalls that so many of his colleagues had fallen into. The sort of thing they now called harassment. The comments, the pinchings, the endless catalog of minor sexual impositions that men had for so long practiced with impunity. Jack had avoided them all. He was recognized universally as a gentleman, and, while others of his generation had found themselves demonized by the new morality, Jack had prospered.

"I've always loved you, you see, Polly," he said. "I still do."

Again the circle came round. Polly could see that Jack was struggling with something inside himself but she did not know what it could be. Perhaps it was just the fact of an unhappy and unfulfilled life. Perhaps he was not so different from her, after all.

"What about your wife?" she asked gently. "You must have loved your wife when you married her. Did you love us both?"

"I thought I loved her, Polly. God help me, I thought I did, but now my true belief is that I married her because I was trying to get away from you."

It was cruel, so very cruel for Polly to hear this now, after so many years of having lived under the shadow of Jack's rejection. Yet difficult though it was, her heart soared at the dawning realization that he had suffered as much as she had. That perhaps, after all, he had truly reciprocated her love.

"Jack. Oh, Jack. You tell me all this now. After all the years I've grieved for you."

"I have to, Polly. Because . . ."

But Polly put her finger to her lips and breathed a "shhh." She had had enough talking now. She would put up with no more. It was her flat and she was going to take control of what went on in it. For the second time that night she crossed the room to stand over Jack, and again, as she walked, he watched the movement of her thighs, brushing against each other as she walked. Polly again took the glass out of Jack's hand and put it down.

"No more talking," she said.

"Polly. I mustn't," Jack replied, but his eyes were filled with a misty longing.

Polly shushed him again, this time putting a soft finger to his lips. His tongue momentarily brushed the tip. Then she cupped her hands around Jack's face and gently pulled him to his feet. Then they kissed again, long and passionately.

"No, Polly, we mustn't. That's not what I came here for." Jack spoke almost into Polly's mouth as she continued to kiss him. Again he succumbed to her embrace. For the time being his passion for her was stronger than the guilt he felt.

Polly unbuttoned her shirt. She did it herself this time, purposefully and quickly. Having done so, she broke off their embrace and stood back, her mouth shining. Then she opened her shirt fully in order to show Jack her body. It was what he had longed for all evening, a proper sight of her, her breasts and her stomach and her neck, her navel and her legs, clear and unencumbered, with only the crimson triangle of her knickers still to be removed.

Jack felt weak with longing. "We can't do this, Polly," he heard himself say.

Polly did not reply. She had done with conversation. He could say what he liked, but she was now controlling the agenda. She could feel his desire even in the air between them. She knew just how much he wanted her. She took his hand. For a moment there was the faintest tug of resistance, but after a moment Jack allowed himself to be led to her bed, as Polly had known he would.

She lay down on the bed beneath Jack's gaze, and spread her shirt wide open on the sheet. Looking up into Jack's eyes, she could see that they were glistening and wet. He was crying! Not much, hardly at all, there were no actual tears, but she was sure he was crying. She had never seen him cry before. Reaching down to her hips, Polly raised her knees for a moment and slipping her thumbs under the elastic of her knickers took them off. Relaxing her legs again, she lay entirely naked save for the shirt at her arms and shoulders.

"Make love to me now," she said firmly.

"I can't, Polly," Jack replied, his voice cracking.

Polly reached up and took his hand. "Jack. Stop this nonsense. I said make love to me now!"

"I . . . I . . . can't." Still Jack resisted, although he could scarcely find the words to deny her.

"Yes, you can, Jack. It's why you came."

Jack closed his eyes to shut out her beauty, to shut out the magnet of eroticism that lay inches from him. As his eyes closed tears formed at the corners.

"It's not why I came, Polly." He said it firmly, dragging the sentence from deep within him. Then he pulled his hand from hers and returned to his chair and drink.

[49]

Peter's mother picked up the phone.

"Camden Police," said a voice at the other end.

Peter's mother had anguished long and hard about informing on her son. She was absolutely loath to do it and shuddered to imagine how he would react when he found out. However, she felt that she had no choice. He had been hanging around that woman's street all night, he was wet through and not himself, and he was messing about with that dreadful knife.

She knew the terrible things her son had written to the girl after she had rejected him. They'd been read out in court. Many times he had threatened to stick a knife in her and worse; sometimes he'd been specific in his threats, talking about cutting bits off her, all sorts of horrible stuff she felt sure he'd got from videos.

He wouldn't do it, of course. She knew that, she was certain of that. On the other hand, he'd looked so very desperate. But Peter's mother would rather have her son arrested for breaking a court order than for murder, which was why she had decided to call the police.

"He's been told not to go there but he couldn't resist it, I'm afraid," she said to the duty officer at the police station. "He's just hanging about in her street in the rain . . . and . . . well, I know he's taken his knife with him . . . Just against yobs and muggers, you understand! I mean, he wouldn't actually harm anyone with it . . . not her, I'm sure, but perhaps you could send someone down to talk to him anyway—tell him to come home."

The duty officer promised that they would send a car round.

"Thank you, officer. Thank you. He's a good boy, you know."

[50]

For perhaps a minute afterward Polly lay staring at the ceiling. She had pulled her shirt around her but apart from that she had not moved. The only sound in the room was the milkman's radio and a faint clatter as he made his breakfast in the room below. Polly felt foolish, angry. She had stripped herself naked in front of Jack. She had practically begged him to make love to her. He had let her do it, too. Oh, there'd been no doubting the way he'd looked at her. Jack had certainly allowed Polly to undress for him, and then he'd walked away.

She got up and put her knickers back on, buttoned up her shirt, and put on the plastic raincoat again. Up to this point she had not looked at Jack once. When she finally did so she found that he was not looking at her but had returned to his old habit of staring into his glass.

"I think you should go now," she said.

Jack did not move. "I can't go," he said.

"I don't care what you can and can't do, Jack." Polly's voice was cold with hurt. "I want you to leave."

Still Jack did not face her. "I can't leave, Polly."

"You rejected me before, Jack. I got over it. Now you come back and reject me again. I'm not strong enough for this."

Jack attempted to explain, but he could not. "It wouldn't have been right for us to—"

"Is it your wife? Is that what's stopping you?" Polly asked. She had not intended to discuss it any further, but she knew that he wanted her as much as she wanted him. She could see it in the despondent way in which he sat.

"No."

Polly felt she had no more dignity to lose. "I'm lonely, Jack."

Jack did not respond.

"I'm lonely," Polly repeated.

Again he did not respond, except perhaps for the smallest of shrugs. Polly finally decided that she really had had enough. Loneliness was better than this. The evening was over.

"I want you to leave. Now, Jack," she said. "And this time don't come back. Not after sixteen years, not ever."

Polly walked over to the door and opened it.

Outside the door Peter froze. Terror and excitement in equal proportions deprived him of the means to move. He'd returned to Polly's floor and had been trying to listen, not very successfully what with that damn radio music, his ear pressed to Polly's door. Then suddenly, more quickly than he would have thought possible, he had heard her footsteps approach, her hand on the latch, and the door had opened.

He had had no time to move even had he been capable of such a thing. He stood transfixed, a knife in his hand, blood still dripping from his nose onto his mouth and chin.

"Good-bye, Jack."

Peter heard her voice through the open door. One thin sheet of paneled wood separated them. In two steps he could be inside her flat, facing her, facing him. He held his knife. He held his breath. He could see the shadow of Polly's arm on the latch through the crack between the open door and the frame. He could see partly into her flat, the carpet, the edge of the table, a shelf with all sorts of stuff on it.

"I'm not going, Polly. Not yet."

It was the American's voice, the despised voice of his hated rival. Peter wondered about running in then and there. He wondered whether he would have the chance to stab the man before he fought back. Peter knew that his enemy was assured, he remembered that from the confrontation at the phonebox. He did not wish to find himself beaten to his knees again, shamed and at the man's mercy in front of Polly. He decided against such a full-frontal attack. Much better to leap out of the shadows at the man later when he left. Instead Peter remained dead still, now more excited than scared, luxuriating in the exquisite tension of the moment, scarcely able to believe that he was almost inside her flat, that she was hardly a foot away from him. For sheer, tense, sensual pleasure this certainly beat swearing at her over the telephone.

"What do you mean, you're not going? You'll go when I bloody well tell you, and I'm telling you to go now," Polly said from behind the door.

It dawned on Peter that Polly was ordering the American out. They must have had a row and now he was being told to go. Peter raised his knife. The blade was already crusted black and crimson with his own blood.

"There are things I need to tell you, Polly," Peter heard Jack saying from within the room, "and something I need to do. Unfinished business."

The door closed millimeters from Peter's face. He stepped back from it, limp with the tension.

Inside the flat Polly turned on Jack.

"Hey, Jack. Look at me," she said. "Don't tell me what's what in my own place. This is today Polly, not yesterday Polly, not twenty-years-ago Polly. Not a little girl who you can screw and screw up. Not a vulnerable, exploitable fucking teenager. This is my place, right? It isn't much, but it's mine and while you're here you will do what the fuck you're told. And right now what I'm telling you to do is leave."

"I'm not going, Polly."

Polly looked at Jack and she did not like what she saw. She felt a surge of resentment. Who the hell did he think he was? She'd got by without him for sixteen years and she was happy to continue to do so.

"Yes, you are going, Jack, because I don't want you as a part of my life anymore. What's more, I want you to forget about what we talked about earlier, about hurting that man. I don't want your help with that. I can fight my own battles, and if anyone's going to hurt him it's going to be me."

"Whatever," said Jack, and Polly despised his tone. He did not believe her. He did not believe she could defend herself.

"You think you're pretty tough, don't you?" Polly said.

"Tough enough," Jack replied.

Polly took her time before replying. "Jack, I've known a hundred men tougher than you. Men who don't need a uniform and an army to give them strength, because their strength is on the inside."

"That's nice," Jack replied.

Polly went back to her bed, kneeled down, and dragged a bag from under it. This time Jack refrained from studying her legs as she did so. He had allowed himself to be distracted for too long. It was time to get on now.

She stood up and put the bag on the bed. "I could kill you right now," she said, looking Jack in the eye.

"Yes, I imagine you could," Jack replied with the same old charming smile. "You've certainly got cause."

Polly could see that Jack had misunderstood her. "No, Jack, I mean really kill you. You could be dead at any moment. I have the means."

The smile still had charm but probably only to a person who liked being patronized. "I doubt it, Polly."

"You doubt it."

"Well, you know," said Jack. "Killing people isn't easy, not unless you know how."

"But I do know how."

Jack did not believe her, of course, but there was something assured about her manner that put him on his guard nonetheless. He wondered what she was getting at.

"You know how to kill people?" he asked.

Before speaking Polly reached into her bag and seemed to fiddle with something or fix something up; whatever she did required both her hands to do it.

"Oh, yes, Jack. I know how to kill people. After I left the peace camp I became a traveler in a convoy. Ever hear about those? Loose wandering collectives of people who didn't fit in, people who didn't like the rules. I mentioned my friend Ziggy earlier. He was one of them. We struck fear into the heart of the British countryside a few summers back. People thought we were going to squat in their gardens."

"Well, you know the British and their gardens," Jack said, watching Polly closely, trying to figure out what she was getting at.

"Despite their scary reputation," Polly went on, "most of the travelers were entirely peaceful, more peaceful than conventional types by miles, the hippies you despise, but at the center of it all there was a core of real anarchists."

Jack laughed. "Anarchists?"

"That's right. People who wanted change and were prepared to fight for it. Road protesters, animal liberationists, that sort of thing. I joined them. I'm still with them. I'm not a traveler anymore, but I'm still part of the struggle."

Jack could well believe it. Polly had always been a hellcat. He could well imagine her seeking out the crappiest people in society and joining them.

"So what do you do? Smear aniseed on hunting dogs and throw paint at doctors' cars? Chain yourself to the cosmetics counter at the chemist?"

Polly looked Jack straight in the eye. She wanted him to understand her very clearly.

"Next Tuesday we're going to blow up a veal truck. I'm the bomb maker. I got the recipe off the Internet. This is the bomb."

Polly motioned to the bag in which she had been fiddling. Jack would have found it hard to deny that he was a little taken aback at the abruptness of Polly's statement. He smiled nonetheless.

"It doesn't look much like a bomb, Polly."

"Oh, yes it does, it looks exactly like a bomb. Maybe not like the sort of bomb you boys chuck about in the army, but it does look like a bomb. Any copper in Northern Ireland would recognize it quick as anything."

Polly peered into her bag, almost as if to check that she was not exaggerating the case. She seemed satisfied.

"Besides," she continued, "it will blow your head off, so it doesn't really matter what it looks like, does it? It's based on chemical fertilizer; I've bags of the stuff. I've made three bombs in all. The first two worked perfectly—we let them off on Dartmoor. This one's my best yet, I think. All I have to do is flip the switch."

And with that Polly reached into the bag. Despite himself Jack jumped. He glanced down at the floor where the sack of fertilizer still lay.

"Polly, if that is a bomb then you know better than to play with it."

"I'm not playing with it, Jack," Polly replied calmly. "I think it's wasted on veal, don't you? I mean, now that I've got a real animal to protest about."

She was so cool, so assured. Jack watched her face, trying to locate the lie, but he could not. He began to feel a little nervous.

"Don't be ridiculous, Polly. You're not going to blow us up."

"Why not? I've got a chance now to really make a difference. I spent years of my life protesting against the military and suddenly here I am with the opportunity to blow up a genuine four-star general. In a split second I could rid the world forever of an agent of mass slaughter."

"Plus one council worker," Jack said, leaping on a salient point.

"Yeah, well, maybe I don't care about that, Jack. Didn't you say that the only true morality was to remove yourself? To end one's exploitative parasitic existence?" Polly was shaking. Jack wished she would take her hand from the bag.

"Besides," she went on, "I'm going nowhere. I've got nothing and I'm not going to get anything. My life went wrong when I was seventeen, but you'd know all about that, wouldn't you, Jack, you fucking bastard. Well, now's my chance to make it all right again. This bomb's big enough to trash my flat completely. When I flip this switch we'll be together again, forever, our flesh will be as one. Entwined, mixed, and blended, never to be parted, as I once dreamed it would be."

Polly gently picked up the bag, one hand still inside it. Holding it to herself she advanced on Jack.

"You should have gone when I told you to, Jack. Now we fucking well go together."

"Polly, please."

"I'm sick of you and I'm sick of life. So fuck everything."

"Polly, you can't," Jack pleaded as she stood over him.

Her face was drawn and weary, her upper lip was quivering, the arm inside the bag was shaking. Jack wondered if he could be quick enough to grab that arm.

"No, you're right I can't," said Polly, "because actually this is a bag full of dirty knickers. Had you going, though, didn't I, you bastard?"

Polly laughed, rather a hard laugh, and tossed the bag back onto the bed. Jack had been completely thrown.

"But . . . the fertilizer . . . ?" he said.

"I told you," said Polly. "It's for my window box. Don't you remember, Jack? I'm into peace, that's my life. I don't approve of killing people. Even people like you. People who turn up in the middle of the night and try to break a girl's heart a second time. Well, I've had enough now. It's after four in the morning. I'm up at seven-thirty and this time you really do have to go."

Still Jack did not move. "I'll be gone soon, Polly. Very soon. But I have to finish saying what I came to say. I have to explain."

"Jack, it's over, gone, many years ago. I don't want to talk about it."

"I don't mean explain what I did, Polly, but what I have to do."

[51]

Outside, a police car turned into Polly's street and drove slowly toward her house. Both the officers inside the car knew the man they were looking for, having often been called out by Polly in the past to deal with him. As they searched they agreed that it was a crying shame that a nice girl like Polly should be harassed in such a way, and they resolved to give Peter the fright of his life if they found him.

They did not find Peter, but they did notice that the light was burning in Polly's flat. This struck them as strange, seeing as how it was only just after four in the morning. They concluded that either the milkman had woken her up again (they knew most things about Polly's life by now) or Peter was about and had already been pestering her.

They decided to check that Polly was all right.

From his position in the hall Peter could see the silhouettes of the police officers through the window panels of the front door. He had retreated to the bottom of the house after his shock at nearly being discovered and had been sitting on the bottom stair considering how best he could attack the American. Seeing the shadows on the window, Peter thought that the game was up. The hated peaked caps outlined clearly by the streetlights surely meant his arrest. He was, after all, inside her house, caught red-handed. For a moment Peter thought about using his knife, but there was no way he was going to stab a policeman. There were a couple of bicycles leaning against the wall. Peter leaned forward and put his knife into the saddlebag of the nearest one. If they found him with that it would be prison for sure.

Upstairs in Polly's flat the intercom buzzer went. Someone was at the front door.

Jack was on his feet in an instant. "It's him. He's back," he said. "And this time he isn't going to get away."

"What do you mean?" said Polly. "What're you going to do?"

"I'm going to deal with him."

The buzzer went again.

"You keep him talking," Jack continued. He was at the door now. "I won't be long."

"No, Jack, I don't want you to—"

The buzzer was insistent. Not for the first time that evening Polly was torn. So much of her wanted to let matters take their course. If Jack wanted to confront the Bug then why not let him? On the other hand, what if Jack got carried away? What if Jack killed him? The buzzer sounded again. Gingerly Polly picked up the receiver, half resolved to shouting a warning to her hated enemy below.

"Polly, it's Constable Dewison," the receiver said.

Jack stopped dead, his hand on the door. "Cops?" he hissed.

"Oh, hello, Frank," said Polly. "This is a surprise."

"We had a call from your admirer's mum, Polly. She said he was hanging about. I'm sure there's nothing to worry about, but she did say that he had a knife. We just wanted to check that you were all right."

Polly assured the officers that although the Bug had indeed been about earlier in the night she had heard nothing from him for an hour or so. Constable Dewison asked if she would like them to come up and take down the details of the harassment for an official complaint in the morning. Polly glanced at Jack. Somehow she felt that the presence of a four-star American general in dress uniform in her flat was a conversation that she did not wish to have.

"No, it's all right, officer. I think I'd rather try and get some sleep."

Downstairs in the hall Peter watched as the silhouettes of the policemen retreated. His relief at escaping arrest was entirely overshadowed by the fury that was consuming him. Peter had heard every word that the policemen had said. He could scarcely believe it! His own mother had turned him in! She'd even told them about his knife! Peter's blood boiled at her betrayal. Well, she'd regret it, that was for sure. Peter would deal with his mother later.

For now, however, he was still inside the house. Inside her house. Even the police hadn't found him out! Surely this was a sign that fortune was on his side. Surely now he could do exactly as he liked.

[52]

Polly laughed. It seemed the only thing to do. "I wonder who'll turn up next," she said.

But Jack was not laughing. Quite the opposite, in fact. His face was like stone. The last thing he had expected was to find the police at the door. It reminded him as nothing else could of the vulnerability of his situation.

Polly caught the look on his face and stopped laughing. She remembered the last thing that Jack had said, before the police had called.

"Jack," she said. "What did you mean before, about what you have to do?"

Jack could not look at her. "Did you ever hear about an army general named Joe Ralston?" he asked. "He was in the news a year or two back."

Polly did not want another endless, pointless conversation. "Tell me what's on your mind or bugger off."

"I *am* telling you," Jack said quietly. "Joe Ralston was all set to become the chairman of the U.S. joint chiefs of staff. The most powerful soldier on earth. Employing about half a million people and spending an annual budget of trillions of dollars."

"Which is totally obscene," said Polly, unable to restrain herself.

"You know where he is now?" Jack continued.

"No, and I don't care."

"Well, I don't know either, because he never stood for that top job. He withdrew his candidacy and retired from the army. Because fifteen years ago he had an affair. Fifteen years ago, while separated from his wife whom he subsequently divorced, General Joe Ralston had an affair. That is why the best soldier in America could not pursue his destiny."

Polly remembered the case. It had indeed been on the news in Britain.

"Your people made that happen, Polly," said Jack.

"My people? Which people would those be, then?"

"Your people, your kind. You see, around the same time that Joe Ralston's application was being considered, a young lady combat flier called Kelly Flinn got caught fucking the civilian husband of an enlisted woman. She was forced to resign her commission, but not before the whole damn country had had a crisis about whether the army would have hit her so hard if she'd been a man."

Polly recalled this case also. The British press always gleefully reported any example of America in the throes of self-torture. But she still could not see what it had to do with her.

"You know what you people have done, don't you, Polly?" Jack continued. "You've created an ungovernable world."

Polly had had enough of this.

"What people? Who are 'my people'?"

"Your kind. Liberals. Feminists."

"Oh, for Christ's sake, don't be so pig ignorant!"

Jack poured himself more whiskey and tried to refill Polly's glass, but she had had enough to drink. He took a gulp of bourbon and continued.

"They tried to indict the president of the United States for dropping his trousers! Are you pleased about that?"

"I don't care, Jack! I don't give two tosses! What does any of this have to do with me? What the hell are you talking about?"

Jack took a breath. He did not want to shout. He wanted her to understand what he was saying.

"The president of the United States, Polly. The most powerful man on earth. The commander in chief of the most formidable army ever known. The person responsible for weapons of destruction that could obliterate life on this planet a thousand times over. That man had put the world on hold, in order that he could prepare to be taken to court to decide whether or not one night six years ago he showed his dick to a female employee. Do you think that is a good thing or a bad thing?"

Polly shrugged. "If the president's a nasty little shag-rat that's his problem."

"Plenty of guys are nasty little shag-rats."

"Yes, well, maybe it's time they started facing up to the consequences."

Despite his efforts to remain calm and reasonable Jack's frustration bubbled over and he banged his fist down on the table.

In the room below, the milkman looked up from his cornflakes.

Four twenty: Shouting and banging, he noted piously in his little book.

"Traditionally women have been aware of what men are like," Jack continued, "which is why they didn't tend to go into guys' rooms in the middle of the night!"

"A woman should be able to go where she damn well pleases!" Polly snapped back, unwilling to be lectured on gender behavior by the likes of General Jack Kent.

"That's right!" Jack snapped back. "And on this occasion one did and in the process she claims she got to see the then governor of Arkansas's dick! Late one night she accepted an invitation to his hotel room, he proffered his penis, she declined, retreated, and there the matter rested for six years! He didn't beat her up, he didn't rape her, he showed her his dick. Then suddenly the whole world was discussing this episode, the whole world! My God, there was a time when a girl would have been proud to see a future president's dick! She would have told her grandchildren! 'Hey, kids, did I ever tell you about the time the president showed me his dick?' "

"Yes, and there was a time when millions of women suffered endless abuse and harassment in silence."

"For Christ's sake, can we get a sense of proportion here? It's like a witch hunt! Oh yeah, except we deserve it, don't we, we guys? Because every horny guy is a rapist, isn't he? I forgot that."

Jack could still remember vividly how during the Helga trial in Bad Nauheim it had seemed as if the whole army was on trial, like they had all gone to that hotel together.

"Jesus! There are women in the States—college professors!— saying wolf whistling is rape! That seduction is rape with flowers!"

Polly pointed her finger straight at him. "I don't know anything about that, Jack," she said, "but I do know that you know something about rape."

For a moment he could not believe what she had said. It was just too surprising.

"What?" was all he could say. "What?"

Polly's voice was suddenly quiet again. "That last night, the night you left me. In that guest house. You made love to me like your life depended on it. You made love to me like a beast . . ."

Jack could scarcely believe what she was suggesting.

"You too! You wanted it! You were totally involved! What are you *saying* here? That I raped you? When you wanted it every bit as much as I did?"

Polly nodded quietly. "Yes, of course I wanted it, Jack. I gave myself utterly and completely and happily."

"Thank you!" said Jack.

"But do you think I would have done that if I'd known? Known that you were leaving? That your ticket was booked? If you'd taken me to your little hideaway that night, a seventeen-year-old girl, Jack, and said, 'What I'm going to do now is fuck you for two hours and then walk away without a word and never see or speak to you again,' do you think I'd have let you have me?"

There was silence for a moment. "Well, no, but—"

"That's rape, Jack. Not big rape, maybe, but rape of sorts. You took me by deceit and manipulation. You took something I would never have given had I known the truth."

For a moment it almost sounded convincing. Except that it wasn't—it couldn't be. Jack did not believe that the world could be run that way.

"Hey, Polly, people get dumped. It happens, you know. Get the fuck over it. What, you think you have a right not to be hurt? Not to be unhappy? I was a shit, I admit it, but a guy sweet-talking a girl into bed is not rape. Little girls getting gang-banged in alleyways, that's rape."

Polly smoldered for a moment and then gave it up.

"Get out, Jack. You just don't get it and you never will."

"No! No!" Jack simply would not let the argument end. "*You* don't get it! The world is not civilized and you can't make it so."

There was nothing Polly could do. If Jack did not want to leave she could not force him. She could call the police, of course, but she had no desire to do that. Besides which, despite herself Polly was beginning to become rather interested in Jack's obsessions. It was obvious to Polly that Jack had some deep, deep problem inside himself. A problem that for some reason he had sought her out in order to deal with. In some ways it was quite fascinating.

"They let the first women into the Citadel this year," Jack said, producing what appeared to be a non sequitur.

"The citadel?" Polly inquired.

"It's a military training facility. They let in forty women who want to be turned into shaven-headed, desensitized grunts."

"How depressing."

"Is that what you wanted, Polly?" Jack snapped. "For women to turn into men?"

"Why are you asking me this stuff? Don't you have therapists in the army?"

But Jack was not listening to Polly. "Truth is they can't do it," he continued, almost to himself. "They're not up to it. Ladies can't run as fast, punch as hard, or lift as much as men. At the Parris Island training center forty-five percent of female marines were unable to throw their grenades far enough to avoid blowing themselves up. Female trainees are twice as likely to get injured, five times as likely to be put on limited duty! These are the facts, Polly. But facts don't matter, because this is politics. Politics decides on its own reality, and if anybody objects they will be condemned as sexist Neanderthals and their careers will be over. It is a witch-hunt, Polly. Leftist McCarthyism. We're living through the fucking *Crucible.*"

"And you see my problem, Jack, is that I don't care," Polly replied. "Don't you understand? I don't care!"

Jack was pacing the room now. "The U.S. military manual has

been changed to accommodate the equality lie. It's called 'comparable effort.' Women get higher marks for doing less. They do six press-ups, the guys do twenty; they only climb halfway up the rope. Assault courses are called 'confidence courses' and you get to run around the walls if you can't get over them. What happens when there's a war? You think the enemy will say, 'It's OK, you're a girl, we'll go easy on you'?"

Polly tried once again to get at whatever it was Jack was trying to tell her.

"Why are you projecting all this onto me, Jack? This is pathological. I'm an ordinary Englishwoman living somewhere above the poverty line in Stoke Newington. I knew you when I was seventeen! This has nothing to do with me! Yet it's almost as if you've come to me tonight to blame me for what you think is wrong with the world—"

"Well? Well! Aren't you pleased we're falling to bits? Aren't you pleased we don't know who the fuck we are anymore? Gender politics is rendering the Western world ungovernable!"

Polly had been interested for a moment, but her interest was over.

"It isn't, but if it was I wouldn't care! Do you understand? I don't care about it either way, all right? What happens to your army and who you choose for president is a matter of supreme indifference to me! Because tomorrow morning I have to go to work and wade back into a sea of people who have been abused, cheated, demeaned, and destroyed all for reasons of race, sex, sexuality, and poverty. They don't have much hope, but if they have any I'm it, so please, Jack, leave, because I have to get some sleep."

"OK, OK, I'm going."

Jack got up and started to put away his bottles, and Polly sat back down on the bed feeling terribly, terribly sad.

[53]

The milkman had finished his breakfast and brushed his teeth. It was time to go to work. He wondered about going upstairs on his way out and speaking to the woman above. He decided against it. She still had someone with her; it would be embarrassing. He'd have a word that evening, just to let her know that two could play at the complaining game.

He turned off his radio, switched off the lights, and let himself out into the hall.

At the bottom of the house, sitting in the hallway, Peter heard the door open and close and then the sound of a heavy footfall on the stair. This Peter knew was his best chance. The man above him, the man coming down the stairs, was the American. It was only minutes since Polly had ordered him to go, and now that was what he was doing. Besides which, who else would be walking out of the house at four-thirty in the morning?

Silently Peter retreated into the shadow behind the stair. His enemy was on the floor above him now, the footsteps descending fast. The dark shape of a man appeared at the bottom of the stairs. Peter leaped out of the darkness and plunged his knife deep into the man's back. He heard the man try to cry out, but there was only a muffled, gurgling sound.

The milkman sank to the floor without a word and lay there gulping his last blood-sodden, strangled breaths beside the bicycle. Looking down at him, Peter noticed that one of the tires of the bicycle was flat. He also noticed that whoever he had killed it was not the American.

[54]

Jack and Polly had also heard the milkman leave. Jack was relieved; he had no wish to encounter the other residents of the building. He finished putting away his bottles, then collected Polly's glass from the bedside table where she had left it and drained his own.

"I'm sorry about going on so much," he said. "It's just that I had to tell you all that stuff."

"That's OK," Polly assured him. "Actually I'm glad. I'm glad you did."

Jack did not ask her why, and Polly did not tell him. The truth was that the things Jack had talked about, the feelings he had displayed, had made Polly feel better about herself and, more important, better about not being, or wanting to be, any part of Jack's life. It seemed to her that he had been right in a way about linking her with the ideological struggles he found so frustrating. The world had changed a little and for the better. Big tough guys like Jack couldn't quite have it all their own way anymore. Power was no longer an absolute defense against bad behavior. Bigotry and abusive practices were not facts of nature; they could be challenged, they could be redressed. And perhaps, in her own small way, Polly had been a part of that change. She and a few million other people, but a part nonetheless.

Jack had stepped through into the kitchen area and was washing up the glasses.

"Jack, please, you don't have to wash up," Polly said.

"Yes, I do, Polly. I have to wash up," Jack replied, drying the glasses thoroughly with a tea towel.

"My God, you're a new man and you don't know it," Polly laughed.

Having cleared up the drinks Jack took a look around the room. He seemed to be checking that everything was in order.

"So General Ralston dropped his candidacy for the chair of the joint chiefs," he said. "The Kelly Flinn scandal had put so much heat under the issue of sexual morality in the military that he had to withdraw rather than further provoke the liberal feminist lobby."

Polly went and got Jack's coat. "Good-bye, Jack."

He put on the coat, still talking, still explaining. "Since then they had two other tries to find the right guy. An air force guy and a marine. Both superb officers, both unacceptable. I don't know why. Probably stomped on a bug during basic training and offended the Buddhist lobby. We have a world so full of people ready to take offense it's tough to find a fighting man, any man, who never offended anybody."

Polly was trying not to listen, but she could not ignore the significance of what Jack was saying.

"I presume what you're getting at is that they're going to ask you to stand," she said, impressed despite herself. "That you are going to be chairman of the joint chiefs of staff. Is that what you came here to tell me? Am I supposed to congratulate you?"

Jack stood staring at Polly. He was gathering his thoughts. Then he stepped across the room to where Polly's answering machine was still blinking out news of the various messages of the evening. Jack pressed the erase button. The machine clunked and whirred in response, wiping clean the tape upon which Jack had announced his rearrival in Polly's life.

"What are you doing, Jack?" Polly felt a chill of fear shiver across her body, enveloping her like an icy cloak.

"Surely you know now why I'm here, Polly," he said.

"No, Jack, I don't," Polly replied although suddenly she was not so sure.

"People die every day."

Polly was cold to the bone now. "What do you mean?"

"What I say. People die every day. Famine, war, accident, design. Death is commonplace. A modern fiction has developed that life is precious, but we know it isn't so. Governments sacrifice thousands of lives every day. At least in the old times they were honest about it. There was no hypocrisy. To be a king or a conqueror you had to kill; no one ever got to the top any other way. Sometimes you even had to kill the things you loved, wives, children . . . many kings and rulers did that. They still do."

Polly could not credit the suspicions that were beginning to flood into her mind. Surely this would turn out to be just another monologue, going nowhere.

"Jack—"

"You were an anarchist, Polly," Jack continued. "A sworn enemy of the state. When I met you your life was dedicated to the confusion of the military policies of your own country and also those of the United States. You were, to put it as I fear the press will put it, as my detractors in Congress and the Senate will put it, a foreign Red. An enemy of the U.S."

Jack could not be implying what it sounded like he was implying.

"I was seventeen, Jack! A teenager! It was so long ago."

"Exactly. Seventeen, that's four years underage in my home

state. An anarchist and a child to boot! Twenty years ago people would have laughed and said I was a lucky guy. These days you get burned at the stake for that stuff. If our affair ever came to light it would finish me for good and ten times over. You know it would. A soldier on active duty consorts with juvenile pacifist anarchist? I wouldn't last ten seconds in a Senate hearing."

Polly struggled to come to terms with what Jack was saying.

"But only you and I know, Jack!"

Jack had taken his gun from his pocket and was attaching some kind of metal attachment to the end.

"That's right, Polly. Nobody else knows about us and nobody knows I came here tonight. I'm a NATO general, in Britain for a few hours, asleep in his hotel room. There is a spook called Gottfried, the guy who traced you for me, but he got promoted to our station in Kabul. Nice job for him, convenient for me—the Taliban don't tend to take the London *Evening Standard.*"

Jack leveled his gun at Polly's head.

"I love you, Polly, but I'm leaving you again. This time for good."

"Peter!" Polly shouted.

"Who?"

"The stalker! He knows, he knows an American was here. He saw you! He could describe you!"

"That's right. He could, Polly, which is a pity for him because you told me where he lives."

Jack's finger was taut on the trigger.

"Jack, no," Polly whispered.

"I'm sorry, Polly, but you do see I have no choice, don't you?"

Jack meant it too. As he saw it he had no choice. In fact it was his duty. He saw himself as the best remaining candidate to lead the army he loved, and it was his responsibility to ensure that nothing compromised his ability to command. Jack had already sacrificed Polly once to the oaths he had made when he had joined the service. Now he had to find the courage to do so again. And this time he would have to do it while looking Polly in the eye.

Polly was still sitting on the bed. Jack stood before her, his arm outstretched, the gun leveled between them, his target pale but somehow calm, calmer than Jack had expected.

"We have a child," she said.

[55]

Jack had been about to shoot. At the very moment that she said it he had been about to shoot.

"What?"

"When you left me I was pregnant, Jack."

Every well-honed instinct of self-preservation within Jack's icy soul told him to shoot and shoot immediately, but somehow he could not, not yet, not for a moment.

"I don't think so, Polly."

"Well, what the fuck would you know, you bastard!" Polly snarled. "You left me pregnant! That was why I always waited for you . . . That was why I couldn't forget you. How could I?"

If she was acting, and Jack was almost sure she was, then she was very good at it; the sudden and bitter venom of her statement was uncomfortably convincing.

It was convincing because it was true. Jack had left Polly pregnant. She realized about three weeks after he had walked out on her. It was not his fault. He could not have known; those had been in the days before AIDS, and Jack had never used condoms because Polly had been on the pill. Unfortunately, like many a young girl before her, Polly had been made careless by love and the result was that she suddenly found herself alone and carrying the child of a man who had had his way with her and then gone.

Polly stared at Jack over the vicious snout of his pointing gun, her eyes teary with angry memories.

"How could I have got over you, Jack?" she said. "You were still there with me, growing inside me every day."

Jack knew that this was nonsense. He tried to shoot, but still he could not. Because if it were true, although it could not be, but if it were true, it would be so . . . Jack shut the thought from his mind. He had come to kill this woman.

"It was a boy, Jack," Polly whispered. "We have a son."

All Jack's life he had wanted a child, and being a soldier, of course, he had particularly wanted a son. He and Courtney had not had children; she'd been young and ambitious for her career and they'd grown apart so quickly. But to have a son with Polly! Jack had often daydreamed of exactly that, imagining what a wonderful spirited boy such a union might create. Jack struggled to regain control. He had no business to be indulging in fantasies of this sort at such a time. Imagining Polly as the mother of his child reminded him of how much he was still in love with her, but he could not afford to be in love with her. He had a higher love to answer to—his love of power, of ambition, his love of self.

Yet still he could not pull the trigger.

"What's his name?" Jack asked, allowing himself to relish the dream.

"Misty Dawn," Polly replied instantly.

"Misty fucking Dawn? You called a boy Misty Dawn?"

"He changed it to Colin when he was at school."

"What was wrong with Jack?"

"Everything was wrong with Jack, you bastard."

Jack knew that he was talking too much. He knew that it was time to get on, time to do the deed. The deed that was the heavy duty of men who would be leaders of men; those who sought to command must know how to sacrifice.

Polly could see Jack's hesitation. "You can't kill me, Jack," Polly said slowly and clearly. "I'm the mother of your child."

This was madness. Jack knew it was madness. "You were on the pill," he said.

"I lied to you. I knew you were paranoid about anything that might damage your precious career, so I lied. I don't approve of putting chemicals into my body. I was using a natural sea sponge and it leaked."

That sounded convincing. Polly had been just the sort of over-confident, illogical, ideological young nut who would have deployed a sponge as a barrier to a liquid. Just the sort of cocky idiot who would have considered her principles more powerful than the laws of physics. On the other hand, she had not mentioned anything before. Jack struggled to think, not an easy thing with Polly's eyes burning into him, pleading for her life, a life he held so dear.

"Fifteen years old, Polly," Jack said. "That's all he'd be."

"That's right, he's fifteen."

With a tremendous effort of concentration Jack began to get over his initial shock and doubt, and began to regain control.

"Then where is he?" Jack asked. "Doesn't a young boy need his mom?"

"He's at his gran's!" Polly replied, perhaps a shade too quickly, too desperately. "She spoils him. Lets him drink alcopops."

Jack knew now. "One photograph, Polly," he said.

"What?"

"I don't see one photograph. Not one. Show me a photograph of our son, Polly. As a baby, as a toddler, now. One photograph, Polly."

Polly could see that the game was up. She'd known that she could not keep up the lie for long, long enough for a course of action to present itself, long enough perhaps for her to find a way to reach across her bed and press the panic button on the wall. But it was not to be.

"I . . . I don't have any," she replied.

Polly had not wanted the abortion. She'd loved Jack so much and suddenly she had found herself still carrying a part of him. But at the time she'd felt that she had no choice: a seventeen-year-old girl with a fatherless baby? There'd been a girl like that in the year above Polly at school. How Polly had pitied that girl, old before her time, her whole youth sacrificed for a single moment of passion. Polly loved Jack, despite what he had done to her, and she had wanted to keep his baby, but not in exchange for her life, and that was how she had seen it at the time. At seventeen she had thought that having a baby would be the end of her life. What cruel and terrible irony to know now that had she kept it, it might have saved her life.

"I'm sorry, Polly," Jack said.

And he was sorry, so very sorry that she had no child to give him. Sorry that they had not shared their lives together, sorry that he had ever left her in order to serve a cold, ungrateful country. Most of all, sorry that despite all that, he would still have to kill her.

Polly sensed his resolve hardening, sensed her life slipping away.

"You said you still loved me," Polly pleaded, dropping to her knees.

"I do still love you," Jack replied, and for the second time that evening there were tears in his eyes.

"Then you can't kill me," she begged.

"Polly," said Jack, and it was almost as if it was he who was doing the pleading. "Try to understand. If I make chairman of the joint chiefs, do you know what the next step could be for me?" Polly had started to sob. "President. Yes, president. Leader of the world's only superpower. There was a time when men waged war all their lives over a few square miles of mud and huts. They sacrificed their sons and grandsons to defend a paltry tribal crown. People have fought and murdered in pursuit of power since the dawn of time. Rivers of blood have flowed for it. For little power, for nothing power! I have before me the possibility of being the leader of the world! The world, Polly! Your existence severely compromises that possibility. Are you seriously suggesting that with such a destiny within my grasp I should shrink from the killing of just one single soul?"

Well, there was a foolish question. Polly could see that, even through the blind terror of her tears.

"Of course I am, you bloody fool."

"Because I love you?" Jack asked.

"I don't care why."

"Love is the enemy of ambition, Polly," Jack said. "I made that decision sixteen years ago, in the early hours of the morning in a hotel room. There's no point going back on it now."

"Jack!"

But Polly could see in Jack's eyes that her time was up.

"Like I said," and his voice seemed to come from somewhere else, "people die every day."

Jack was a stranger to Polly now. She no longer recognized him. Whatever it was that she had loved in him had simply disappeared; all that remained was pride and ambition. It was as if he had shut down his heart and soul, had removed himself emotionally from the scene. He had gone over this moment in his mind a thousand times and knew that he could not trust himself to say good-bye, he never had been able to say good-bye to Polly.

And so in his mind at least he stood apart. It was not his finger squeezing the trigger but some other self, a separate personality too strong to be denied. He watched himself as the story unfolded, knowing the sequence of events exactly, like a series of stills from an old movie.

The soldier shoots the girl in the forehead. The girl falls back upon her bed, stone dead. The soldier wipes his eyes on the sleeve of his coat (he is surprised to discover how upset he is) and takes a last look round. Confident that there is nothing of his left in the room save for a single bullet, he picks up his bag and without looking again at the dead girl he lets himself out of her flat. Ensuring that his overcoat entirely covers his uniform, the soldier descends to the front door, and, having checked that there is nobody about in the street outside, he quietly leaves the house. He then drives himself back to the private hotel in Kensington in which he has been staying, parks his plain rental car in the private car park, and returns to his bedroom. The following morning he is collected in an army car and begins his journey to Brussels in order to continue with the business of NATO.

That was what was supposed to happen, anyway.

One bullet between the eyes and leave.

But Jack did not shoot. He had meant to, he had been about to, but he had talked too long and he had missed his chance. Because in what was to have been Polly's final second on earth, at the point when Jack began to draw his finger back on the flimsy resistance of the trigger, there was a knock at Polly's door. More than a knock— a bang, a thud, the crash of a body throwing itself against the solid panels.

[56]

The Bug had remained frozen for some time after killing the milkman. He had stood on the sodden, sticky stair carpet, gaping at the corpse that he had made, wondering what on earth he could do now. He could, in fact, do anything, because it was all up for him. He had stabbed a man to death and there was no hope of escape from the consequences. The police knew that he was about and that he had a knife; his mother had made sure of that. They would put him away now, that much was sure, not just for a month or two but forever. His life was over and it was so unfair. All he had been trying to do was protect her. He had acted always out of love.

And now he would never have her, not even once. He would be locked away from her, never again to feast his eyes upon her beauty. Even if they ever did let him out, which he doubted, she would have long since grown old and ugly.

Then a wicked thought began to grow in Peter's mind. He would have her, he would have her that very night, before the police arrived. He would go upstairs, kill the American, and make love to Polly, rape her if she resisted. Why not? He had nothing left in the world to lose now. He was a murderer already and hadn't he earned his moment with her, earned it with his love? Surely even her cold

286

heart would not expect him to go to prison without even once knowing that for which he had sacrificed his life.

Peter turned away from the dead milkman and bounded up the stairs, all caution forgotten. He knew that the corpse could be discovered at any moment and the alarm raised. He knew that if he was to act it must be immediately. If he was to have time to force himself upon Polly and justify the life of incarceration that he faced then it must be now.

At the top of the stairs the door to Polly's flat was closed as Peter had known it would be. He hurled his body against it, hammering with the fist of his left hand. In his right hand he still held the knife, his fingers clenched around the bloody hilt, sticky with his own blood and that of the milkman. Peter was no longer afraid of the American. He had killed once, he could kill again. The moment the door opened he would stab his hated rival and then force Polly to his will.

"Let me in, you slut!" he shouted. "You've let him do it to you! Why not let me?"

Inside the flat Jack leaped to the door. Whatever it was that was going on outside, the noise would surely wake the whole house. There would soon be irate figures in the stairwell and one of them would be bound to ring the police. Jack had only moments in which to silence this new menace.

He flung open the door. Outside stood the Bug, knife in hand. Peter was caught momentarily by surprise, but then lunged forward with a shout of triumph. But the Bug was no more of a threat to Jack than if he truly had been a bug. Jack stepped neatly aside and Peter stumbled forward into the room. In some ways even this pathetic circumstance was a small triumph for Peter. He was inside Polly's home for the very first time. He glanced round, trying to take it in, store it up, memorize more of Polly's life.

But Peter had no more need of memories.

Jack raised his pistol and shot the Bug, as he intended to shoot Polly, straight between the staring, gaping eyes. Peter was dead before he hit the floor. Jack then turned back to Polly in order to complete his self-appointed mission.

But it was too late. The Bug had foiled Jack's plan, providing Polly with a tiny window of opportunity in which to defend her life. For as Jack turned back toward her Polly was already reaching up to the head of her bed; her finger was already on the panic button. Instantly as she pushed it the room was filled with the noise of jangling bells, and outside the open door the stairwell began to glow a jarring intermittent red as the alarm light installed there began to flash.

Jack met Polly's eye, a surprised look upon his face.

"It's connected to the police station!" Polly shouted, having to raise her voice in order to make herself heard above the jangling of the bells. "They'll be here in two minutes at this time of night."

Jack stood, gun in hand, and for the first time that night he seemed at a loss.

"Go, Jack!" Polly shouted. "Run, get out now!"

But it was too late to run. Jack had killed a man; the bloodied corpse lay at his feet and the forces of the law were almost upon him. Even now he could hear a faint siren amidst the shrieking of the bells. They would be in the street in moments. There was no escape. Yes, he had killed Peter in self-defense, but there would still have to be a police investigation. Even if Polly stood by him, and there was no reason why she should, even if she kept his terrible threat to her life to herself, the whole story of their past must eventually come out. Then would come the suspicions and the whisperings. Why had he been in her flat that night? Why had he been carrying a gun? Despite what Jack had said to Polly, it was not common practice for

American soldiers to go about London armed. At the very best, Jack's career would end in pathetic and contemptible disgrace, and at worst he would be imprisoned for manslaughter. What a mess.

Downstairs, a shrill woman's voice joined the chorus of complaint now ringing round the building. The whole house had been aroused.

"Run, Jack!" Polly repeated desperately. "Get out! Get out now!"

He loved her more in that moment than he had ever loved her. He had tried to kill her and yet still she cared for him. Such was the power of love, love that he had denied all his life, love that he had tried that night to murder. But he had failed and it was love, not him, that would survive.

The police were at the front door now. In a moment they would be in the house.

"I love you, Polly," said Jack, "but I don't deserve you and I do not deserve the trust of my country. I have failed in my duty and brought disgrace and dishonor upon everything I care for."

Then, like a Roman general of old, Jack fell upon his sword. He raised his gun to his head and pulled the trigger. As his body fell toward her Polly tried to scream but found that she had no voice. All that she could do as he came to rest on the floor before her was silently mouth his name.

[57]

Nibs and her husband had made an uneasy peace. She would stand by him, even lie for him, and in return he had promised that this sordid little affair would be his last. He tried to kiss her to say thank you but she was not yet ready for that.

They had just ordered coffee when a knock came at the door.

"I said we weren't to be disturbed," Nibs's husband said as his principal private secretary entered the room.

"I'm extremely sorry, Mr. President, but the State Department felt that you should know this. I'm afraid that we have bad news from London. General Jack Kent seems to have shot himself. It looks like some kind of sex thing. He was in the apartment of an Englishwoman. Another man is dead also. We have no further details at present."

The president and the first lady were horrified. They had both known Jack quite well. Nibs in particular knew Courtney Kent and could only imagine how she was feeling.

"I'll call Courtney," she said, and left the president with his aides.

"Jack Kent of all people," the great commander said. "We were going to propose him for chairman of the joint chiefs."

The president was truly sorry to hear the news, but he was a politician and already he could see that from a personal point of view there was an upside to this tragedy. Jack's suicide would be enormously newsworthy, particularly if it did turn out that there was a sexual angle to the case. Anything that diverted attention from the president's own problems was to be welcomed.

"In the meantime there are practical considerations," the president added. "This is going to hit the army hard. We need to fill this gap and quickly, and, for Christ's sake, can we please try to find a clean pair of hands."

A few days later, to his utter shock and abject terror, General Schultz, Jack's blundering, indecisive colleague, whose anonymous career had shadowed Jack's for so many years, was appointed chairman of the joint chiefs. He had turned out to be the only senior officer in the armed forces who had never done anything that anybody considered suspect. The reason for this being, of course, that General Schultz had never done anything.

Two years later Schultz's name would be spoken of as a potential presidential candidate for exactly the same reason.

"It isn't a case of who's most qualified these days," the Washington power brokers had wearily to admit. "It's a case of who's least likely to be disqualified."

[58]

Despite the dreadful memories of that violent night, Polly decided to stay on in her flat. At first she had intended to move. The image of the Bug's corpse bleeding on her floor was not a pleasant one, but in the end she decided that the Bug had not managed to drive her out while he was alive and she was not going to let him do so now that he was dead. Besides, there was the memory of Jack to consider. He had died in that flat, and despite the awfulness of what he had planned Polly wanted to be the keeper of that memory.

Over the weeks that followed the night of Jack's return Polly tried to come to terms with what had happened to her. It was not an easy thing to do. Three men had died, and although she knew that none of their deaths was her fault she could not help but feel in some way responsible. The milkman weighed particularly upon Polly's mind. He had died at the hands of a man who was obsessed with her. Even now Polly was the classic stalker's victim, feeling guilty, taking the blame. Polly was in truth no more connected to or responsible for Peter's madness than had been the poor milkman, but she felt that she was. She wrote to the milkman's family saying how sorry she felt for what had happened and they wrote a polite but unfriendly letter back. She also wrote to the Bug's mother, expressing her sympathy and thanking her for alerting the police when she did. Peter's mother did not reply.

Then there was Jack, for whose memory there was to be no private grieving. His death and his past with Polly were now public property. What had remained so intensely private for so many years was now worldwide news. Both the American and British media bore down upon Stoke Newington like an invading army. The British were particularly excited; it is not often that a story comes along that is front-page in the U.S. but has a genuine British connection. Polly could have made a fortune but instead she resolutely turned down every request for an interview. It all came out anyway. The press even tracked down Ziggy, who was living in a tepee in Anglesey. He told them what little he could remember in exchange for seven pints of cider and an ounce of rolling tobacco. In the end, of course, the furor died down, and the ringing and knocking at Polly's door became less and less frequent until finally it stopped altogether and Polly was left alone.

Not surprisingly, Polly did not recover easily from the horror of that night. She often found herself weeping. Though fine at work, when she got home at night the sadness returned and she would lie on her bed and cry. Of course, she knew that in one spectacular way her life was better than it had been for years: the Bug was dead and he would never harm her again. But Jack was also dead and before he had died he had killed their love. The memory of his betrayal, which had haunted her for so long, was now made tiny by his second and more terrible rejection. He had tried to sacrifice her for his ambition and when he had failed he had sacrificed himself. Polly's love for him and his love for Polly had not been enough to save him and now she was truly alone.

She was alone on the evening when the phone rang.

Polly never picked up the phone directly. Despite the fact that she no longer felt in any danger she always let the answering machine stand as a barrier between her and callers. If nothing else it shielded her from having conversations with Telecom sales staff about their various incomprehensible discount schemes.

"Hello," said Polly's voice. "There's no one here to take your call at the moment, but please leave a message after the tone. Thank you."

Then Polly heard Jack.

She had been midway through a slice of toast, but her jaw froze in horror as those soft mellow American tones emanated from the machine.

"Hullo, this is a message for Polly. Polly Slade."

Except it wasn't Jack. It was only nearly Jack. This voice was a little deeper, sleepier, almost.

"Look, you don't know me, Polly, but I know you, a little, at least I think I do. My name's Harry, Harry Kent. I'm Jack's brother. I found your number among his effects . . ."

Harry was not in London when he called, he was in his little home and workshop in Iowa, alone, like Polly. They talked for a very long time, and when the time came to hang up they found that they both had more that they wished to say. Harry asked if Polly felt it would be appropriate for him to come and visit her in London when he had finished the kitchen sideboard on which he was currently working. Polly said that she felt it would be.

A week or so after that Polly was sitting alone in her flat, wondering why she felt so nervous, when the expected buzz came. Harry was at the door. She let him in and waited for him to climb the stairs. She was wearing her nicest dress.

Even through the little spyhole in her door Polly recognized Harry immediately. He was like Jack but different, thinner, she thought, leaner, and his hair was longer. Polly opened the door. The eyes were just the same; that same sardonic twinkle. He smiled. She knew that smile also. It was not the same as Jack's, but similar. Perhaps Polly was fooling herself, but it seemed to her that it was kinder. She stepped back into her flat and let him in.

BEN ELTON is one of Britain's most popular and successful comedians. In addition to his stand-up work, his television credits include *The Young Ones, Blackadder,* and *The Thin Blue Line.* He has written three West End plays—*Gasping, Silly Cow,* and *Popcorn*—and four previous bestselling novels—*Stark, Gridlock, This Other Eden,* and *Popcorn.* Ben Elton is married and lives in London.